A Certain Magical Index 2

KAZUMA KAMACHI

ILLUSTRATION BY
KIYOTAKA HAIMURA

"Okay. Then I'm that."

Unidentified shrine maiden **Aisa Himegami**

"What?! What the heck is that supposed to mean?!"

Nun managing the Index of Prohibited Books **Index**

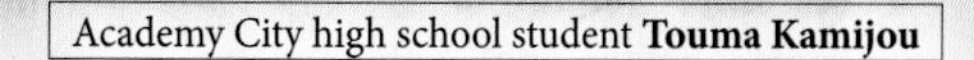

Academy City high school student **Touma Kamijou**

"Don't smile at everything. Are you ready to die?"

Sorcerer **Stiyl Magnus**

“We meet again, Index. I am most pleased to see you haven’t changed.”

Alchemist **Aureolus Isard**

“Are you…maybe…the golden Ars Magna?!”

"Actually. I'm a magician."
"Err, which part of you is a magician?"

"My right hand…is being cut off?!"

contents

1
PROLOGUE *DAYS LIKE USUAL*

11
CHAPTER 1 *THE FORTRESS OF GLASS*

83
CHAPTER 2 *WITCH-HUNTING WITH FIRE*

135
CHAPTER 3 *THE MASTER, LIKE A CLOSED WORLD'S GOD*

170
CHAPTER 4 *THE SEVENS OF MURDER*

201
FINAL CHAPTER *DEEP BLOOD ENCROACHES*

VOLUME 2

KAZUMA KAMACHI
ILLUSTRATION BY: KIYOTAKA HAIMURA

NEW YORK

A CERTAIN MAGICAL INDEX, Volume 2
KAZUMA KAMACHI

Translation by Andrew Prowse and Yoshito Hinton

This book is a work of fiction. Names, characters, places, and incidents are the product of the author's imagination or are used fictitiously. Any resemblance to actual events, locales, or persons, living or dead, is coincidental.

Edited by ASCII MEDIA WORKS
First published in Japan in 2004 by KADOKAWA CORPORATION, Tokyo.
English translation rights arranged with KADOKAWA CORPORATION, Tokyo, through Tuttle-Mori Agency, Inc., Tokyo.

Yen On
Hachette Book Group
1290 Avenue of the Americas
New York, NY 10104

www.hachettebookgroup.com
www.yenpress.com

Yen On is an imprint of Hachette Book Group, Inc.
The Yen On name and logo are trademarks of Hachette Book Group, Inc.

First Yen On edition: February 2015

ISBN: 978-0-316-259422

10 9 8 7 6 5 4 3 2

RRD-C

Printed in the United States of America

PROLOGUE

Days Like Usual

The_Beginning_of_the_End.

They say you can tell someone's personality by looking at their bookshelf.

"...There's nothing but comics here..."

It was the eighth of August, and Touma Kamijou saw nothing but manga in his bookcase, much less anywhere else in the room. For appearances' sake, he decided to go out to the Academy City station to buy a study guide.

...That's what he'd *wanted* to do, anyway.

"Man, I didn't think it would cost 3,600 yen...," Kamijou grumbled to himself with all the enthusiasm of a straggler from a defeated army. On top of that, the clerk had informed him that just the day before, there'd been some kind of summer exam study fair. Study guides had apparently been half off.

What rotten luck.

What unbelievably rotten luck.

Unfortunately, this was par for the course for Touma Kamijou. After all, he was a man prized by those who kept him close at hand as a lightning rod for their misfortune, all of which he would inevitably absorb.

Still, he couldn't just pack it in and leave after coming all that way.

Whatever the cost, he had to tear the manga-exclusive fantasies, his scarlet letter, off his bookshelf. It was abnormal. He didn't know

if the notion of deducing someone's personality by what was on their bookshelves was based on science or superstition, but normal people wouldn't have put so much weight on such a trivial platitude.
He, however, had serious cause to devote so much thought to the matter.

Touma Kamijou had amnesia.

It wasn't as if he was completely clueless, though. Things like how to cross the road or how to use a cell phone weren't subjects of confusion.
The only thing he'd lost had been his memories. His knowledge was still alive and well.
Even though he knew how to use a cell phone, he found himself wondering things like: *Huh? Where'd I leave my cell? And when did I sign up for one in the first place?* That was his predicament.
A person's knowledge is like a dictionary.
For example, he understood that an apple came from a deciduous tree in the rose family that blooms in the spring and produces round fruit. But he didn't know whether it was delicious or not unless he actually tasted one. This was because he had no photo diary–esque memory to tell him something like "on X day of X month, I ate a delicious apple."
The source of his quandary was that between his episodic memory, in charge of those experiences, and his semantic memory, which stored information, apparently only his episodic memory had been destroyed. But putting that aside for now…
Regardless of the cause, Touma Kamijou wanted to know what sort of person he'd been before his amnesia.
He was desperate enough to cling to the silly idea that looking at his bookshelf would provide that insight.
However, he didn't come across as frantic or as if he was at the end of his rope.
He hadn't been dropped into the middle of the world all alone and wasn't caught in some intrigue where he was being hunted. For now,

he had clothes, food, a roof over his head, and an acquaintance upon whom he felt he could rely.

"Touma."

As he headed back home along the summer roads, ready to die from exhaustion at his unforeseen expense (in general, he considered any impulse buy over one thousand yen to be suicide), he heard her whine.

He turned to look, and indeed, there stood a single girl giving him a sullen, pouting face.

She looked around thirteen or fourteen years old, and he could tell she was a foreigner at a glance: Her waist-length hair was silver, her skin was white as snow, and her eyes were the color of emeralds. Above all, though, the thing that smelled most foreign about her was her outfit. It was a habit, the attire worn by sisters and nuns of Crossism. However, this habit was pure white with gold-laced embroidery here and there. It managed to possess the characteristic look of an ostentatious teacup.

The girl's name was Index.

That wasn't her actual name, of course, but everyone in the world seemed to be calling her that.

They had met in the hospital.

Actually, Kamijou *thought* they had become acquainted there, but apparently they'd known each other before he lost his memory. However much he struggled to remember the girl, he couldn't recall anything about her. He wasn't about to reveal that, though.

The day he'd met her in that hospital room...

As he lay in his bed, she'd looked at him, happy enough to burst into tears.

Her expression now wasn't directed at the Kamijou here, present in this moment, but rather at the Kamijou from before his memory loss.

He couldn't bring himself to break her heart. In order to protect her heart's warmth, he needed to continue playing out the role of Touma Kamijou as if he still possessed his memories.

It was a complicated feeling.

It gave him the impression that there were two Touma Kamijous.

So, without noticing what Kamijou was thinking (having her notice would cause problems), the girl with the false name, Index, looked up unhappily from a head shorter than him.

"Touma, what could we have done with that 3,600 yen?"

"...Don't even go there."

"What could we have done with it?" she pried.

Kamijou was about to repeat "Don't even go there!" with more force before plugging his ears and shutting his eyes to escape from reality, when suddenly, he realized that she wasn't looking at him.

"?" He followed her upturned eyes, which led him to notice the signboard of an ice-cream shop, spinning around and around.

... Well, after all, it is *August eighth, we* are *walking around under the blazing afternoon sun, there* are *evil-looking mirages seeping up from the asphalt, and Index* is *wearing long sleeves, but...*

"...I get it, but you can't possibly eat 3,600 yen's worth of ice cream. Normally, anyway."

"Mgh." Index returned her gaze to Kamijou, frustrated. "Touma, I haven't uttered a single word of complaint that I'm hot or tired or weary, okay? Furthermore, I don't remember thinking about using someone else's money, and in conclusion, I wasn't considering eating any ice cream, even a little bit."

"...Okay, I get that you aren't allowed to lie, since you're a nun, so stop making abandoned puppy eyes at me while you're all covered in sweat. You should really just say you want to go in a store with air-conditioning and eat some ice cream. If you keep wearing that totally out-of-season, ostentatious habit in this ridiculous heat, you're gonna collapse."

Touma Kamijou made this assertion as if he had enough cash to spare, but that didn't change the amount of money in his wallet. Well, just getting some ice cream wouldn't cost *too* much, but it would decimate the train fare they needed to get back home. Academy City was so big that it occupied a third of Tokyo. The journey would be too far for Kamijou, who was still convalescing, and Index, who was a girl. Some people would probably feel that the "girl" part was discriminatory, but if she *did* trek straight across a third of Tokyo under the boiling-hot afternoon sun in the middle of summer without batting an eyelash—well, that wouldn't have been quite in line with Kamijou's image of "feminine appeal."

In the meantime, Index's frown was deepening with her discomfort.

"Touma, these clothes are the visualization of the Lord's protection. I would never, ever consider them too hot and stuffy or complain that they make no distinction between a summer outfit or a winter outfit, okay?!"

"...Uhh." *Wow, honesty and kindness are two totally different things, huh?* reflected Kamijou in a bit of an adult-level epiphany. *And one more thing. Why are a bunch of safety pins stuck in that ridiculous habit?*

"Moreover, despite these clothes, I'm still in training. Alcohol and tobacco go without saying, but all other indulgences, like coffee, tea, and fruit-flavored dessert icicle pops are forbidden, too."

"Huh. I see. I figured feasting on ice cream right about now would feel *really good* and be a *totally in-season* way to deal with this sweltering heat..."

People can't say anything when they're told something is for religious reasons.

He looked back at the ice-cream store's signboard one last time.

"Then let's not. I won't force you to eat—"

—*anything.* He'd been about to finish when his shoulders were grabbed at supersonic speed. Unable to endure the viselike grip of her fingers, Kamijou turned around to face Index.

"I-it's true that, based on the fact that I'm still in training, ingesting any kind of indulgence is restricted..."

"Then you can't, right?"

"But I *am* still in training after all, so there are still easy times and hard times to act like a perfect saint, you know! Therefore, there is a possibility in this case, albeit a small one, that ice cream could be placed in my mouth by mistake, Touma!"

"..."

He was about to make a witty retort, but her fingers dug into his shoulders even harder. Apparently, she didn't want him to say anything. What she didn't seem to grasp was that sometimes maintaining silence is more exhausting for everybody than allowing a comeback. It spoke to her inexperience.

Just then…

"Heya, looks like you're havin' a pretty nice conversation there, dude, and by the way, who's the kid, Kami?"

He detected a weird voice, speaking in a fake Kansai accent.

When he turned, he saw something even more suspect: a man standing 180 centimeters tall, sporting blue hair and an earring. Well, he was an unusual person, but even for a weirdo, he was far too strange.

Was I really friends with this guy before my amnesia, though? Kamijou wondered. His people-related memories were entirely eradicated, so he had no clue. *But anyway, your taste in friends sucks, Touma Kamijou!* He cursed at himself as if he were a different person.

"Eh? What's the matter, Kami? You're spacin' out, dude. Why ya actin' all distant toward me? The summer so hot it wiped your memories or somethin'?"

"Wha—?!"

Kamijou froze in fear, but Blue Hair waved a hand around. "Yeah, yeah, just kiddin'. Amnesia's that thing mysterious crazy girls get, right?"

Blue Hair looped his arm around Kamijou's shoulders (making him hotter in the process). "So, Kami, seriously, whozzat? How do you know such a tiny little thing? She your cousin?…Nah, can't be, since there's no way Kami genes are mixed in with that silver hair."

Well, I guess one of his negative qualities is that his voice is so loud that everyone can hear him when he whispers, thought Kamijou.

The "tiny little thing" bit gave him a slight start. Uneasily, he pondered if the girl next to him would overreact and throw a fit at that phrase…but she didn't look as if she would.

"…Okay, anyway, real talk here. You givin' a lost, scared kid directions? Must be pretty tiring for you, what with your English grades sucking so much you're not allowed to leave the country... Wait, does she even come from somewhere they speak English?"

Kamijou didn't really know, but maybe Index was used to being called small. She was listening relatively calmly. Actually, she glared up at the sun flinging killer heat down on them. She looked too hot to want to feel like talking.

"...Well, Kami, I dunno where the heck you found that girl, but it's too soon to relax! I mean, we've been the proven and trusted unpopular loser squad for sixteen years now. Don't tell me you don't know how big a contradiction it would be to trigger a 'meeting with a normal girl' event, aight? Look, it's in romantic comedies and stuff. 'The person you liked was actually a married woman with a baby face! Aha-ha-ha, your dreams have been crushed!' Y'know, *that* kind of ending. Same thing, dude!"

Well, thank goodness it didn't turn out like some overused rom-com plot, Kamijou reflected, sighing with relief.

"Is it gonna be one of those endings where she's actually a boy dressed up like a girl? I mean, look at her. She's totally flat."

Criiick. That moment, Kamijou could swear he heard the blood vessels in the girl's head throbbing madly.

Aagh?! He desperately bit down on the shriek that was halfway up his throat. She apparently tolerated people referring to her as "little" or "young," but it didn't look like she had any patience for someone mistaking her for a boy. She maintained her smile and ground her back teeth together loudly enough for him to hear it.

What rotten luck! Kamijou wanted to hold his head in his hands.

"What? But Kami, there's no way we—members of the proven and trusted unpopular loser squad—would ever meet a real-life, three-dimensional girl! So there's gotta be a crazy ending in store for ya! Ahh, I can see it, I can see your future! It's the eighteen-plus scene you've been waiting so long for. You remove her last piece of clothing, your hands quivering. Suddenly, you realize the truth, and you fall right out of the bed in complete surprise! I can see it!"

"...You're joking, right? You actually understand, and that's why you're joking, right?"

"Huh? So it really is a girl? What a bore," Blue Hair answered, though he still had a playful grin on his face. "Then your meeting wasn't normal, huh? Look, Kami, even though you're part of the proven and trusted unpopular loser squad, you can't go around kidnapping little girls, y'know? It don't take much for your barbaric bravery to race all over the Internet!"

"Wha...Shut up! That would be insane!" Kamijou didn't actually remember how he met her. "She's just a freeloader, sir! Everything has been mutually agreed upon, Sergeant!"

"A freeloader? A freeloader?! Did you call a girl *just* a freeloader, Kami?! What are you, an elementary schooler who's eaten so much candy he no longer appreciates the value of rice?!"

"Shut up already! She isn't anything else, so of course, I called her *just a freeloader*! No one is just sporadically firing random rom-com events here! Do you have any idea what the Kamijou residence's wallet looks like because of her?! It would have been better off if a *zashiki-warashi* or something had rolled into my house inste—" And then, after shouting 80 percent of that at the top of his lungs, he suddenly realized something.

Index, walking next to him, could obviously hear the whole conversation.

"..Uh."

He looked at her. With much trepidation, he glanced to his side.

She was smiling. She was beaming so warmly her smile could have been that of the Virgin Mary herself. All the while, blue veins popped out of her face, reminiscent of a cantaloupe.

This wasn't good. He wondered if the old Touma Kamijou possessed the talent to coax Index into a good mood even when she was like this. If he had, then he seriously thought he had lost an important memory.

"Touma," said Index, wearing the most beguiling smile he'd ever seen.

It's over, he thought. He responded anyway. "What is it, O Great Sister?"

"I am a nun of the English Puritan Church. If you have anything for which to repent, don't hesitate to tell me now, okay?"

The holy girl crossed herself and folded her hands.

Her smile was perfect, which let him know it was feigned.

He wanted to hold his head in his hands.

She's a bomb. No, she's a dud; she hasn't exploded yet. If I mess with it any more, my story will end right here, right now! he instinctively deduced.

What do I do, what do I do?! Ah, that's right! Ice cream! I should get out of this with ice cream!

His mind at the very pinnacle of panic, Kamijou pointed stiffly at the automatic door at the entrance to the ice-cream shop, as if he had forgotten how to speak. "Hm?" Index followed his finger, puzzled, and then stopped abruptly. "Hmm...," he heard her mumble.

I dodged it..., Kamijou thought with relief. Then, in his relief, he saw it.

There was some sort of piece of paper hanging on the door to the ice-cream store.

This was what it conveyed:

"To all customers.

"We will be temporarily closed for renovations. We greatly apologize for the inconvenience."

Scrape. With a premonition of an ultimate "bad end," Kamijou slowly turned to the girl beside him.

Her smile immediately disintegrated.

He didn't even have time to cry out, "What rotten luck!" before he was set upon by Index the raging beast girl.

They ended up compromising on milk shakes at a cheap-looking fast-food restaurant.

Of course, Index wasn't satisfied with just that. Thus, Kamijou thought to throw in some relaxation time in a place with an air conditioner as a bonus to sate her, but...

...it was afternoon, and the restaurant had no empty seats.

"..."

She was completely silent. In her hands was a tray, upon which were three milk shakes—one vanilla, one chocolate, and one strawberry. He wanted to make a jab at her—*did you really want ice cream that much?*—but had a premonition that doing so would mean certain death for him, so he couldn't mess with her carelessly.

What rotten luck, he thought earnestly.

With three milk shakes all to herself, her mood was steadily improving to some extent, but it was an afternoon during summer break, so every seat was taken. However, anyone going back outside right now was out of the question. He didn't think a soul would be inclined to leave his or her long-desired oasis of air-conditioning to wander back into the desert roads under the blazing sun.

He started overhearing the lazy gossip of a few high school girls, who were completely ignorant of his despair.

"Yo, yo. By the way, are those rumors about Anzai using mind reading during finals true, yo?"

"I did hear that a faculty meeting got called about it, and that the odds are ten to one it's true. But apparently they all unanimously agreed that since powers are part of what's taught in class, it didn't constitute cheating."

"Urk. How dirty, LOL! If I knew that, I'd've used my power during the test, yo?"

"...Don't you specialize in combustion?"

"Yeah, I'd light some fire behind the teacher and get him to tell me all the answers, yo!"

...This may not have sounded the faintest bit like normal gossip, but that's how life in Academy City was. This was a single, large Ability Development organization, where all 2.3 million residents of the city were awakening some kind of supernatural ability within them.

Kamijou was one of those same espers. He possessed a right hand that could nullify any abnormal powers, even divine miracles, the Imagine Breaker.

"...Touma, I would like to sit down and take a rest by any means necessary," stated Index. Her voice was absolutely devoid of emotion for some reason.

He was scared—scared of the nun's eyes, which told him that she would bite him if he didn't listen.

"Right away!!" he exclaimed, dashing over to an employee who was sweeping the floor.

"I see. I guess you're going to have to share a booth with someone else, then, huh?"

With a businesslike, almost cruel smile, the employee pointed toward a corner near a window.

Share a booth? Kamijou's gaze followed along to the spot indicated by the employee's finger.

"Urk?!"

Despite the restaurant being as full as a train station at rush hour, there was a single four-person table with free seats, like a black hole gaping wide in the crowd of people.

And there...

...at the table...

...was a shrine maiden.

A shrine maiden was sleeping with her face down on the table.

Her long black hair was spread out like the tentacles of a beached jellyfish and completely hid her face.

What...

What the hell is that?! Kamijou screamed to himself.

It was strange. It was *too* strange. His bad luck sense was tingling: *Don't get involved with that. If you get involved, it will bring you misfortune for sure. Losing your memories has got nothing on this.*

Touma Kamijou was an unfortunate person, but he wasn't playful enough to jump into misfortune of his own accord.

He closed his eyes once and made up his mind.

...Okay, let's go home. I'll take Index biting me over getting mixed up with that any day, he concluded. But when he turned back, he noticed that the other two weren't anywhere to be found.

"...?"

He looked around the place.

"…Geh!"

A different employee had suggested that Index share a table, and she was indeed already sitting directly across from the unfamiliar shrine maiden. *Does she have no sense of danger? Or is she just that philanthropic? I don't even care, but seriously, Blue Hair, I'd like to ask, is the combination of a nun and a shrine maiden really amazing enough to make your eyes sparkle like that?*

I want to run away.

But he couldn't. If he turned his back on Index here, she'd kill him and eat him like a lion, and it was too dangerous to leave the starry-eyed Blue Hair with the two girls.

But above all…

Index, sipping from her strawberry shake, was beckoning him over with a fantastically happy expression. *Somehow that face seems like the one thing I absolutely can't ruin*, thought Kamijou.

That said, there was still an unknown priestess asleep on the table.

When Kamijou fearfully approached, the shrine maiden's shoulders twitched.

"Ai—"

Her mouth moved. The shrine maiden's mouth moved. Kamijou got a bad feeling about this. He got an *extremely* bad feeling about this. *I wonder why?* As an amnesiac, he shouldn't have had any memories of anything from before his accident, but for some reason, he couldn't help but get the sense that this wasn't the first time this sort of thing had happened.

He gulped audibly and waited for the priestess to speak.

And she did.

"—I binged."

CHAPTER 1

The Fortress of Glass

The_Tower_of_BABEL.

1

In this room, there were no windows.

There were no doors, no stairs, and no elevators or hallways. This "building"—which served none of the functions of one—was an impenetrable citadel, accessible only by a Level Four teleportation ability.

This Curriculate Fortress was easily tougher than a nuclear shelter. Inside it stood a single sorcerer.

His name was Stiyl Magnus.

Stiyl was both the flame-specialist paragon of runic magic and a priest of English Puritanism. At the young age of fourteen, he was an exception among exceptions: **an expert at sorcerer-killing magic.**

Normally, he was not someone who should have been here.

Not *here* in this building, but *here* in this city. He was a member of the occult Necessarius, the Church of Necessary Evils and the 0th parish of English Puritanism, a denomination of Crossism. Right now, he was within the borders of the completely *anti*-occult Academy City, a factory for the mass production of espers via drugs, biostimulation, and sleep learning. He stuck out like a tarot card in a fifty-two-card poker deck.

There was a reason he was in this place he shouldn't be.

He was currently present as a delegate of English Puritanism, and his goal was to conduct a dialogue with the *humans* of Academy City, who differed in principles and position. However, considering he was representing an organization, his personality was possessed of a striking flaw.

He was not a man who felt any hesitation in killing others.

He wouldn't even twitch an eyebrow at setting a living being awash with flames.

"..."

Despite that, though, he would never grow accustomed to the sight before his eyes, no matter how many times he witnessed it.

In this room, too wide and vast to call indoors, there were no sources of illumination. Nevertheless, the room was overcome with starlike lights. Completely covering all four walls were innumerable monitors, buttons, and other such things, each blinking on and off. From the thousands of different machines of various sizes came tens of thousands of cords, cables, and tubes, all sprawled across the floor like arteries, gathering in the area at the center of the room.

In the middle of everything was a giant beaker.

Four meters in diameter, and more than ten in height, the cylindrical container was made of tempered glass and filled with red fluid. Although it had previously been explained to Stiyl that the liquid's hue was that of a weakly alkaline culture solution, scientific concepts were well removed from his own field as a sorcerer.

A person in green surgical garments floated inside the beaker.

The word *person* was the only way to describe the figure. They looked both male and female, both old and young, and both holy and sinful.

Was this person a superposition of every human possibility or had they abandoned them all?

Whichever the case, there was no word to use except *person*.

"Every man and woman who comes here has the same reaction when they observe my state of being—" began the person submerged in the beaker. In a voice that could be heard to both male and female, adults and children, and to saints and to sinners.

"—but there really isn't a need for humans to go out of their way to do what machines can."

That summed up this person.

One can compensate for all biological activities using machines. Therefore, there was no meaning in doing those things yourself. The outer limit of humanity, with an estimated life span of 1,700 years, was staring Stiyl in the face.

Stiyl was terrified.

He wasn't scared of Academy City's scientific prowess and how it could replace all human biological processes with machines. **No,** what made him tremble was this human's very perspective—the willingness, the lack of hesitation to abandon their flesh and give their life over to machinery just because they *could.*

A *human*...

...The thought of a human warped to this extent was what frightened him so intensely.

"I believe you know the reason I called you here—" asserted the Academy City general board chairman, the *person* named Aleister, while floating upside down, "—but things have gotten troublesome."

Stiyl frowned at that. He couldn't have imagined the person before him would complain about something "troublesome."

"Would you be referring to Deep Blood?"

He normally stayed away from speaking in a formal tone of voice, but things were different here.

He **wasn't** doing so because of his position as representative of the Church. It was because he knew that if Aleister felt even a moment's hostility toward him, he would tear him to pieces before he could blink. It didn't matter if Stiyl himself ***had*** **any hostility**. A simple misunderstanding or misinterpretation on Aleister's part could cost Stiyl his life.

Because this was the enemy's base...

...and this was a place with control over 2.3 million espers.

"Hm." Aleister watched over the shivering Stiyl. "If it were just an esper, there wouldn't be a problem. **It** was one of the espers originally in my possession. If it were an incident caused in this city, by this city's residents, there would be 70,632 different methods we could use to resolve it or cover it up, but—"

"..." Stiyl didn't have any particular thoughts on the matter. He didn't care what sort of fail-safes Academy City had set up, nor would he understand this world of science if it was explained to him anyway.

"—the problem is that one of your sorcerers has involved himself in an incident that he should have stayed out of."

Therefore, Stiyl focused his thoughts on this one point.

The Bloodsucker Killer, "Deep Blood." He knew the name not from Academy City's data banks, but from the archives of the British Library. As the name implied, it was said to be the power to kill a *certain creature* whose very existence was uncertain. Both the details of the ability and its authenticity were unknown. At any rate, he had only heard that there lived a young woman named Deep Blood.

The girl in possession of this Deep Blood was currently imprisoned by a sorcerer.

That one piece of information encapsulated the incident.

"Hm. Them being someone from *outside* this city makes things a tad complicated," Aleister explained, still flipped over. "It isn't like it would be *difficult* for a city with the strength of more than 2.3 million espers to crush one or two sorcerers. The problem lies elsewhere: It has to do with *us* killing one of *you*."

Both Academy City and Necessarius commanded their own worlds.

Things were the way they were right now because each of them held complete control over its own art: the scientific and the occult, respectively. If Academy City, with its supervision of espers, was to threaten a sorcerer, those on the side of the sorcerers would not take kindly to it.

The situation was very much akin to a top-of-the-line aircraft going down behind enemy lines. It could possibly let the enemy army gain information about your technology.

"I suppose that means it would be difficult for you to request reinforcements, then," said Stiyl in an uninterested tone.

A combined force of espers and sorcerers could spark conflict for the same reason. There might be struggles over who would lead the team, because it would be easy for one side to steal the other's technology under the pretense of ascertaining their combat abilities.

That raised another question. Stiyl had come to Academy City about two weeks ago and had fought an esper. When he considered it calmly, why had that battle been an exception and overlooked? There might have been some kind of deal made between Academy City and the Church that he wasn't privy to. Or that the city treated that young man as having little importance, since he was a Level Zero, an "Impotent."

But this current case was different.

The espers and sorcerers involved in this turmoil were all *important people*, and all of them had great power.

"**I see—that's why you've summoned an exception: me,**" Stiyl replied, maintaining his expression. He said this just to affirm the facts.

In other words, Stiyl Magnus himself was a special case here. There would be a problem if a sorcerer was killed by an esper. However, there wouldn't be any problem if Stiyl took down a sorcerer, since he was a sorcerer himself. And when he gave a thought to his superiors, he knew they would probably want to deal with their own embarrassment by themselves. They wouldn't consent to anything unless someone from the Church dealt with the sorcerer.

"Now then, here is what we must consider. A miniature of the *battlefield.*"

By some kind of contraption, a direct image suddenly swam up in front of him in the darkness.

It was a wireframe-like drawing done in CG. It displayed a sketched map of a completely normal building, which would be the field of battle this time.

The words "Misawa Cram School" were written in a trim font on the edge of the sketch.

"We've analyzed its interior using satellite imagery, as well as its construction blueprints." There was no emphasis in Aleister's voice.

"Whether there are any sort of magical traps inside is unknown. It's outside my field, after all."

"…"

"This Misawa Cram School has a somewhat unique background."

Aleister's explanation went like this.

Academy City had always been a large teaching establishment that gathered hundreds of schools of all sizes into one place. Among its Curricula, it included the preeminent "Supernatural Ability Development" program.

The Misawa Cram School was a prep school with locations all over the country. The original reason a branch of it had been placed in Academy City was more than likely so it could be used as a giant corporate spy to **steal the city's teaching techniques**.

Unfortunately, the Misawa School dabbled only halfheartedly in Ability Development and came under bad influence. In what could be referred to as scientific worship, they have been enslaved by the cultlike idea that they were "chosen ones" for being the only people who knew about Ability Development.

Eventually, the city's branch school even started to ignore the orders of the Misawa School Group and ran amok. As a result, it had ended up taking the girl named Deep Blood prisoner in accordance with its "teachings."

"But why might Misawa Cram School have placed Deep Blood in confinement? Does their doctrine contain the objective of sacrificing themselves to the descendants of Cain in order to achieve immortality, like some sixteenth-century cult?"

"No. The school has no particular attachment to Deep Blood. I suspect they would have done the same to any esper whose power was unique and couldn't be reproduced."

"?"

"The student ranking in Academy City is separated into two factors: a student's academic ability and their abnormal powers. Because of this, they must have considered it meaningful to acquire Deep Blood and conduct research on her. If they were to announce that they can mass-produce an amazingly rare ability, it could effectively bait in Level Two "Adepts" and Level Three "Experts," since they usually have a complex regarding their own more widespread abilities.... But for heaven's sake, it's impossible to change an already-awakened ability into a different one, even with a brain transplant."

But Stiyl found this odd. Say it was a rule in this city that less common abilities granted higher societal status, but he couldn't believe that anyone in such a science-ridden place would believe in something like the occult *creature* in question.

As he pondered it, Aleister answered him casually. "In any case, if you acknowledge the value in the power's rarity, the story makes sense. There are plenty of other espers with unidentified abilities, not the least of which is Imagine Breaker, as well as espers who have never had the opportunity to show the true extent of their power in combat because of their enormous power."

In any case, things would be easy if it was just that Deep Blood was being held captive. As an internal affair of Academy City, they could have used any one of the 70,632 methods Aleister had mentioned of dealing with the case.

That wasn't the problem.

Just before they *had* handled it, an outside sorcerer came to Misawa School seeking Deep Blood. On top of that, he didn't destroy the school—he hijacked it, which is what made this all so intricate.

"..."

Stiyl silently gazed at the map of the school building.

He couldn't tell how much it had been magically "remodeled." He felt nervousness run down his spine a bit. It was the sort he got when he was blindly diving into a situation he couldn't predict. While the sensation was familiar to him, it didn't feel good. It only meant that a battle of life or death, of zero or one, was inevitable.

However, the city had a combat potential of 2.3 million espers. The thought that he'd be alone for such a fight was a little enjoyable.

"No, not really," assured Aleister, appearing to read his mind. Perhaps there was some kind of equipment in the room that could detect a person's thought patterns. "Lest you forget, I am in possession of one of *your* worst enemies."

Stiyl stiffened and gulped.

Imagine Breaker. That was the name of the boy he had engaged in deadly combat with two weeks ago. It was the name of a unique boy, one which implied something beyond the realm of common sense and possibly beyond even the realm of the strange. It could cancel out any unnatural power, from sorcery to supernatural abilities to divine miracles; all he needed to do was touch it with his right hand.

"Will it not be an issue to utilize a supernatural ability to defeat a sorcerer?"

"That isn't an obstacle, either," Aleister responded, as if they had prepared what to say in advance. "First of all, he is a Level Zero with no valuable information. We don't need to fear our information leaking to you if he was to act in conjunction with a sorcerer."

"..."

"Secondly, he doesn't have the intelligence to understand your techniques. Therefore, none of your information would leak to us if he acted in conjunction with a sorcerer, either."

This fox... For the first time, Stiyl felt a grudge toward Aleister.

He couldn't discern this person's intentions. He understood from experience, down to the very marrow of his bones, that Imagine Breaker was *far* from useless.

Of course, that power wasn't something Stiyl could understand the mechanics of at a glance. In addition, it was probably impossible to steal that technology and return to the Church with it. But he thought that Academy City was in the same boat as him. Well, he wanted to *believe* they were, because if something like that could be mass-produced, the Church would find itself in quite the predicament. He could, after all, smash thousand-year-old sacred treasures to pieces just by poking them with his right hand.

The Imagine Breaker was so rare and so valuable, and yet Aleister handled it so carelessly.

Like Aleister was giving him various trials, molding a man walking the path of a saint.

Like Aleister was pounding heated steel with a heavy hammer, forging a true blade.

"..."

And, above all, shouldn't the 103,000 books at the young man's side be taboo?

Aleister's true intent and spoken intent were at odds with each other. Stiyl harbored doubts about it deep in his heart but didn't let it show on his face.

He took caution to disallow it. He didn't want even the slightest bit of trouble coming to that girl.

"...Deep Blood."

Stiyl muttered, exhaling. His face was that of a scholar with a question he couldn't find an answer to. "Deep Blood. Does something like that really exist? If it did, then that would—"

Stiyl stopped, unable to complete his sentence.

Deep Blood, the Bloodsucker Killer...The fact that she was called this meant that those certain creatures to *be* killed must exist. The ability wouldn't make sense otherwise. In other words, acknowledging the existence of Deep Blood proved in and of itself the reality of that certain *creature*.

"Hm. The occult is more your domain than ours, I think. I suppose that means even *your* sensibilities cannot accept it, then."

Of course not, Stiyl thought, digesting it in his mind.

The mana used by sorcerers worked like gasoline. The user's life span and life force were the crude oils from which it was created, while the user's breathing, blood flow, and meditation were what refined it into an easily usable source of fuel, "gasoline."

That was why sorcerers were not omnipotent in the slightest. However far one made it in his pursuit of sorcery, he only has so much gasoline to work with.

However, this *creature* didn't have that limitation.

Because this creature had the ludicrous characteristic of *immortality*, it would boast an infinite amount of mana—**even in spite of the fact that the very resources of the planet seem limitless but still have a bottom.**

The descendants of Cain—vampires.

They weren't the simple things from children's stories that could be dealt with by a cross or the sunlight. Just one of them could present a threat to the entire world rivaling that of nuclear bombs.

"Well."

The person upside down in the giant beaker looked at Stiyl disinterestedly.

"Do you know why what we call *supernatural abilities* exist in the first place?"

"...Why?"

There was no reason Stiyl would have known, nor did he think Aleister would tell him the truth. Granting confidential information to an enemy would mean he'd have to abandon all hope of leaving this place alive.

However... "They're nothing more than **blurs** in one's cognition," answered Aleister, not seeming to care. "Have you heard the story of Schrödinger's cat? Well, it *is* the most famous tale of animal cruelty in the world."

"...?"

"I shall spare you the details, but in essence, it implies that the nature of our reality is to distort itself to align with the thoughts of the one observing it. Though with the laws of physics of micro- and macroscopic scales being at odds with each other, it's not a general rule."

This world consists of two different sets of laws of physics—one for microscopic sizes and the other for macroscopic ones. Just where did the "tiny" world end and the "huge" world start? Aleister told him that this problem was one of the things he researched.

"...I am having difficulty understanding what you mean."

"You need not attempt to. If you did, I would be forced to kill you here," Aleister answered him, still without a care. "...Though even I do not understand it. The existence of Deep Blood is more than likely a mere trifle, just like the cat inside the box."

Aleister explained that an esper was like a piece of litmus paper that had changed color.

Rather than being overjoyed at a piece of red litmus paper changing color to blue, they would ask: Why does the color change at all, what makes it happen, and furthermore, can it be manipulated? Even with the power of 2.3 million espers at their disposal, and despite that potentially being enough to take on the entire world, this person was actually claiming that it was all just a means to an end.

Stiyl felt himself shiver.

The person in front of him was a human who would assert that there is no reason for a human to do what a machine can.

But just what exactly was *machine*...

...and what was *human* to this man?

"However...," the *human* said, visible to all males and females, adults and children, and saints and sinners, making a face that looked like a smile.

"Well, then. If Deep Blood proves the existence of vampires, then I wonder, just what does Imagine Breaker prove?"

2

What's up with this? wondered Kamijou in bafflement.

He was currently in the completely full nonsmoking area on the second floor of a fast-food restaurant. He was sitting at a four-person table in the corner by the window with Index and Blue Hair.

Right, I've got that much.

"—I ate too much."

And, for some reason, there was a shrine maiden slumped over the table at this vulgar place, and moreover, she had flung these mysterious words at him...?!

The priestess was around his age. With the standard red-and-white outfit combined with black hair reaching down to her waist, she looked like the mold from which other shrine maidens were created.

"..."

"..."

The air felt odd, like the inside of an elevator. As Kamijou was working out what to do next, he suddenly realized that Index and Blue Hair were staring at him in unison.

"...Wh-what?"

"...C'mon, Kami. She's talkin' to you, so go ahead and answer her!"

"...That's right, yeah. Touma, it's wrong to judge a book by its cover. 'The hand of God's salvation extends to all humankind,' right? Amen."

"...What, no! That's stupid! This is where we play rock-paper-scissors for it! Wait, Index, you already assumed I'd lose, didn't you? Quit making that docile face and crossing yourself!"

With all this, they decided that whoever lost the game of rock-paper-scissors would be sacrificed.

Rock, rock, then scissors—Kamijou was the only loser.

In conclusion, Touma Kamijou did indeed have rotten luck.

He held his scissors out there by themselves, still in disbelief. For now he attempted an "Umm, excuse me?" to the shrine maiden face-down on the table. Her shoulders gave a start. He made up his mind that he'd bring up a safe topic first.

"Uh, err...what do you mean, you 'binged'?"

After all, this was a shrine maiden talking. She probably wanted someone to hear her out, right?

"I had a lot of discount coupons. One hamburger for fifty-eight yen."

"Uh-huh." With no memories to speak of, Kamijou was oblivious to what a hamburger tasted like. He did have knowledge, though, and it explained that it was an emergency food meant for those low on cash and that it was just a flat piece of meat and some wilted lettuce in a bun.

"So I figured I'd ask for thirty to start with."

"That's too much of a saving, stupid."

He shot back on reflex. Right then, the shrine maiden ceased any and all movement. Her silence tipped him off to a somber aura emanating from her body, like she had been very hurt by it.

Well, that was embarrassing. I think she actually took it seriously. Wow, this is really embarrassing.

"Ah, no, I didn't mean it like that. What I meant to say was, 'That's stupid, but why would you do something like that?' but I was trying to move the conversation along smoothly, so it ended up sounding rude, and, well, you know, sounding rude is a sign of affection, and *definitely* not one of malice, and also, public service announcement to the nun and the blue-haired guy, I'd like to see you outside for a moment later, quit looking at me like that!!" Kamijou ended with a wail, unable to stand the silence any longer.

"I ate my emotions."

She made this declaration abruptly, deathly still.

"Huh?"

"The return train fare. It's four hundred yen."

The heap of shrine maiden replied, sighing. Kamijou forced himself to absorb her words. Though he didn't remember ever having been on a train, he *did* possess the knowledge that the train and bus fare in Academy City was expensive.

"So, why did you splurge on hamburgers when you needed four hundred yen for the train back?"

"Total possessions. Three hundred yen."

"...May I ask why?"

"Bought too much. Didn't plan ahead."

"..."

"That's why I stuffed myself."

The word *stupid* made its presence known in his throat again, but he just barely managed to force it back down.

Instead, he chose his words carefully.

"Wait, why didn't you just ride the train with that three hundred yen? Then you would only have to walk for about one hundred yen's worth. And besides, can't you borrow the fare from someone?"

"...Good plan."

"Why're you looking straight at me? Wait, don't point those hopeful eyes at me!!"

Kamijou leaned backward, startled, as if trying to distance himself from the priestess. To make matters worse, he had spent a whole 3,600 yen on that (useless) reference book. On top of that, he had bought three milk shakes for Index to cheer her back up. It was honestly an inconvenience to spend any more, even if it was just one hundred yen.

But aside from that...

The shrine maiden was showing her face for the first time since they arrived. Contrary to his expectations, she was extremely good-looking.

She had the white skin of a Japanese person, in contrast to the foreigner's skin color Index had. Her darkly colored eyes and hair made it stand out even more. Her eyes looked sleepy and devoid of energy, but in return, he couldn't feel any aggressiveness from her. She seemed strangely openhearted, even, like it would be safe to get as near to her as he wanted.

Then...

"..."

...Index was glaring at him quietly, and...

"Th-this can't be real. Kami's talkin' to a girl...He's talkin' normally to a girl he just met! It can't be!"

...Blue Hair was raising his voice in terrible slander for some reason.

"Shut up, you blue-haired, pierced 2-D lover! Public service announcement, please come to the gymnasium later! Also, shrine maiden, supply yourself with the one hundred yen you need and then go home immediately! That's all, briefing over!"

"What is this? Kami, I'm not done talking, man! You've been part of the proven and trusted unpopular loser squad for sixteen freakin' years, but in just two weeks you've gotten to know people with strong characteristics like a nun and a shrine maiden! What's goin' on?! Huh? Is this some kinda dating sim, Teach?!"

Blue Hair was deranged and half-crying over something or other, and Kamijou really wanted to give him a good right straight to shut him up. Unfortunately, he was located diagonally across the table, so he was too far away. His rotten luck had even determined the seating arrangement.

"One hundred yen," stated the shrine maiden. She had a difficult expression, like she was worrying about something, and then she raised her face.

"No?"

"No. I can't lend you what I don't have."

"..." She deliberated on this for a moment. "...Tsk. Can't even lend one hundred yen."

"...You're the one not even *carrying* one hundred yen, stupid," responded Kamijou hotly.

"Kamiiii, how can you answer her so *casually*? You're a member of the proven and trusted unpopular loser squad! When faced with a beauty like this, you should be totally nervous and not even able to give her an answer! As a member of the loser squad, it's your destiny!!" Blue Hair sounded like he was struggling to crawl up out of the depths of hell.

"...Beauty."

The priestess's gaze wandered strangely, thinking about something. Then she went, "...For this beauty. Another one hundred yen."

"Argh! Be quiet, you evil woman! A witch who uses her face to get money is not called a beauty! Besides, I already had to buy three milk shakes for no good reason, so I don't have any money left!"

"Th-thank God, Kami! You still believe that all beautiful women have kind hearts, so can I take that to mean your two-dimensional nature is still alive?!"

"...Wait, Touma. If you didn't buy these milk shakes, you'd just hand over one hundred yen and everything would be fine...Is that what you want to say? Hmmm."

The voices flying at Kamijou from all directions were approaching the upper limit of what his brain could deal with at one time. *Aw, jeez, where do I even start?!* he wondered frantically, scratching his head. Index, chomping on the straw of her milk shake with enmity, shot the shrine maiden an inimical gaze.

"Hmph. From your red hakama, I can see you're of the Urabe style. Do Urabe priestesses even use their looks to get by? You know,

I think 'shrine maiden' used to be slang for 'prostitute' during the Heian period."

Kamijou couldn't help but sputter at that one. For now, he figured he'd get Blue Hair to shut up. He seemed to be extremely excited; his eyes were practically shouting, "Aha-ha! This is great! A battle between a western nun and an eastern shrine maiden!"

"Actually. I'm not a shrine maiden."

"Huh?"

Everyone at the table stopped and stared at the black-haired girl. She looked like the picture that would be in an encyclopedia under the entry for *shrine maiden.*

"Umm, if you're not a shrine maiden, then who and what are you, miss?" asked Kamijou, like he was somehow the group leader.

"I'm a magician."

"..."

The table fell silent. He started to hear the television broadcasts in the restaurant coming from miles away. *Wait, what?* thought Kamijou. *I've got amnesia, but for some strange reason, I feel like this has happened before. That's what it feels like. But why is Index shaking like that, is she about to explode?!* he shouted to himself.

Bang! Index passionately slammed the table with both hands.

Before the milk shakes on the tray could spin around and fall over, she demanded, "What do you mean by 'magician'?! Caballa?! Enoch?! A Hermeticist?! Some kind of modern astrologer subscribing to the visions of Mercury?! *Magician* is way too vague! You're supposed to introduce yourself with your specialty, school, magic name, and order name, stupid!"

"???"

"If you didn't even understand any of that, then you mustn't call yourself a sorcerer! Besides, you're an Urabe-style shrine maiden, right? At least brag about being an Asian yin-yang astrologer or something!"

"Okay. Then I'm that."

"What?! What the heck is that supposed to mean?!"

Bang! Bang! Index hit the table a couple more times.

Kamijou sighed and took a look about. The restaurant *was* bustling with activity, but Index's fit of rage was a bit too much. He needed to settle her down and *fast*.

"Okay, fine, the shrine maiden is actually a magician. We get it, so quiet down for a sec—"

"Wha—?! Touma, you acted kind of totally differently for me!"

Index glowered at him like she was about to bite off his head. Unfortunately, without any memories, he couldn't remember what happened in his past. He couldn't just say he didn't recall it, even *if* she was wrong.

"She said it herself, so isn't that enough? Jeez. She's not doing any harm to anyone, and she's not trying to trick us, so leave it alone."

"...Urgh. You're the one who went to the extent of *taking off my clothes* to prove I was the real thing."

"Huh?"

"Nothing! I didn't say anything, and I'm not thinking anything!"

Index jerked her head away from him in a huff. It didn't matter, but under the table, his foot was being smashed into the floor by something. Okay, it did matter. There was only one culprit here, no matter how you thought about it.

"Ah..."

Suddenly, Index grunted, like she had spotted something.

At first, he wondered if it was an employee finally deciding to walk over to give them the red card and kick them out for making such an uproar.

Huh?...People?

The moment he questioned it, **he finally caught on to the fact that approximately ten people had surrounded their table**.

"..............."

Why didn't I see them until now?! he puzzled.

Even though there were ten strong staring at them intently at a distance a waitress might stand at to take their orders, all crowded around their one table, he hadn't been able to notice they were there.

And...

Even now, he saw that not a single other customer in this packed restaurant had even realized anything was wrong.

In other words, they had concealed their presence *just that much*, like assassins.

"..."

Each one of them wore the same suit, and they were all males in their twenties or thirties.

They would have lacked individuality to the point you wouldn't be able to tell their faces or names apart in a train station at peak hours. However, their eyes were without emotion. In return, their **perfect lack of individuality** made it seem like it should be impossible for them to melt into the background like this.

Eyes without...emotion? he thought, swearing he'd seen this before. He returned his gaze to the table...

...and to the shrine maiden in front of him, whose name he didn't even know.

She had been surrounded by almost ten people, and yet her eyes were without emotion as well.

"One hundred more yen," she said.

She rose from her seat without a sound. She didn't look like she was on her guard against *them*. In fact, she displayed the ease of someone waiting for another to come.

One of *them* took a step back to yield the way to the priestess. One of *them* took a hundred-yen coin from the palm of his hand and handed it to her, silently and dutifully.

"Eh, um, what? Do you know these people?"

Kamijou asked in bewilderment.

"..." The shrine maiden let her eyes wander for a bit, like she was considering her next words.

"Yes. My cram school teachers."

Her reply was abrupt and without concern.

She walked down the hallway and headed for the stairs leading to the first floor. The men followed, her shadows and her protectors, without a noise or a voice.

He began to hear the familiar bustle and noise of the music on the television from miles away, as if it had faded.

Once *they* had gone out of sight, Blue Hair finally spoke.

"But why are her salaryman cram school teachers lookin' after her? It ain't like she's an elementary schooler or anything."

3

Summer's evening glow was upon them.

Kamijou and the others goofed off for a while and tired themselves out to forget all about the mysterious shrine maiden and the men in suits. Then, like little kids, they made the decision to go home at the five o'clock chime, and they upheld it.

"Bye-bye!" called Blue Hair, waving his arm in the air to them—indeed like a little kid—before disappearing into the city gleaming in the sunset. Blue Hair didn't live in a student dormitory like Kamijou. Instead, he led the relatively uncommon lifestyle of boarding at a bread shop. Apparently, the uniform used by its employees looked like a maid outfit.

He and Index were left alone in the wide street next to the station, in front of a line of large department stores.

He sighed.

The moment the words *left alone* popped up in the back of his mind, some kind of tingling, nervous feeling reached out from the center of his brain, went down his back, and reached into every nook and cranny in his body.

The reason was obvious.

"Touma, is something the matter?"

The girl beside him was innocently smiling at him. He had no choice but to answer that nothing was wrong. He breathed another sigh, this time quietly enough that she wouldn't hear him.

After all, they were living together.

Secretly, in a male dormitory.

To top it all off, she was such a little girl.

A few days had passed since they returned to the dorms from the hospital, and whenever night came around, Index would lay down and sleep next to him as if it were the natural thing to do. And she never slept well, either. Maybe she couldn't stand the heat, but she would toss and turn all night long, causing her feet, navel, and other things to pop in and out of her pajamas. Kamijou had no recourse but to lock himself into the room's unit bath and cause a shut-in incident for a while. This is why he'd been sleep deprived lately.

"...Was I a terrible enough person to be on the news?" he grumbled to himself tiredly. He wondered about how exactly the old Kamijou had handled this "phenomenon." *But wait, the Kamijou that had my memories was the source of us being roommates in the first place! What the hell were you doing at a time I wouldn't remember, Touma Kamijou?!* he silently shouted at himself.

"Ah!" Index noticed something and ground to a halt.

"Eh?" Kamijou gloomily followed her gaze. At the foot of the pillar of a wind turbine, there was a kitten in a cardboard box, crying out with mewing sounds.

"Touma, it's a—"

"No."

—*cat.* He cut her off before she could continue.

"...Touma, I haven't said anything yet, okay?"

"We're not taking it."

"Why not, how come? Why, why? Why can't we adopt Sphinx?!"

"We live in a student dorm, pets are forbidden, and we don't have money, and why did you already give it a name, and why the heck did you call it Sphinx when it's clearly a noisy Japanese calico?!"

<*"Why don't you keep a cat! Do as you are told!"*>

"???...Hah! Blabbering in English isn't going to make me listen to you!"

"No! I want it, I want it, I want it, I want it, I want it, I want it, I want iiiit!"

"We're not taking it, even if you shout like you're doing some Stand attack I've never seen before! Besides, you scared it away already! It just ran into the alley!"

"It's your fault, Touma!"

"Why me?!"

Graah! The two of them stood there in the summer evening, yelling at each other angrily. Kamijou vaguely thought about this. He asked himself how the Touma Kamijou before his amnesia treated this girl. He came to the conclusion that it was probably something like what he was doing now.

He was happy with that.

But at the same time, it felt a little lonely.

After all, she wasn't looking at him. The soothing, relaxing, splendid smile she would give him was for the *old* Touma Kamijou.

He'd be lying if he said it didn't hurt.

But he still didn't think of giving up on the act.

"Hmph. Japanese shamisens are made from binding cat skin, aren't they? Why does this country do so many horrible things to cats!"

"...Don't start insulting our national culture, stupid! Besides, you British people all chase around foxes and bully the poor things!"

"Wha...? Foxhunting is a proud national tradition, and—!!"

Index was about to growl at him, but all of a sudden, she froze, like she just noticed something.

"Wh-what is it? The cat? Did that cat from before come back?!" Kamijou demanded, looking around. He didn't see anything like a cat anywhere, though.

"...I wonder? Touma, it looks like the flow of mana nearby is being controlled," Index murmured abruptly to him. "...Its attribute is earth, and its color is green. This spell...It uses the ground as a medium for mana, and by interfering with one's awareness, it..."

It sounded like her internal musings were coming out of her mouth as broken phrases.

"What is it?" inquired Kamijou, looking at her carefully.

After a moment, Index breathed one word:

"Runes?"

Then her eyes shone as sharply as the edge of a knife. She ran vigorously to the roadside, toward an alley between two buildings.

"Wa— Hey, Index!"

"Seems like someone set up a magic circle. I'll go check it out, you can go home first!"

Before he could blink, she disappeared into the alley.

"I can go home first…?"

Her weird actions sure do stand out, he thought. However, he certainly couldn't just leave her to her own devices and go home. After all, a young girl had just gone into a suspicious-looking back alley by herself. The encounter rate with some incident in a place like that was probably about the same as a poorly made RPG.

He groaned. His rotten luck was making trouble again.

He was about to follow her in, but then—

"It's good to see you again, Touma Kamijou."

A voice came from behind him.

His feet had started for the alley, but he needed to stop them.

After all, he had heard, "See you again." Those words were pretty much taboo for Kamijou. He hadn't forgotten knowledge like how to speak Japanese or how to do first-grade math. However, his *memories* were another story. When did he buy that video game? What were his final exam grades? Those kinds of memories were all gone without a trace.

When faced with someone he didn't remember in the slightest, claiming that they were seeing each other again, the only thing he could do was respond with the greatest Japanese smile he could manage.

Because to protect the wishes of a certain girl…

…Touma Kamijou must never make anyone aware that he lost his memories.

He turned around.

"Um."

As expected, he didn't have any recollection of the man there.

Actually, he was a young man—a boy, even. The word *boy* seemed a little off, though, given his towering stature of more than two meters tall. Like Index, the man had pale skin that couldn't have belonged to someone Japanese. He was clad in a jet-black habit.

The smell of perfume wafting from this "priest" was over the top, though. His long hair was dyed scarlet, he wore earrings in his ears, he had a silver ring on each of his fingers, and under his right eye, he had a tattoo that looked like a bar code. It all felt *corrupt*, like he was a priest of war or a religious traitor.

There was no reason Kamijou should have recognized him.

In fact, he didn't really *want* to have memories of a man like him.

"Hmph. It's been a while, but you don't even want to greet me, eh? Right, right, that's fine. That's how our relationship *should* be. Just because we fought together one time doesn't mean you can let your guard down."

Despite that being what the perfume-stinking priest *said*, he was smiling quite amicably.

Who the heck is this guy…?

The strangeness of the priest in front of him was one thing, but he felt stronger confusion at the old Touma Kamijou being acquainted with a person this suspicious.

And he had something else on his mind.

Kamijou quickly glanced around toward the alleyway. Index had dove straight in all by herself. He didn't have the time to spare chatting it up with a totally unknown wannabe priest, but…

"Oh, don't worry about the girl. I've engraved Opila runes in that area. She probably just went to locate the flow of mana."

Kamijou didn't know what to say.

Rune magic. Magical Celtic symbols dating back to the second century. Simply put, they were *characters that held power*, so if you wrote "Kenaz" on a piece of paper, then just as the word entailed, flame would spring forth from it.

…What is this?

His throat tightened.

Not because the priest in front of him was talking about this enigmatic runic magic.

But because that enigmatic knowledge was flowing freely out of his own mind, and it didn't even feel out of place.

It was clearly bizarre. It was an odd sentiment, like a rusty bike dropping into the middle of a clean, pure lake, leaving a gaping hole in its wake. Right alongside extremely commonplace knowledge like "you cross the street at a green light" or "it costs money every time you send a text message on a cell phone" was an... **abnormality where magical nonsense was mixed in with his everyday life as if it was natural!**

The Touma Kamijou before he lost his memories...

Just what kind of world did he *live* in?

For the first time since it happened, Touma Kamijou shuddered at his own situation.

"Hmm?"

The priest reeking of cologne shut one eye and grinned slightly like he had noticed something in the color of his face.

Kamijou didn't know what was going on. He didn't have time to spare having a conversation with someone, so for the moment, he smiled vaguely and tried to force back the peculiar feeling.

Suddenly, the red-haired priest took out what looked like a single card.

"Don't smile at everything. Are you ready to die?"

The red-haired priest's grin grew wide, as if it were melting across the face of a waxen puppet.

He shook.

The knowledge inside Kamijou from before his amnesia was warning him of danger, like it sent electricity through him.

"..."

His right hand moved before he could think about it.

He immediately positioned it in front of his face. As it blocked the sunlight pouring into his eyes, a flame burst forth from the palm of the priest's right hand. Like gasoline had erupted from his hand, he created a shining sword of crimson fire in the blink of an eye.

The priest didn't waste a second.

He didn't show a shard of hesitation nor a trace of mercy as he swung the flame sword down mightily toward Kamijou's face.

When the fiery sword made contact it expanded, and flames shot out in all directions like a balloon popping. The fire made a brutal noise as it absorbed oxygen. The hellfire, more than 3,000 degrees Celsius, whirled out and utterly violated their surroundings.

Roar! went the flame, its strength unceasing.

Whoosh...went the flame going out. It was like it had been frozen and smashed in the blink of an eye.

"Hah...hah...!"

Without letting down his right hand he was using for defense, he started breathing raggedly and rapidly.

The Imagine Breaker.

The aberrant ability he knew nothing about that dwelled in his right hand was said to be able to cancel out any irregular power just by touching it, even if it was the power of a miracle.

"Hah...hah...!"

After seeing Kamijou stiff, trembling, and unable to move properly, the priest finally smiled in satisfaction.

"That's it, that's the face. This is the relationship between Touma Kamijou and Stiyl Magnus, right? Don't make me say it again—if you let your guard down just because we fought together one time, you'll be in trouble."

The priest's smile ripped across his face again, melting it, stretching it out.

But Kamijou was unable to answer. It wasn't because he was afraid of the unnatural power his body contained, much less of the priest he was facing down, Stiyl Magnus.

Yes, if it was one thing, it was this:

His own knowledge, his common sense. It had stopped the attack out of reflex, without thinking much at all, and as if it was the obvious solution...even though some crazy flame sword or something had been swung at him.

That was scary.

"Wh...at, are—" Kamijou promptly took two, three steps back. His knowledge—the old Touma Kamijou—had warned him of the threat to his life.

I don't have time to deal with ***the enemy within***, Kamijou thought. *Right now I have to do something about* ***the enemy without***.

"—you trying to do, asshole?!"

Kamijou roared, lowering himself steadily into an unconventional fighting position, a stance so used to brawling it even surprised *him*. Maybe it was thanks to the knowledge soaked into him, too.

In response, the sorcerer in priest clothing smirked.

"Hm? I just want to tell you a secret, why?"

What is he saying? wondered Kamijou...But as he did, Stiyl removed some kind of big envelope from his clothing. It was large and seemed like really important documents were inside. *Is he seriously telling me a secret here?* Kamijou frowned. He wanted to tell him a secret *here*, on this six-lane road wide enough to be an airplane runway, after causing a racket with all those explosions...?

...?

Once he thought that far, he finally realized it.

Even though that explosion had made noise, there was absolutely no sign of commotion.

...?!

No, he thought a step later, looking squarely at the reality.

It wasn't that there was no commotion. There was nobody here in the first place. This six-lane road, with big department stores lined up on the left and right, had emptied of both people and cars without him noticing. No one but he and Stiyl were there.

The *clatter-clatter* of the wind turbine propellers resounded throughout the uninhabited street like the sound of a laughing skull. From extremely far away, he noticed he could hear the sound of a warning siren reaching him from an equally uninhabited railroad crossing. The silence was like the middle of a lake at night.

"I already said—"

Quietly breaking that silence, Stiyl smirked.

"—I engraved runes for Opila, and it's been keeping people away.

"Ehwaz," came Stiyl's voice. He flung the oversize packet he was holding from his index finger like he was flicking a postcard. The thick envelope spun around and around like a Frisbee and slowed as it settled into Kamijou's hands.

A strange symbol was inscribed on the mouth of the envelope like it was some kind of seal.

Stiyl muttered.

"Gebo."

Suddenly, the symbol on the envelope lit up. The seal split to the sides as if cut with a knife.

"Have you heard of a cram school called Misawa?"

Stiyl asked in a singsong voice. The necessary documents flew out of the envelope, and each indeed appeared to have a rune inscribed on it. They floated together in the air before Kamijou's eyes like a flying carpet.

"Misawa...?"

Touma Kamijou had amnesia.

Having precisely zero memories, he could only draw conclusions from the knowledge he had. However, he still didn't have any recollection of a Misawa Cram School. It seemed like the old Touma wasn't too interested in taking university exams.

"At the least, it's apparently the prep school with the most market shares in the nation, but...?"

Stiyl made the suggestion disinterestedly.

A prep school was, as its name suggested, a school for preparing for exams. Think of them as cram schools meant for the "wandering students" who had failed university entrance exams.

In Academy City, the definition of a university preparatory school was a bit more contrived. **It could also refer to a prep school made for people who *were* good enough to get into a university, but who would purposely become wandering students for a year in order to advance to an even *better* university and study for *its* exams instead.**

One of the documents flew nimbly up to Kamijou's eyes.

It seemed that this Misawa Cram School was both *that* kind of university preparatory school *and* it had students who weren't yet wandering. In other words, it also acted as a prep school for normal high schoolers trying to take entrance exams in their senior year.

"...So, what do you want with this Misawa Cram School? Do you get a discount on your student fees if you refer a friend or something?" Kamijou looked at Stiyl with clear distrust; the priest in front of him seemed a bit removed from the concept of prep schools.

"Ah, well—" Stiyl answered in a bored voice.

"—there's a girl being held captive there. It's my job to go and get her out."

Kamijou stared at him, speechless.

Not at the bothersome words *being held captive*. He was doubting this man's *sanity*. No, wait, if Stiyl was simply insane, there wouldn't be a problem. Except there was, because he had the power to freely control magical flamethrowers.

"Hmph. I think you'll figure it out if you take a look at the documents."

Stiyl poked his index finger up again. One after another, more sheets of copy paper flew out of the envelope Kamijou was holding, and like a blizzard they danced around Kamijou and surrounded him.

——This one was a sketched map of Misawa Cram School.

However, there were apparently inconsistencies when compared to a full-scale map measured externally via infrared and ultrasonic waves. There were clearly crooked, hidden rooms in various places on the image, looking like leaves nibbled on by a worm.

——This one was a list of its electricity utilization expenses.

However, the cost didn't add up when all the rooms and electrical appliances were accounted for. Someone somewhere in the building was clearly using a large amount of electricity, away from prying eyes.

——This one was a checklist of people entering and leaving the school.

However, a very large amount of food was being bought in bulk, even considering all the students and teachers. Even if you dressed up like a garbage-collecting janitor and investigated all of the trash cans, the quantity wouldn't add up. It was clearly being eaten by *somebody* in the building.

——And the final sheet.

One month before now, a single girl was witnessed entering the Misawa School building.

As far as her student dormitory caretakers could tell, she hadn't returned to her room since then.

"It seems like the school has turned into a new religion centered on scientific worship," said Stiyl disinterestedly.

Scientific worship...? Kamijou frowned in puzzlement.

"Oh, you mean like those guys who think God is really an alien that came here in a UFO, or like the people who are trying to clone the DNA of saints or what?"

The idea that science and religion don't mix is illogical. There were plenty of followers of Crossism among doctors and scientists in the western world.

At the same time, though, it was true that scientific religions with their backs against the wall caused horrible incidents. After all, they possessed cutting-edge technology. Formulating poison gas or bombs would be simple for them.

Academy City, which was both a place on the leading edge of technology and a place for learning and teaching, was particularly cautious of these scientific religions. This was because, of course, it was an environment for *teaching things*. Even a small slipup in this regard could transform a teaching establishment into a brainwashing factory.

"Well, we don't know what it is they're teaching. And honestly, I don't care a bit about what sort of cult Misawa Cram School has been perverted into. It's already been flopped, after all."

"...?"

"To be frank," Stiyl spat, "the school's been hijacked. A science-crazy scam religion has been hijacked by a genuine, bona fide sorcerer—well, by an alchemist of the Zurich school."

"A bona fide…?"

"Yeah, even as a sorcerer, it sounds dubious… Hey, wait a second."

"What is it?"

"…Aren't you being a little *too* understanding? You're not just letting everything go in one ear and out the other just because you come from a different field, right?"

Kamijou froze.

Not because what Stiyl said hit the mark or anything. Kamijou had been listening to him urgently and seriously, and he was trying to break down words he didn't understand so he could take everything in honestly.

But that's where he felt strange.

He felt like the sorcerer had pointed out a gap between the Touma Kamijou now and the Touma Kamijou then.

Don't let him realize, don't let him realize…!

The Touma Kamijou *right now* didn't know anything about the relationship between the sorcerer in front of him and that girl. But he didn't want anyone to know about his amnesia, no matter who it was.

Kamijou had seen it. He had seen it in the hospital room. He had seen the girl wearing the white habit on the verge of tears. He had seen her face of salvation after **he made her think** the man in front of her was the same Kamijou.

He couldn't bring himself to destroy that salvation.

So Kamijou would trick the world. He'd even try and lie to himself.

"Tsk. I try listening seriously *one time*, and this is what I get? What are you, a masochist? Is that it? Are you the type that can't stand it unless someone interrupts your conversation over and over again?"

But the Touma Kamijou now didn't really understand *how* he was different from the Touma Kamijou then. When you're walking along a road with a map and realize that you've gone astray, and then you look around and get a 360-degree view of a desert, you don't know which direction you should go.

Stiyl stared at Kamijou doubtfully for a moment, but replied.

"Well, whatever. I have no problem with the discussion proceeding smoothly."

Finally, he collected himself and returned to the topic at hand.

"The things that are important are the reasons the alchemist had for hijacking the school. Well, one of them is obvious—he was probably thinking he could reuse the school's original fortresslike systems. Most of the students, or *followers*, haven't even realized that the head of the principal—or *guru*—changed.

"But..." Stiyl drew in a breath.

"The alchemist's original goal is Deep Blood, who was being held captive by Misawa Cram School."

Deep Blood?

Kamijou didn't remember that name, and he didn't appear to have any knowledge of it. But the meaning hidden behind those words was incredibly ominous.

"It seems that she was originally confined there so they could make her act like a shrine maiden. Well, I suppose they're drawing out the high levels using a girl as a pretext, so the term 'shrine maiden' is actually fitting."

"..."

"The point is, the alchemists had been aiming for Deep Blood for some time, but the school was one step ahead of them. Why, it must have been quite a nuisance. Their plan was to steal Deep Blood secretly and flee the city, but then the school made a bold move and ruined everything."

"In other words, they forcefully stole the credit back from the school...?"

So it's like... If a master thief was about to break into a museum after extremely thorough preparations, and then as he was about to steal the painting, the entire museum was suddenly taken over by super-flashy terrorists? Is that it?

The barbaric terrorists wouldn't know the value of art. If the master thief was able to protect that painting from the terrorists, the museum would end up under siege by the police. He wouldn't have any alternative, and he would have to barricade the entrances and hole up in there... Something like that?

"Yeah. Acquiring *it* would be the highest aspiration for an alchemist.... No, if we're going that far, then it would be the greatest wish of all sorcerers. Or perhaps that of all humanity maybe."

"???"

Kamijou gave him a blank expression.

"Deep Blood is an ability meant for killing a *certain creature*. Well, that's not all it is. It's also the one and only chance at capturing one of those *creatures* alive, even though we don't know if they exist."

He still didn't understand.

"In our jargon, these *creatures* are called the 'descendants of Cain,' so."

Stiyl grinned a little, and then made a declaration, conspiratorially this time.

"Putting it simply, I'm talking about vampires."

"Are you serious?"

That was the first thing he thought of to say when he heard the words coming out of Stiyl's mouth.

Vampires. Kamijou didn't know where the legends originated, but he knew a bit about them from video games and manga.

Vampires were weak to crosses and sunlight.

Vampires die when stakes are driven through their hearts.

Vampires turn into ash when they die.

Vampires turn other people into vampires by biting them.

...That was about all he knew. And for some reason, the manga and video games in Kamijou's knowledge were, without exception, the punk-action variety where the slightest respect wasn't paid to the cross.

However, Stiyl grimaced and averted his gaze, saying, "...Things were happy and easy when we could still joke about it."

Despite the sorcerer being able to control flame like that, he almost seemed *afraid*.

"Hmph. Deep Blood is a power for killing vampires. Since *that* exists, it wouldn't make sense unless those vampires *also* existed. It's like that vicious cycle where a villain is required for someone to be a hero of justice, but anyway, this one thing is definitely true.... Even I'd deny it if I could."

"...Wait, what's that mean? Are you saying those vampires from picture books actually exist?"

Kamijou's brain denied it.

But for all his rejection, this man was giving off an air that was far too grave.

"No one has ever seen one..."

Stiyl Magnus sang, as if he was a big ball of confidence.

"...because anyone who does, dies."

"..."

"Of course, even I won't believe this blindly. No one has seen one, and yet the existence of Deep Blood proves them. That's the problem. We don't know how strong they are, or how many there are, or where they are. We don't know, we don't know anything. And we can't do anything about something we don't understand."

Stiyl repeated like he was singing, but Kamijou couldn't process the word *vampire*, so he wasn't really getting the sense they were real. *Well, I guess it's like trying to take on unseen terrorists scattered around the world*, he translated for himself.

"But for everything we don't know about, there are also unknown possibilities." Stiyl grinned cynically. "Touma Kamijou, have you ever heard the term Sephirothic Tree— No, I suppose you wouldn't have."

"...You know, you're not gonna get on my nerves by saying stuff like that."

"Fine. The Sephirothic Tree is a hierarchical diagram that displays the spiritual rank of God, angels, and humans. In a few words, it tells you things like where a human can ascend to if one trains hard enough, while anything past that is unattainable."

"...Look at you, belittling people like that. What are you trying to say?"

"Did that get to you? What I want to say is that **there is a height that humans cannot reach, no matter how hard they try**. But human nature is to want to reach it anyway. Sorcerers exist precisely because of that. So what should we do?"

Stiyl's cynical grin widened across his face like it was tearing it in half.

"It's simple. We just have to borrow the power of something inhuman."

Kamijou couldn't say anything.

"Vampires are immortal, after all. Even if you were to gouge out one's heart and implant it in a magic sword, it would keep living. I guess it would be kind of like a living magic item?" Stiyl explained. "Whether or not it's true doesn't matter. Scholars will try it if there's even the slightest possibility," he growled.

In other words, this is what Stiyl was trying to say.

It didn't matter whether or not vampires actually existed. What was important was that there were people who would cause trouble because they believed in them. And now that an incident *had* occurred, someone had to resolve it. That was the important part.

"So then we still don't really know if vampires exist?"

He felt like there were a ton of action flicks with people going around fighting over ancient treasures they were uncertain of. But when presented with this in real life, he couldn't think of a more stupid story.

"It's originally our job to handle occult things whose existence is uncertain, so." However, Stiyl flashed a bitter grin. "Both Misawa Cram School and our alchemist seem serious, you know? They're *seriously* playing a game over these vampires. Someone like Deep Blood is necessary because they need a trump card."

"..."

"And do you know Deep Blood's background? The kid apparently used to live in a mountain village in Kyoto, but the village was wiped out one day. The last reported villager was apparently deranged, saying that he was going to be killed by a monster. After that, the story is that people who rode out to the village found it deserted save for a single girl, standing there alone, and white ash, blowing around like a blizzard and blanketing the village."

Ash.

Vampires turn into ash when they die.

"I mean, vampires are things we're not sure exist, after all. But think about it. Deep Blood is the power to kill vampires. Therefore, Deep Blood must first meet a vampire. If one wishes to encounter a vampire, regardless of how pure one's intentions were, the best thing to do would be to first gain control over Deep Blood, right?...Of course, I think actually *controlling* the owner of a power immense enough to kill vampires would be a big problem in itself."

This conversation might as well have been taking place on an alien planet at this point.

Kamijou's instincts informed him that it would be dangerous to hear him out any longer. *I feel like if I listen to this guy anymore, it's gonna screw with my common sense real fast.* He even got the distinct feeling that the conversation proceeding like this would mess things up beyond the point of no return.

He quickly asked a question so he could cut the conversation short.

"So, you've been talking about all these *secrets* for a while now, but what exactly did you need to tell me?"

"Ah, right. Neither of us has much time, so let's finish up here." Stiyl nodded twice to himself, pleased. "...Well, frankly, I'm in a situation where I must go raid Misawa Cram School now and get Deep Blood out of there."

"Okay," nodded Kamijou easily. However...

"I wish you wouldn't nod so easily. You're coming along, too."

....

....

"Huh?! What did you just say?!"

"The simple truth. Oh, and that before was the briefing. You remember everything we talked about, right? As for the documents, they have Kenaz runes on 'em, so they'll burn up after you finish reading them. You'll get yourself into trouble if you slack off on memorizing them."

"Wha—?!"

Is this some kind of joke?! he thought. This Stiyl person wouldn't hesitate to kill a man, and he had the most suitable power to do it. If Kamijou snuck into the headquarters of this enemy "alchemist" or whatever the hell it was, he could end up getting involved in a murder incident.

"Oh, and one more thing," said Stiyl in an emotionless voice. "I don't think you have the right to refuse. If you don't obey, things will move in the direction of my taking Index away from you."

"!"

Crunch. For some reason, he could almost hear those words stabbing into his heart.

His knowledge—the remnant of the old Touma Kamijou—was terrified of something.

"The job Necessarius has handed down to you is to be her leash, to prevent her from turning traitor, since her 'collar' was removed. But if you don't obey the will of the Church, then they can't trust that to work." Stiyl sighed. "But, well, personally, if the Church considers you *unnecessary*, then it helps me out. I'd be grateful, even. Thank you! Because a leash that doesn't work means nothing. I would be able to recover her with no worries."

That was a threat.

Blackmail that the girl close by him would be harmed if he didn't obey.

"..."

Thump. His own pulse violently pounded on his heart like it was a hammer driving a nail. Touma Kamijou had no memories. Even if the old him was the one who met that girl for the first time, it didn't have anything to do with him now. His heartbeat was acting up, and he was losing the ability to think. It must have been because of what remained in him from before his amnesia. It shouldn't have been related to him *now* at all.

So then...

Why?

"...Are you freaking serious, asshole?"

Why could he have so much faith that the fury he felt was *justified*?

He wondered about it.

He had certainly met Index before he lost his memories. The Kamijou who Index trusted and smiled at wasn't the Kamijou who was here now.

But he thought that was okay.

The girl he had met in that white hospital room had looked at the wounded Kamijou and cried...

If it would prevent her tears, then...

He swore to uphold his lie, even if he had to fool the world and deceive himself...!

"...Hmph."

Stiyl looked away, disinterested.

His face looked like someone whose job had been stolen. Kamijou would be lying if he said it wasn't weird.

"If it's killing each other that you want, then let's leave it until we deal with the alchemist lurking in Misawa Cram School. Also, I forgot to mention something. Deep Blood's real name is Aisa Himegami. There's a photo of her in there, so make sure you know what she looks like. You'd be at a loss if you didn't know the face of the person you were trying to rescue."

A single photograph slid down out of the envelope.

Supported by Stiyl's runes as well, it fluttered through the air and came to a stop right in front of Kamijou's face.

He looked at it.

He thought about what the face of Deep Blood, an esper with such a dangerous-sounding name, looked like.

And there was the face of the shrine maiden he had met this afternoon.

* * *

"Huh...?"

Kamijou caught his breath.

The picture looked like a blown-up student ID photograph or something. It was definitely the face of Aisa Himegami, the priestess from this afternoon.

Kamijou remembered what Stiyl had said.

"It seems that she was originally confined there so they could make her act like a shrine maiden."

Kamijou remembered what the girl from this afternoon had said.

"Actually. I'm not a shrine maiden."

Kamijou remembered what the sorcerer had said.

"There's a girl being held captive there. It's my job to go and get her out."

Kamijou remembered what Aisa Himegami had said.

"Yes. My cram school teachers."

"...!"

But why..., he thought. From what Stiyl had said, Aisa Himegami would have been imprisoned in the school. If that shrine maiden *was* Deep Blood, then why on earth was she hanging out in a fast-food restaurant, passed out from overeating?

"The return fare. It's four hundred yen."

Could she have been running away? he asked himself. She was supposed to be locked up, so if she was outside, then she must have been fleeing from Misawa.

"Total possessions. Three hundred yen."

Thinking of that brought him to Himegami's lack of money on hand. She had hurried to escape with only the clothes on her back. If she continued to take public transportation like trains and buses, her money would obviously run low.

But then why was she in a fast-food restaurant? he thought. If she had run out of there like hell, what reason could she have had for relaxing in a place like—

"I stuffed myself."

"Ah!"

Suddenly, Kamijou remembered her saying that.

What if her money had already run out, and she couldn't flee any longer? What if she was just trying to have one last good time at the end?

She had said she wanted to borrow one hundred more yen.

Was that because she had a chance of getting away for good if she only had one hundred more yen?

That's why... Her one and only wish. Who was the moron who ruined it for her?

"That's why I stuffed myself."

"Damn... it..."

On top of that, Himegami hadn't shown any resistance at all when she was hemmed in by the teachers from her cram school. She obviously must have *wanted* to resist. She had run in desperation away from the school, so she couldn't have been okay with being brought back like that.

The first thing a normal person would do is run away.

If running away alone wasn't going to work, then they would ask another person for help.

But...

Asking someone for help would have meant getting them wrapped up in trouble.

"Goddamn it... !!"

He was angry. He was so angry he could barely think. Angry at the Misawa Cram School for imprisoning a girl like some sort of object, angry at the alchemists who had come to snatch her away, and angry at Stiyl who had said Deep Blood was a trump card to put a collar on vampires.

But the thing he was the most mad about was that Aisa Himegami had ignored her own well-being to protect him.

Because that was wrong. If Kamijou had paid her just one hundred yen, it could have changed her whole life. But she chose to be dragged back to the school in order to save him, the one who destroyed her last hope. That was wrong.

He hadn't the faintest idea what kind of new age religion it was.

But she was just one girl. He couldn't imagine what kind of treatment she was getting, imprisoned somewhere like that. He didn't *want* to imagine it, either.

Kamijou should have been the one to feel that pain.

Why did you go and—

Kamijou bit his lip. He tasted blood clinging to his front teeth.

—put someone in your debt like that?!

That was what made him the angriest when he thought about it. His head felt like it would boil over just because of it.

There were no "memories" in Kamijou.

But that way of life... The belief that it was okay to be treated as an object by everything around you... The pattern of thinking that said there was true happiness in saving others while disregarding your own pain...

The lone girl suffered for the sake of others and smiled anyway.

Before...

He had a feeling he had met a girl like that before, and he got frustrated with himself for not being able to remember it.

There was no way he wouldn't go and save her.

Because he felt like... He had to punch Aisa Himegami hard once for all the selfish things she'd done.

INTERLUDE ONE

——A girl was standing in an ocean of ashes.

It happened ten years ago.

The First Lancers, one of the thirteen knight brigades of English Puritanism, departed for a mission to "inspect the enemy headquarters faster than anyone else" in accordance with its founding principles.

This time, the designated "enemy headquarters" was a small village on an eastern island nation, in the mountains of Kyoto. Their routine mission was to determine the identity of abnormally inflated mana flows, and if there was malicious intent behind one, to eliminate it.

——Six hours after all communications from the mountain village in Kyoto had ceased…

——Three hours after the police officers who went to check on it went missing…

Everyone knew the village in question here was probably already completely destroyed. At the same time, however, that wasn't anything extraordinary. In England was the British Museum, or the Arsenal—a blood altar onto which the divine treasures pillaged from all over the world were gathered. Compared to the angered ancient kings who dwelled in those treasures turning against their captors, the danger level was low.

Their provided equipment was light as well, including only the usual Surgical Armor and cross lances, without even any Longinus replicas. A sacred suit of armor, the Surgical Armor could direct mana throughout itself and heighten the wearer's mobility by twenty times. It could be called a first-class Soul Arm, but it was clear to everyone that the big shots involved didn't feel any sort of threat from this situation.

But even that was but a trifle. There was something to bother them.

Something like this had been in the final message of a survivor who had used a telephone:

"Pl—se, he—. That thin—isn't huma—it's a—."

No one believed, of course.

Even the higher-ups in the Church didn't treat it as true, which is why they hadn't given them decent equipment.

But a somehow unpleasant, heavy pressure was growing in every member of the First Lancers, which had a long record of service.

The creature. Though there were at least old records remaining in the British National Library, no one had ever seen this particular *creature*, and the very concept of *capturing* one was nonexistent. Why had the presence of this uncertain *creature* been denied until today? The answer to that was the clear reason for the pressure they felt themselves under.

It was because the world would have ended long ago if a being like that existed.

It wasn't this *creature*'s physical strength that was scary. If an enemy's physical strength is unmatchable, humans will use something other than physical strength to defeat it. That's why humans had created many different kinds of tools, weapons, and armaments.

It wasn't this *creature*'s immortality that was scary. If an enemy doesn't die when killed, then one just had to find a way to defeat it without killing it—for example, by imprisoning it below the permafrost of Antarctica or by dismantling its invulnerable body into two hundred pieces and bottling it up.

These things weren't the problem.

The problem was the vast amount of mana these *creatures* were implied to possess.

Mana, in terms of sorcery, could be compared to simple gasoline.

You would refine the crude oil in your body—your life span and life force—into gasoline that was easier to use. Humans possess only a limited life span to begin with, so the difference between someone with strong and weak magical power was nothing more than whether the person was good or bad at this refinement.

However, that didn't apply to these *creatures.*

The life span and life force that acted as their crude oil was on a fundamentally different level. No, not on a different level—their life force was literally *infinite.* Naturally, this also created a difference in the magic they can use. There is no way that a handgun with a limited number of bullets can rival an uncountable number of missiles attacking you.

Therefore, the First Lancers laughed off their unease but were unable to wipe it away completely.

And when they pushed their way through the vegetation and arrived at the mountain village left behind by the ages, what they saw crushed their hearts in a death grip.

Pure white ashes as far as the eye could see.

A blizzard of white ash was raging in the eastern village left behind by the ages. The roofs of the houses, the soil of the paddies, and the slender farm roads were all covered in a thin, thin layer of ash.

Ash.

Was it... the remains of that *creature*?

However, that wasn't what surprised them. If they *were* remains, there were enough for more than just ten or twenty, but even that couldn't stand up to the scene before them.

In the center of the tempest stood a single girl.

If they were to guess at her age, she must have been no more than five or six, and she had the black hair characteristic of Asians. But despite seeing her sweet face, the very souls of the knights who came to destroy the heresy were frozen.

Even those *creatures* plaguing the village had been annihilated and turned into an ashen maelstrom...

But despite being in this hell, the girl didn't have a scratch on her.

The wind danced, and the ashes fluttered.

As if there was a sanctuary surrounding her, the ashes didn't come close to her, despite the turmoil storming about and burying the mountain-encircled village. It was as if the ashes, though dead, were avoiding her out of fear.

"I—" said the girl…

"—I killed again, didn't I?"

…in a voice as though this was normal for her.

CHAPTER 2

Witch-Hunting with Fire
By_the_Holy_Rood...

1

He decided to think about the girl named Index.

Kamijou's "knowledge" said that she had a trait called perfect recall, where she would never forget anything she learned. Using that trait, she had recorded 103,000 grimoires in her brain.

It was a double-edged sword. Never forgetting meant that she would also never forget anything she *wanted* to. From a three-year-old supermarket flyer to each and every face of the people she passed by at the station during rush hour, every meaningless memory constantly accumulated in her head, since she couldn't remove them from her brain.

To deal with this, she had to use magic to erase all her own memories once a year. If she didn't do that, her brain would blow out and she'd die.

However, right now she was somehow relaxing next to Kamijou, smiling and such.

According to her story, it was Kamijou himself who'd saved her from that hopeless situation. But he didn't understand what he had felt at the time, and he didn't know what he had done.

Now then, thought Kamijou.

He and Stiyl had parted for the time being. Kamijou had brought Index back to his dorm, but he had to leave again to head to the Misawa Cram School battlefield. Taking Index along was out of the question, so the smarter option would be to hide the fact he was going there altogether.

But if he said he was going out for a while and didn't give a reason, she would suspect something was up. She might insist on coming with him.

"Touma?"

Sweat was beading up on his palms.

He might not return alive. Obviously, he could never, ever bring Index somewhere like that.

"Hey, Touma?"

So things were simple.

For the moment, he swallowed his anxiety and made up his mind to start ranting like crazy.

"I have to go to a super-high-tech primary culture institute for a bit. What, you want to come? You'd better not; you're hopeless with machines, and you probably don't even know how to work a super-magnetic cerebral cortex detector. Which would mean you would get trapped in there by the auto-locking doors, since they're security Level Four. Plus, if you investigate basic solutions without registering the exons first, you'll get shocked with electricity, like a zapping negative ion beeeeaaam!!"

Just as he expected, Index let out a yelp, overloaded at the flurry of technical terms.

It was understandable. This was Index. She had so little modern sense that she would involuntarily bow to the ticket vending machines at the station, saying, "Welcome!"

"Then I'm going out. Dinner is in the refrigerator, so nuke it later to eat. And don't stick your spoon in the microwave and play with the sparks, or open the fridge door to cool yourself off, or anything like that."

"Huh? Oh, uh...I think I might be bad at microwaves."

Some people might not understand what a person could possibly do wrong when using a microwave. Index, however, had shown him various ways of messing this up, like blowing up the dressing packet in a convenience store bento box by microwaving it while still in the wrapper, exploding soft-boiled eggs while trying to prepare them, melting a bento box by overheating it…Anyway, it always ended with a *bang*. Maybe she had mistakenly taught herself that microwaves are machines for making things blow up?

…At least it doesn't look like I need to worry about seeming suspicious.

Kamijou sighed at Index, who was having a staring contest with the microwave, as if to say that this time she wouldn't fail.

And then he realized something.

"Hey. What's that you've got in your clothes? More precisely, around your stomach."

"Huh?" Index looked at Kamijou, startled. "I-I'm not hiding anything, okay? I promise you, in the name of our father in heaven, and nuns can't tell lies, after all!"

As soon as she finished saying that, he heard a kitten's mew from Index's stomach.

"Graah! And you call yourself pious?! You totally just broke your promise! Whatever, just take out that stray cat you're hiding in your clothes!"

He hadn't noticed it at the time because of the excitement during his talk with Stiyl, but now he got the feeling that Index had been in the alley for kind of a while. She had said something about runes, but she must have switched her mission to searching for the stray cat partway through.

"Mgh. T-Touma, these clothes are called the Walking Church, okay?"

"So what?"

"Churches extend the hand of salvation to lost sheep without expecting anything in return. Therefore, I took in Sphinx, who was adrift in the streets, by the hand of the Church. Amen!"

"…" Kamijou's lips pulled back. "…So you're gonna raise a stray

cat inside there, then. Okay, got it. So I just pour the cat litter down your collar, I take it?"

"..."

"..."

"I-it's fine! I already decided that the Church will give shelter to Sphinx!"

"Whoa, you really can't plan anything, can you? At least think about your duty to another living creature's life!"

"If we raise it like family, then it'll be fine!"

"That cat has no right to call me Daddy!"

It'll leave a bad taste in my mouth, but I'll probably have to dump the stray cat on my way to Misawa School, reflected Kamijou... But he was pretty sure if he did that, Index would 100 percent come after him in order to get the stray cat back.

"Stupid! Stupid Touma! I already decided I'm definitely going to take care of this cat!"

"... You should wait until you can earn money on your own to say dumb stuff like that."

"But don't worry! You're only stupid in hiragana!"

"Listen to me! Wait, what the hell does that mean?!"

On the other hand, though, he got the feeling that Index would back off if he decided she could keep the cat.

... How should I put this... What rotten luck.

Kamijou sighed in defeat. When he thought about what the stray cat's food would cost, he realized he would have to go with one less dish at dinner per day from now on. He was seriously exhausted. *Really, of all the things, of all the times, why did she pick up a stupid stray cat?* he thought.

"..Okay."

"Huh? Touma, did you say something?"

"... I give up, so you can keep it, okay?"

But, well...

Index looked happy enough to shed a tear at that simple sentence. That made him think that, well, maybe it was okay.

"O Lord in heaven! It seems that your warm light has finally reached the heartless, cruel, sadistic, snake-like Touma. I will never forget your blessing that saved this single cat's innocent soul!"

...That's what he was *thinking*, but for some reason, he didn't quite find this satisfying.

2

When he left his room, he saw Stiyl hanging up things that looked like trading cards around the hallway, even though he thought they had gone their separate ways earlier.

"Uh, what are you doing?"

"As you can see, I'm spreading a barrier and building up a temple here," answered Stiyl without stopping his work. "Since we can't be certain that some other sorcerer won't make a move on Index while we're preoccupied with Misawa. Well, I think it's merely *temporary* peace of mind, but optimistically, leaving Innocentius here should at least buy her time to escape."

Innocentius, the Witch-Hunter King.

Kamijou had no "record" of it. But his *knowledge* spoke of it. An ultimate weapon in the shape of a person, it had an automatic pursuit ability, and its form was made from flames burning at more than 3,000 degrees Celsius. Its weak point was—

"—you can't use it unless it's inside the 'barrier' of the runes you spread, and it will fall apart if they're destroyed, right?"

"...Let me tell you something." Stiyl's ears twitched. "That definitely doesn't mean that my power is inferior to yours. There just happened to be a geographic problem. If it had been somewhere without sprinklers..."

"Huh? Have we gotten into a fight before?"

Kamijou only possessed knowledge, not memory. He understood how to defeat Innocentius but not where he learned that information.

"Ugh...It wasn't even worth remembering in the first place? Is that what you're saying?" Stiyl moved along the conversation, having misunderstood something. "Well, fine. Once I put up one last rune, the barrier will be fully prepared, and then we can head for our primary objective....Man, what a pain. This is an anti-sorcerer barrier, but if I make it too strong, she'll end up noticing it."

Despite Stiyl griping to himself, he looked pretty happy for some reason.

That made Kamijou realize something.

"Wait, are you in love with Index?"

"Bwha?!" Stiyl's face went beet red like his heart had been flipped over. "Wh-wh-what are you talking about all of a sudden?! Sh-she's an object to be *protected*, a-and definitely not an object of romantic interest———!"

"Is that so?" Kamijou cut off the topic, grinning.

He stopped because he detected that prying into this carelessly would mean his ruin. It wasn't a matter of how Kamijou thought of Index right *now*, but he'd end up in a tight spot if there was a discrepancy between that and what he thought prior to his memory loss.

He hadn't the slightest idea how he'd felt about Index before his amnesia or how he'd treated her.

If he was to say something carelessly and there was an inconsistency between that and what the old Touma Kamijou had said, it could reveal that he had lost his memories.

It's like there're two of me..., he thought, agitated. "Two of himself" didn't quite have the right connotation, either. He actually felt a sense of *comedy*, like he was a fake who had been swapped in, who was desperately pretending to be the real thing.

"All right, then before we head for Misawa Cram School, I should fill you in on the *enemy*," continued Stiyl, who might have been trying to redirect the conversation away from that topic to avoid further questioning.

They exited the dormitories. As they walked through the streets in the evening light, Kamijou decided to hear him out.

* * *

"The enemy's name, see, is Aureolus Isard," began Stiyl.

"There's only one person named Aureolus, but...Yes? What, surprised because it's such a famous name? This one is only a descendant, though. He doesn't have the kind of power you hear about in legends."

"? Wait, so who is this Arr-ray-oh-lus guy?"

"...I see. I forgot you were completely oblivious to *our* affairs. But surely you've at least heard the term Paracelsus, right?"

"???"

"Argh...! It's the name of one of the most well-known alchemists in the world!"

Stiyl explained, exasperated.

Kamijou listened as they walked through the dusky roads.

"So, does that mean he's crazy strong?"

The windows of the buildings and the propellers on the wind turbines, along with everything else, were painted in orange, as if the August twilight were burning into them. *Looks kinda like a faded photograph*, Kamijou noted, perhaps because their own conversation was so out of this world.

"It's not a big deal in and of itself...But he did get his hands on *something* that's letting him suppress Deep Blood, after all. And I don't want to think this...but in the worst case, he might be using her to tame the *creature*."

That seemed to worry Stiyl more than Aureolus Isard.

Kamijou couldn't accept that, though. However unique this situation was, he didn't feel like it was right to consider their actual *enemy* to be only secondary.

"Hey, is it okay to think like that? I dunno how irregular these vampires or Deep Blood are, but shouldn't we be focusing on the enemy leader? Say you're fighting someone with fire all around you. If you let the fire distract you, you'll get your face beaten in."

"Hm? Ah, no, that's actually nothing to worry about. The Aureolus from myths might be top class, but his strength has waned.

Alchemist isn't a profession in the world of magic in the first place," Stiyl pointed out, bored. "Astrology, alchemy, summoning... In your words, those are just language, mathematics, and history. Even language teachers study *some* math, right? If you're a sorcerer, then first you sink your teeth into everything and then find a specialized field that suits you. That's basic.

"However, Aureolus Isard is only called an *alchemist* because he has no other talent besides that," Stiyl said.

"And also... alchemy itself isn't even a completed field of study to begin with."

"..."

Even after this explanation, Kamijou only had sort of a point on a historical time line about alchemy in his knowledge. It was a method of fraud used widely in the sixteenth century, where people took in large amounts of money by playing tricks on royalty and nobility.

"Alchemy, particularly that of late Zurich, is an imitator of a subject called Hermeticism. In general, though, people know it as more like... something to turn lead into gold or to synthesize an elixir of immortality."

Stiyl didn't sound interested. Maybe because it wasn't his own vocation.

"**Those were nothing more than experiments.** The reason scientists constantly consult testers is because they want to know about whatever theorem or law. Those testers aren't in it to create something, right? Alchemists are the same—their essence isn't one of *creation* but of *knowing*."

"... So it's like how Einstein's goal was to study the theory of relativity, and the nuclear bomb was just an extra by-product?"

If that was the case, he felt like scholars were an arrogant bunch. They create things, and yet they never consider the effect they would have on the world. The term for that was *madman*.

"That's about right. But beyond studying formulas and theorems, they have another, ultimate goal." Stiyl paused for a breath. "———It's to simulate the entire world inside their mind."

"..."

"If you understand every law of the world, then you can create a perfect simulation in your brain. Of course, if you get even a single massive law wrong, it'll distort your internal image."

"??? What? You mean like theoretical modeling?"

Something like, for example, how on southern islands like Fiji or Melanesia, a requirement to become its chief was to have the talent to accurately predict the next day's weather.

At first glance, this "weather forecast" seems like a supernatural ability. In reality, though, the person is unconsciously sensing wind currents, the shapes of the clouds, the temperature, the humidity, and other things. The forecast is simply the result of repeating massive calculations in your head. The island chiefs are totally ignorant of these unconscious measurements, so they accurately predict the next day's weather just by "listening to the voices of the wind."

Stiyl was definitely saying something along those lines.

The island chiefs were perfectly simulating the next day's weather. However, the world they envisioned was imaginary—one which would crumble if those perfect calculations were even the slightest bit off.

"...But what use would something like that have? Do they want some calculator that predicts the future? Like weather forecasting?"

"Nope, that's not it," Stiyl said angrily.

"What do you think would happen if, hypothetically, you could drag what you pictured in your head into the real world?" he asked.

"Bringing something you picture in your mind into the real world, such as ectoplasm or using a telesmatic image to summon an angel, isn't really an unusual method in the world of magic." Stiyl folded his arms. "Therefore, the power to imagine an accurate world has huge consequences. In simple terms, you'd be able to use everything in the world like your own hands and feet, even gods and devils."

"...Wait."

"Of course, it is extremely difficult. The flow of water, the flow of clouds, the flow of people, the flow of blood—the universe contains an endless number of laws governing such important things. If you get just one of those wrong, you can't construct the world in your mind. A warped world is the same as a warped wing—as soon as you summoned it, it would destroy itself and vanish."

I guess that part is like a computer program, thought Kamijou. *However beautiful the program is, forgetting to write just one line will cause an error and it'll crash.*

"But on the other hand, **wouldn't we be completely helpless if he perfected it?** You sure as hell can't win against the entire *world.*"

He could only state that opinion with relative ease because deep down, Kamijou didn't believe any of this.

However, a human doesn't have the power to win against the entire world. Not because gods or devils are overwhelmingly strong or anything.

It was because **the entire world includes you, yourself, who lives there.**

It was a simple fact. Imagine a mysterious mirror that you could drag reflections out of. However strong Kamijou was to become, if he pulled out an exact copy, they'd just end up defeating each other.

But despite that, Stiyl didn't look that tense.

"I already told you, it's fine. **As a field of study, alchemy is still incomplete.**"

"Huh?"

"For example, consider everything in this world...from every single grain of sand on the beach to every last star in the night sky. If you wanted to talk about them all, how many years do you think it would take you? I don't think it's something you could finish doing in one or two hundred years."

"..."

"That's what I mean. **The incantation itself is complete.** But a human's lifetime is too short to recite the whole thing," Stiyl hissed. "Though there are people trying all sorts of things to accomplish it. For example, by trying to omit needless parts to shorten it as much as they can. Or by dividing one hundred spells into ten parts, then passing those down from father to child, and child to grandchild, chanting it a little at a time."

Despite that, there were apparently no examples of success.

No needless parts exist in a finished spell in the first place, and passing it from parent to child and child to grandchild would **distort the incantation** like a game of telephone.

"On the other hand—" For the first time, Stiyl seemed to be showing a spirit to battle. "—**a creature without a life span can chant spells that are too long for humans.** Yet another reason this *creature* presents an imposing threat to sorcerers."

Perhaps that is why he wanted a vampire, thought Kamijou.

For scholars, it was probably agonizing to know the answer but not be able to prove it.

And if it was a wish a person's body wouldn't grant…

You just had to insert something outside the category of *person* into the magic.

"Well, alchemy is certainly a threat, but Aureolus Isard doesn't currently have the capacity to master it. The best he can do is make stuff… He's got his hands full just fortifying Misawa School, the setting for all this, and setting up a million traps to deny intruders."

"…?"

Stiyl said that with an awful lot of confidence. Kamijou got the feeling something was odd.

"What, do you and Isard know each other?"

"Well, yeah. We both belong to the same religion, after all," he snarled. "I'm with English Puritanism, and he was with the Roman Orthodox Church… We belonged to different denominations, but we're acquainted. We're not friends, though."

The way *church* and *sorcerer* sounded didn't quite fit for Kamijou.

The Church of Necessary Evils, Necessarius, which Stiyl and Index belonged to, aimed to kill sorcerers by studying magic. But that was completely heretical. Even if English Puritanism recognized it, he didn't think a different denomination—Roman Orthodox—would have the same kind of agency…

When Kamijou expressed all this, Stiyl raised an eyebrow slightly.

"Necessarius is an exception among exceptions. It'd be impossible for other churches."

Stiyl sighed as if bored.

"If we're an exception among exceptions, then he's a special case among special cases: a Cancellarius. To sum it up, a Cancellarius is someone who writes grimoires for the Church. He's creating the same kind of books, but they're used in the opposite way. They're instruction manuals that say things like 'lately, witches have been using this sort of spell, so to combat it, read whatever page of the Bible.'" Stiyl fluttered his hand in the air. "It's not strange for people of the Church to write books to warn people about these things. The grimoires of Pope Honorius III and James I are a couple of the really famous ones, I think."

"...I get it. So that's why you keep on saying Aureolus Isard's ability is no big deal."

"Right. He has knowledge in abundance, but none of it is suited for actual combat. He's a bookworm, not a jock. But at the same time, he's also an annoying opponent. He's one of the few Cancellarii even within Roman Orthodox, and he has a lot of influence. The Roman Orthodox Church is actually getting up at arms in order to punish his *betrayal.*"

"No, not that. Aureolus is, like, as important as popes and kings, right? Could you maybe be jealous of him?"

"...So, in other words, you're trying to pick a fight with me?"

"I love myself a good brawl, but don't mistake who we're fighting here." Kamijou looked ahead. "I can see the battlefield."

The two of them stopped.

The building was prepared for them, illuminated by the evening glow.

3

"But, well...," murmured Kamijou, looking up at the building.

An "irregularly shaped building" would be a good way to put it. Well, the building itself was a perfectly ordinary, rectangular, twelve-story tower. However, there were *four* of them. An intersection sat in the middle, and the placement made the entire structure a square

with a cross in the middle when looked at from above. Raised passages straddled adjacent buildings, connecting them to one another.

That's gotta be in violation of the Land Plot Town Planning Law, thought Kamijou as he viewed the aerial walkways. In general, the rights to the sky belong to the possessor of the land underneath. In other words, anything above the road should be public property.

"Well, not like any of that matters," he thought aloud, running his eyes over the four-building Misawa Cram School Academy City branch school again.

Based on what he heard, as an outsider, it didn't give him the unconventional impression he thought a scientific religion would. It was a totally normal university prep school, pure and simple. Even the students entering and exiting from time to time didn't present anything that seemed out of the ordinary.

"In any case, our first destination is the fifth floor in the south building—next to the cafeteria. There's apparently a hidden room there," grunted Stiyl, relaxed. The map sketches had been lit on fire after Kamijou had looked over them. Did that mean he had the whole thing all up in his head?

"A hidden room?"

"Yeah. I think that more than likely, it uses illusions or trick art to conceal itself from the people inside. That building has more holes in it than a house of building blocks made by a child." Stiyl stared at the building. "...There're seventeen, just from checking the plans. I'm trying to say that the closest one is on the fifth story of the southern building, beside the cafeteria."

"...Hmm. It doesn't *look* like a suspicious ninja mansion or anything," Kamijou grunted without any real reason. Stiyl muttered to himself alongside him, annoyed.

"...It doesn't look suspicious, huh."

"Yeah?"

Kamijou looked at Stiyl. His eyes were on the buildings piercing up through heaven and earth, but he finally shook his head, like he was taking a breath.

"Don't worry about it. Even though I'm a specialist, I can't spot anything dubious. I can't spot anything dubious, even though I, a specialist, am looking at it *quite* carefully."

Despite saying that, Stiyl didn't look too happy as he watched the school. It was like he was a doctor, clearly looking at something abnormal in an X-ray and yet unable to find the affected body part.

"..."

That was weird. He didn't really know why, but it was really weird.

Stiyl was saying, "I can't spot anything dubious," but that didn't mean he was asserting that there *were no dangerous places in this building.* He actually couldn't tell one way or the other. There could be tons of unseen land mines buried in there, or maybe there wasn't anything at all. It was a black box.

But if this facility was dangerous enough to light a fire in a master sorcerer's heart, then should they really just be walking on in without a care in the world?

"Of course, it's not okay," Stiyl answered quickly. "But we have to go in, don't we? We're here to rescue someone, not kill someone. I mean, if you told me it was okay to just burn the entire building down, that'd be a load off *my* shoulders," he explained, doubtlessly more than half-serious.

"We have to go in... Hey, wait a second. We're gonna go pay them a visit through the front door? Don't you have some kind of *actual* plan, like a way to invade without anyone noticing or a way to safely defeat the enemy?!"

"What. Do *you* have any tricks up your sleeve?"

"...Urgh! You... you actually just want to rush in like this?! We're practically making a frontal assault on a building terrorists are hiding out in! Even characters in cheap action movies come up with one or two plans to outwit the enemy!"

"...Hmm, well, if I inscribed 'Ansuz Gebo' on my body with a knife or something, I could at least conceal my presence."

"Then do that! I don't wanna get hurt!"

"Hear me out to the end," Stiyl retorted. "Even if I suppressed my presence or became an invisible man, I would have *still used magic.* I can't falsify that."

"…Huh?"

"Since you don't seem to be very used to the word *mana*, I'll have to explain fully." He sighed. "Here's an example. Consider a painting done in only red, okay?"

"…That sounds like a psychological nightmare."

"You're not listening to me. Anyway, that red paint is Aureolus's mana, and the whole building is teeming with it. If you smeared my blue paint onto a red painting, it would be clear to everyone, right?"

"…I don't really get it, are you saying you're a walking transmitter?"

"Something like that. It's certainly preferable to being *you*, though."

Before Kamijou could ask why, he continued:

"Your Imagine Breaker is a magic eraser that wipes away the red paint entirely, you know. Anyone would notice their own painting being steadily rubbed out. In my case, I just don't have to use any magic, and he won't detect anything odd. But in your case he'd see a whole flood of oddities!"

"…Then what? Are you saying we're gonna just go up to a building full of terrorists and politely ring the doorbell? Without any kind of plan? When we both have transmitters hanging from our waists?"

"That's why you're here. If you don't want to get shot full of holes, then make sure you shield yourself with your right hand for your life."

"You little— You're saying it like it's completely someone else's problem! Now I'm the one paying the bill for *your* lack of planning, aren't I?!"

"Aha-ha. My, you do say some funny things. Your right hand is the only plan we need against *that* alchemist. It can even block an attack from Saint George's Dragon. Besides, you really can't rely on me for anything. I'm using Innocentius to protect that child, and I only brought along one flame sword this time."

"Whoa! This guy really isn't thinking at all!"

"So, what will you do? You wanna stay behind here or something?"

"…!"

Kamijou looked at the entrance. It was a thoroughly normal automatic glass door.

Frankly, I don't want to set foot in a place like that. Of course not. People in there are trying to kill me, and they booby-trapped the whole place. I don't want to go there. And that's not even mentioning the fact that this is the HQ of some strange cult.

However...

If that was the case, then it was *wrong.*

An adult man would get goose bumps just looking at this entrance, and a single girl with a crazy name like "Deep Blood" is being locked up for a very long time in there. *That* was definitely wrong.

"Let's go," whispered the sorcerer.

Kamijou stood at the automatic door without a word.

He passed through the glass entrance, but a fully ordinary sight greeted him.

Many glass panes were placed throughout the whole lobby to let in a lot of sunlight. The lobby was fairly wide; it was about three stories tall, too. The building was a prep school, and this was its "outward" appearance. It wasn't a facility for the students. It was a place to attract guests looking to matriculate. That made the extravagant decoration understandable as well.

At the back of the lobby was a line of four elevators. The one on the end was a little larger than the others, so it was most likely used for bringing in luggage. A staircase was a few steps away from the elevators. It had few affectations, indicating that it was only there as a basic, minimal emergency stairwell.

It seemed to be a long break period at the moment—about the same length as a normal school's lunch break—the lobby was filled with students going outside to get some food.

Kamijou and Stiyl didn't draw much attention in particular. It wasn't like they were paying attention to the face of each and every student, either. Besides, if the worst case was to happen and the students saw them as *outsiders*, then—well, this was the front lobby. Maybe they just came here to request enrollment information.

...I'm one thing, but **this guy** *doesn't look anything like an exam student!*

Kamijou quietly sighed. The person standing next to him was certainly young, but he was also a ridiculous-looking, perfume-stinking priest whose hair was dyed red and whose ears and fingers were covered with earrings and rings. Preparatory schools were nevertheless businesses, though, so they couldn't exactly refuse service to someone.

For the time being, he couldn't locate anything notable.

Even the people coming and going didn't appear the least bit strange.

"Hm?"

For that reason, there was one gaping hole that stood out uniquely.

The line of four elevators. Between the first and second ones from the right, there was some kind of person-shaped robot thing leaning against the wall. Actually, it was more like it had been set against the wall. Its hands and feet were crushed and broken. Whatever it was, it was lying on the floor, having been reduced to a lump of metal reminiscent of a traffic accident.

Its shape was close to that of western full-body armor. But its streamlined form was somehow more modern—yes, like a fighter jet, it had a calculated and functional beauty. Its silver shine gave him the impression that it wasn't just iron, either.

A giant bow, eighty centimeters in length, had fallen nearby, as if it was also part of the robot's equipment.

The word *Percival* was etched into the wrecked robot's right arm. Maybe that was its name.

However, it was clear to anyone who looked that this robot wasn't performing to its capacity anymore.

The hand and feet parts had been mauled and were bent back and forth, and a thick black oil that looked like coal tar was flowing from its damaged joints.

Kamijou's face instinctively scrunched up at the smell of rust.

What is *that?*

First, he didn't know what that robot was. Security robots, cleaning robots, and other sorts of robots could be seen all over Academy

City, but those all looked like oil drums. He had never heard of such humanlike, utterly inefficient robots wandering around.

Second, he didn't know why that robot was broken. He didn't know how strong it was, but smashing it into something reminiscent of a car accident would take a *lot* of force. What in the world had taken place in this cram school lobby?

And finally…

…*Why the hell is no one making a fuss about it?*

That was what baffled him the most.

No one here was attempting to talk about the robot. They weren't even making eye contact with it. It wasn't like they were averting their eyes from something they didn't want to see or something they didn't want to remember. It felt like the machine was just a pebble lying in the road, something for which there was no need to go and pay any attention to.

It was as if…

…even that broken robot had fused into *normality.*

"What's wrong? There's nothing here. Whether we're looking for Himegami or going to crush Isard, I think it would be wise to get moving," said Stiyl matter-of-factly.

"R-right."

Kamijou finally took his eyes off the robot. No one was paying the least bit of notice to it, so he was under the illusion that he was looking at a ghost only he could see.

But that couldn't be right.

Because that robot definitely *existed* in front of Kamijou.

"What, are you worried about that? Well, I guess it would be unusual for you," Stiyl remarked, finally noticing where he was looking.

"W-well, I guess.…Hey, wait. Robots are our territory, science, aren't they?"

"Hm?" Stiyl frowned at Kamijou's words for a short moment.

"What are you saying? That's just a corpse," he told him.

"Huh?"

I don't...get it.

"Divine protection from a Surgical Armor and a Heaven's Bow replica—he's probably one of the Roman Orthodox Church's Thirteen Knights. It's nice that they came for the traitor's head, but from his condition, it looks like they were all wiped out. For heaven's sake. Knight squads are English Puritanism's forte. That's what you get for plagiarizing it so badly." Stiyl wiggled the cigarette at the end of his mouth. "...Damn. At any rate, that formaldehyde bastard sure did a number on them. That person set it up so they'd attack in a scattered way while members of other churches were all there. Was that guy purposely aiming for them to fail...? Everyone who came to clean up afterward would surely be the Church's best. Thinning those ranks by even one person would probably be a godsend for *that person*, but..."

Stiyl was grumbling something to himself in vexation, but Kamijou didn't understand any of it, so he ignored him.

Instead, he looked at the *thing* collapsed on the wall next to the elevators one more time. At that lump of metal that looked like it was hit by a truck, its limbs all shattered. At the wreckage of the robot, spilling out dark red oil, its silvery metallic body destroyed.

No.

What if that wasn't dark red oil—what if it was fluid of an even deeper color?

No.

What if that wasn't a robot—what if it was simply a *human* wearing armor?

"What are you surprised about?" asked Stiyl, as if it was completely reasonable to see. "This is a battlefield, isn't it? What's so strange about one or two dead bodies lying around?"

"..."

Kamijou searched for something to say.

He had known. He should really have known all along. This was a war zone, where people killed one another.

The *enemy* would set up traps to kill the *intruders* Kamijou and Stiyl and lie in wait for them. Even Kamijou, on the offensive side, wasn't actually thinking that *talking* to an enemy pointing his sword at him would resolve anything...

Yes, he needed to have an understanding of that.

But while he understood it, he couldn't stay silent about it.

"Damn...it!"

He ran. He didn't know how running would help. The most he could do was wrap bandages; real first-aid treatment methods were beyond an amateur like Kamijou. First and foremost, he didn't know whether the person inside the brilliantly destroyed armor was even alive. He also couldn't think of a way to drag the person out of the thing.

Despite all that, there was still no clear evidence that the person inside was *dead*.

So if he hurried, he might manage somehow.

Kamijou dashed across the broad lobby in ten seconds. With the armor covering the person's face, he couldn't even tell what kind of expression they had. However, the faint sound of air escaping from the gap in the lump-like iron helmet reached his ears.

Still breathing...!

As he was grateful of his good fortune, he realized another fact: that meant he couldn't move the person hastily. He thought, *I need to call an ambulance*, but then the elevator doors nearby abruptly made a sound and parted to the sides.

A handful of boys and girls about the same age as him began to alight from it. They paid no mind to the near-dead person right next to them, as if it was an ordinary sight. They were laughing, talking about things like how expensive the school lunches were, how bad they were, how quickly they got tired of them, and how it would be a better idea to buy convenience store bento boxes instead.

"Y...you..."

The most important thing he needed to do was to rescue this smashed armor. He understood that. But while he understood it, he couldn't stay silent.

Kamijou emphatically grabbed the shoulder of one of the students nearby without thinking.

"————What the hell are you doing?! Call an ambulance, right now————"

His words ceased in the middle of his sentence.

Because in return, Kamijou's arm was pulled away from him *really hard.*

No.

It wasn't simply being "pulled away." It was as if his hand had caught on a moving dump truck. The impact was on an entirely different level.

"Wha————?"

He thought his shoulder would come out of its socket.

But that's not why Kamijou was speechless. The student he grabbed hadn't been holding on to Kamijou's arm or anything. The hand he had placed on the student's shoulder had been pulled, like a balloon caught on a car.

On top of that, the student didn't even seem to notice that Kamijou had put his hand on his shoulder. And it wasn't just him. Nobody in the lobby seemed to hear him, despite yelling so loudly.

Just like the smashed suit of armor in front of him.

"————What just happened?"

Kamijou recalled the sensation in the palm of his hand.

The fabric of the student's clothing should have been soft, but it was as hard as if it had been soaked in instant glue that then solidified. **No**—he wasn't even close to pulling on the student's body, **he wasn't even able to press his fingers down onto the fabric.**

"That's what the barrier does. This place is like a coin; it has a front and a reverse side. Those living on the 'front of the coin,' the students who don't know anything, won't notice a sorcerer on the 'back of the coin.' And those residing on the back of the coin—we, the external invaders—can't interfere one bit with the clueless students. Look at that," sung Stiyl, pointing out the feet of a girl coming out of the elevator.

The floor. The dark red blood flowing out of the armor was

spreading like a puddle, and **the girl proceeded over it like she was walking on water**.

"..."

Kamijou kept his eyes on her as she passed by. There weren't any stains on the bottoms of her shoes, nor did they leave red footprints. That sea of blood had been treated like it was hard plastic.

"Hmm."

Stiyl casually took the cigarette from the corner of his mouth and pressed the lit end of it firmly against the plastic button for the elevator.

But it didn't leave a single bit of soot behind, much less any sign of the button melting. "I see. The building itself is on the front of the coin, it seems like. Well, that is more fitting for a bastion of anti-magical warfare. Touma Kamijou, it seems we're no longer able to open even a door with our own strength. Same goes for the automatic door at the entrance, so we're basically trapped in here."

"..."

A barrier.

Kamijou certainly didn't have much familiarity with the term, living in a scientific world. But if it was an abnormal power, then wasn't this Touma Kamijou's time to shine?

He clenched his hand into a tight fist.

The Imagine Breaker. It would even nullify miracles just by touching them. It was the most unusual among the unusual supernatural abilities.

He brought his fist into the air...

And as if to shatter the barrier itself, he slammed it down on the floor with all his might————!

...Well, he slammed it, but all he got was a dull *thud* noise.

"Bah! Myaah! Migyaahhh?!"

"...What on earth are you doing?"

Stiyl sighed in aggravation at the writhing Kamijou.

"It's probably the same as my Innocentius. We can't break this barrier unless we crush the spell's core. And this is just a theory, but...the core itself is probably placed outside the barrier. That way, he can be sure that people locked on the inside can't turn the tables on him. Troublesome, indeed."

"...Damn it." Kamijou was a bit perplexed at how to deal with that but asked, "Then what do we do? There's a wounded person right in front of us, but we can't call for a doctor or even get him out of here..."

"There's no particular need to do anything. He's already dead."

"Quit the crazy talk, and check his breathing for yourself! He's still alive, you know!"

"Yes, well, if we're only going by whether his heart is beating, then yeah, he's alive. But his broken ribs have punctured his lungs, his liver has collapsed, and the veins in his hands and feet are long gone.... These aren't wounds he can be saved from. There's a word for people like him. It's a *corpse*."

Maybe he had investigated that with his runic magic, too. Stiyl's words were mercilessly clear, like a doctor giving the cruel truth to a patient suffering from an incurable disease.

"...!!"

"Why are you making that face? You really knew at first glance, didn't you? Even if he *is* still breathing, he's definitely hopeless."

A moment later, Kamijou was grabbing Stiyl's collar with both hands.

He didn't get it. He didn't understand one bit. How could this man remain so calm? How could he talk like that in front of someone who is about to die———?!

"Move it. He doesn't have any time left————"

However, he simply brushed away Kamijou's hands.

"———We also don't have time to push our one-sided sympathy onto a corpse. Sending off the dead is my job as a priest. Greenhorns should shut up and watch."

"..."

An odd enthusiasm came from Stiyl's words.

Kamijou removed his hands without thinking and finally figured it out. He stared after the priest, who had turned his back to face the crushed and broken "knight," whose flame of life seemed about to be extinguished...

Is he... angry?

It was a face unimaginable from his normal face full of sarcasm and scorn. But it couldn't have been anything else. Right now, Stiyl Magnus was not a sorcerer. That back of his, wrapped in something like static electricity that might repel Kamijou if he touched it, belonged without a doubt to Stiyl Magnus the *priest*.

He didn't do anything special.

" "

He said just one thing. It was in a foreign language, so Kamijou didn't know what it meant.

Those were Stiyl Magnus's words as a priest, not as a sorcerer.

There must have been a lot of meaning in those words. Despite not raising a finger at all until now, the knight's right hand started moving unsteadily. He brought the hand up toward Stiyl as if grasping something floating in the skies...

" . "

...and said something.

Stiyl nodded slightly. Kamijou still didn't understand how much weight those words held. However, the tension in the knight's entire body melted like he had told the priest everything he needed to tell him. There was a contented, satisfied relaxation in him, as if to say that he had given up all his lingering regrets.

The knight's right hand fell.

Gonk. The steel-clad hand rang against the floor like a funeral bell.

"..."

At the end, Stiyl Magnus the priest made the sign of the cross at his chest.

A ritual to send off a single human, regardless of whether they were of English Puritanism or Roman Orthodox.

There, Kamijou finally caught on to one fact...

This was unmistakably a genuine battlefield.

"Let's go———" Stiyl Magnus said in the voice of a sorcerer, not as a priest.

"———It looks like we've got another reason to fight."

4

He felt dour.

Their goal for the moment was to search for rooms hidden in the gaps throughout the building. The closest one was in this south building, next to the cafeteria on the fifth floor, so they were ascending the cramped emergency stairs.

As they climbed, Kamijou got to thinking. At first, he thought it was because of that knight, and then he thought it was because of this dimly lit, narrow staircase.

But there was one physical problem apart from those mental ones.

"My feet…"

He looked down at his legs. They were already showing signs of exhaustion.

The rules of the front and back of the coin. Sorcerers (and himself) who came in knowing everything weren't able to obstruct the residents blindly going about their lives on the front. The building itself belonged to the front as well, according to Stiyl.

What this meant was that every bit of the shock that came from stepping on the floor rebounded back to his feet.

In simple terms, it was like the difference between punching people and concrete. The floor was so overly tough that it was tiring him out two or three times more quickly.

"I guess…we just have to pray…that the enemy's gotta deal with this, too, huh?"

Stiyl seemed to be distressed at the rapid onset of fatigue as well. He had a large body, but apparently he hadn't trained it for jumping or leaping in the first place.

"Damn…If it's gonna be like this anyway, then wouldn't taking the elevator have been a better idea?"

"We're on the back of the coin, so if you know some way of pressing the button on the front of the coin, I'd love to hear it."

"..."

"Even if we mixed in with the students on the front coming and going and slipped in through the open door, where would that lead us? If a whole bunch of people boarded on the next floor, we'd be squeezed to death."

The people on the back of the coin can't interfere with the people on the front of the coin.

Apparently all this meant was that even if a car on the back of the coin rammed full speed into someone on the front of the coin, the *car* would be the one to get wrecked, and the person wouldn't have a single scratch on them.

If they ended up being packed like sardines in the elevator...

Then their bodies would be squashed in no time, just like a raw egg brought on to a train car packed to the limit.

...Ugh, I think I'm actually in full-out depression mode now.

Kamijou sluggishly looked down. Now his dark thoughts were clashing with his accumulated weariness. It made him feel like his mind was about to split in half.

Something fun...Can't there be something fun? Kamijou asked himself, greedily desiring repose.

And there was.

"That's right. What about phones?"

"What?"

"Well, I'm talking about the front and back of the coin. I was just wondering if phones wouldn't be able to connect," he said, bringing out his cell phone from his pants pocket.

Though he said this, Kamijou himself realized it was a facade. Strange things were happening one after the other. He felt like he needed his phone to bring him back to reality lest he would be driven insane.

He didn't hesitate on whom to call.

He would call his room—in other words, the room a girl was waiting in. As he was about to, though, he suddenly thought of something.

"...Wait. The bad guy won't detect me using my phone and come attack us or anything, right?"

"Who knows? But either way, I'm sure he already knows we've invaded. We just broke in through the front."

"So why doesn't he come to get us?"

"Not a clue. Maybe he's got some leeway, or maybe he wants to kill us with one swift, certain blow. Well, this is *that* alchemist we're talking about. He's more than likely setting up preemptive measures to quash our counterattack."

"..."

Then why does this guy have so much leeway? Kamijou pondered dubiously. If the enemy had already noticed them, though, there was no point in trying to be quiet. He boldly decided to make the call.

The ring sounded three times.

So it won't work after all...?

The ring sounded six times.

...Guess I'll give up.

The ring sounded nine times.

Damn it, pick up already! he cursed to himself, oddly enough not in the mood to hang up. While he waited, he had another notion. What if it didn't have anything to do with the front or back of the coin, and Index just wasn't answering the phone? And hypothetically speaking, what if it wasn't that she *wouldn't*, but that there was a reason she *couldn't*?

What if...

What if something happened to Index?

In————!

Goose bumps. The moment after an unfamiliar chill began scraping its way up out of his stomach...

...the phone connected.

"He-hellooo! This, um, this is Index Libror———wait, no, that's not it, this is the Kamijou residence, um, hello! Whooo is it?!"

...And then he heard Index's voice, sounding completely freaked out.

"Umm, I just need to ask something—" Kamijou said with the exhaustion of someone trying out a wrong diet, "—but is this the first time you've ever answered a phone?"

"Yes?! Wait, huh? That's Touma's voice. Huh? Does everyone on the telephone have the same voice?"

Gonk-gonk.

That was probably the sound of Index hitting the receiver, her head slanted in confusion.

"Index, don't start hitting the machine just because you think it isn't working! That's, like, exactly how old ladies fix televisions."

"...That's strange. Only Touma could have said something that dumb."

Hey! Kamijou retorted to himself.

No doubt about it. This was Index's first time using a phone (though she knew to say "hello" and seemed to have **at least seen or heard other people doing it**). She probably panicked when the ringing didn't stop no matter how long she waited. Then, finally, without any other recourse, she prepared herself and picked up the receiver. Something like that.

For a magic specialist possessing 103,000 grimoires, Index didn't even have basic common sense when it came to science or technology. Kamijou thought that trait was charming, but it gave him something to think about at the same time.

He knew from his knowledge...

...that Index had no memories from before last year.

Actions that seemed charming at a glance were actually deformities caused by her amnesia. It was pretty painful when he looked at it that way.

"Nyai? So, Touma, what's wrong? Why are you using the phone—this excessive, gaudy, bothersome thing that's bad for your heart? You must be really worried about something."

"Ah, no———"

Apparently, Index didn't consider phones to be commonplace.

"Ah! There were two things of lasagna inside the refrigerator, could one of them have been for you?!"

"You ate it? Well, whate——"

"Ah!"——*ver.* Before he could say that, she exclaimed again, "There was some pudding inside the refrigerator . . . !"

"You ate it?! You ate it! You really ate it, didn't you!"

"But there was only one in there!"

"Don't you have any regard for your landlord?! Those Kuromitsu House Bakery puddings were seven hundred yen a piece! Gyaah!" shouted Kamijou. "Urgh! W-well, fine. We're getting off topic. Anyway, everything's A-OK if my phone connects."

"? Touma, you didn't need anything?"

"Nah. I just wanted to see if a call got through. I'm hanging up now."

"???"

Kamijou pictured Index, whose head must have been cocked in bafflement. He said, "Oh, right, right. Did you know, Index? Apparently, for every minute you talk on the phone, your life span goes down a day."

"Gyawah!" came a shout as the phone suddenly cut off. She probably slammed the receiver into the cradle.

". . . What a simpleton," Kamijou said to himself as he turned his phone off, his retaliation for the pudding complete.

And . . .

"..."

For some reason, there was a sorcerer looking at him like he *really* wanted to say something.

"Wh-what?"

"Nothing." Stiyl exhaled a sigh. "I was just thinking you lack a bit of tension. Man, this is a battlefield after all, and here you are without a care in the world, chatting it up with a girl, so if pride is your own downfall, then you know what, I don't care, I'd be jumping for joy, but if you start holding me back, then I'll be—"

"Are you jealous?"

"Gh . . . Urgh . . . ?!"

Stiyl fell silent, like 60 percent of the vessels in his body had ruptured. *I feel like I'm steadily figuring out how to manage this guy,* thought Kamijou.

"... Yeah, I am."

Kamijou felt his heart being pierced more than he thought it would at that phrase.

He didn't know why it shocked him so much, but Stiyl continued on.

"... Don't get me wrong. I don't view that girl as an object of affection or anything." Stiyl wasn't looking at Kamijou. "I mean, you know, don't you? Until now, **she had a body that couldn't survive unless all her memories were erased at yearly intervals.** So you get it, right? You at least know that many other people have stood in your position before."

"..."

"There was someone who tried to be her father. There were people who tried to be her siblings. There were people who tried to be her friends. There was someone who tried to be her teacher," Stiyl said as if singing alone. "That's it. That's all it is. In the past, I failed, and you succeeded. That's the only difference between us."

Stiyl looked Kamijou in the eyes.

It was as if he was staring at a dream—a future—that would never again be within his grasp.

"Although, I'd be lying if I said I didn't have any regrets." Stiyl gave another sigh. "**After all, it's not like Index has actually turned us down.** She just doesn't remember. If she did, she'd come jumping to embrace us."

"..."

Kamijou couldn't give him a response.

If he had someone important to him... if that important someone lost all their memories... What if a completely different person was boldly staying at that clueless someone's side?

Would I even be able to stay sane? thought Kamijou. No, it wasn't **just** that there was a total stranger sticking with them.

Wouldn't he feel betrayed by that important person who had forgotten it all?

But right now, he was looking at someone who, despite all that, had faith in himself and was trying to follow through with his convictions.

That was real strength.

Kamijou looked at his cell phone. It was just a five minute or so casual conversation. Someone had given up everything *just for that*, to protect someone precious to him, even though he knew he'd never reach her again.

The feelings of all those people…

Did the current Kamijou have the right to trample on all of those feelings and keep her to himself?

…I don't know.

If that was the one and only thing Index wished for, then he knew he would defend that to the end.

But the Index in question had *only forgotten* about those people. She didn't even know that she had a choice in the first place, so making her choose something was fundamentally unreasonable.

I don't know, but…If they say Touma Kamijou saved Index, then…

…yes, I at least need to fulfill my responsibility for saving her.

Giving food to an abandoned cat on a whim and not taking it home, even though you know it'll die of starvation, was more wicked than the despair caused by rashly giving it the hope of *maybe* being picked up.

However…

The one who saved her isn't the "current" me———

Whenever he thought about it all the way through, it always came back to here at the end.

———*Index is looking for someone else…the Touma Kamijou from before his loss of memory.*

5

After ascending some five flights of stairs, Kamijou and Stiyl stepped out into a hallway.

Stiyl had the sketched map of the Misawa Cram School memorized. There was a proper meaning for them coming up here. It was on this floor that there was an apparent discrepancy between the building's paper blueprints and its actual size measured externally via infrared and ultrasonic waves.

Meaning they thought there was a secret room here.

"According to the blueprints, it should be nearby."

Stiyl lightly knocked on the completely ordinary wall in the middle of the straight hallway.

"...It *should* be, but if it ends up not opening, then we're shit out of luck."

"Yep."

They couldn't open a single door on the front of the coin even if it *wasn't* a secret one in the first place, since the two of them were on the back of the coin. Entering and leaving rooms would require them to slip through the gaps left by students opening the door, but of course there wouldn't be anyone frequenting the hidden rooms.

"But it's best to verify their locations. However strong this barrier is, Aureolus is the one who made it. Dealing with the barrier is as simple as threatening him... We could just kill him if it comes to that."

"..."

Kamijou unwittingly glanced at Stiyl.

He understood that this was a battlefield, and that Aureolus was an enemy they needed to defeat. The situation wasn't frivolous, and all it took to know that were the fallen knight in the lobby and the fact that Aisa Himegami was being held prisoner.

Even so, part of Kamijou couldn't outright assert that he'd "kill" Aureolus, because it was also possible that Aureolus had taken down that knight in legitimate self-defense.

However, this sorcerer was a different story.

He said "kill." He didn't use a vague word like *defeat* or *beat*; he had declared he would *kill* him.

They searched for the room closest to where the hidden room seemed to be. It turned out to be a cafeteria. It was probably an illusion, a psychological trick—you messed with people's perspective by setting up a big room. That way, you could hide the existence of a small hidden space next to it.

The entrance to the cafeteria didn't have any particular doors.

Kamijou and Stiyl entered, cautious not to let themselves be swallowed up by the waves of people.

As it turned out, places with a lot of people were fairly problematic.

After all, those on the back of the coin couldn't intrude upon those on the front. Boys were playing musical chairs as they moved around what few seats there were. Crowds of girls were walking with their trays and talking to one another. They were all basically raging bulls charging at Stiyl and Kamijou. On top of that, the size of the cafeteria made it hard to predict people's movements, compared to in the hallways. They needed to strain their nerves to the limit just to avoid the flow.

It being evening, the cafeteria was filled with students.

No one was looking at him—that sensation was fresh in a way. It was completely different from walking through a bustling train station like normal. When he was faced with this sight, he understood that people unconsciously avoid others normally so they didn't end up running into one another.

There was a counter on the wall behind the hidden room, and over the counter was a cramped kitchen. The industrial-sized refrigerators and cookware made matters worse, forcing the already-tight kitchen to feel even more confined. *I get it. As long as you don't know the original size of the room, that would make it hard to figure out how much open space is on the other side of the wall,* thought Kamijou, impressed.

"...Hmm. This is my first time seeing a scientific religion, but from the looks of it, it doesn't look like all that much. I thought there would be framed pictures of the founder's face decorating the place or something."

Stiyl inspected his surroundings with boredom.

"...It definitely doesn't *seem* dangerous, but..."

Kamijou looked around as well.

In the science world, there was something called a "cultic danger level list." It included, among others, a cult's "income" level, or to what extent it would collect possessions from its followers; its "expansion" level, or how forcibly it made new followers; its "absolute obedience" level, all the way to the point where even suicide bombing was a possibility; and its "dangerous material-refining" level, like poison gas, explosives, and so on. Points would be assigned to each of those items, and the ones with a lot of points would be classified as religions that presented a threat to science.

From a purely scientific standpoint, he didn't think that the Misawa Cram School was all that dangerous. Since its subjects were students, the school couldn't easily collect a large amount of money from them, and prep schools weren't the best-suited places for refining poison gas or bacteriological weapons.

But...

"...No. This place is definitely a scientific religion," he said under his breath with spite.

Strangely, although the cafeteria was brimming with students, there was an oppressive air present in the room, like the kind in an elevator. *That's understandable,* Kamijou thought. Everyone in here **was just making noise—they weren't having enjoyable conversations.** For example, they discussed how much more one's grade had gone up after a mock exam, having outsmarted their fellow schoolmates, or how they just couldn't understand the trash that hadn't been studying whatever subject at this time of year. They could only laugh with one another by saying degrading, scornful things about others.

Kamijou looked at the posters hanging on the walls of the cafeteria.

They were pretty conventional for preparatory schools and university advancement cram schools. Lined up on the walls were illustrated, dichotomous statements along the lines of "Study now, pass the test, be happy. Don't study now, fail the test, be unhappy."

It's like a more positive version of a chain letter, he thought. The sort of thing that would say, "If you send this to seven people within seven days, you'll find happiness." Which, on the other hand, is a threat that **if you don't, you will become unhappy**. That was the part that *really* stunk of cultism.

"...Hmph. The whole 'we're the smart ones for studying here right now' thing is religious belief itself, isn't it? After all, even during lectures, professors are always spouting stuff like 'these are the essential points for this exam that you can only learn here. The only ones who don't study here this summer are unintelligent, inferior beings.'"

It makes me sick, he said to himself.

It seriously makes me sick.

He himself was what made him sick for being able to understand this, if even a little bit.

To top it off, all in all, exams end up involving superstition. People try out weird foods that are claimed to improve your concentration despite a complete lack of empirical evidence, and people bring lucky charms in to pass tests all the time.

The tiny chasm named "anxiety"...

Misawa Cram School was a scientific religion that slid the tip of a knife into that hole.

"Hm. You seem to be stricken by the cult's virulence, but I trust you haven't forgotten our original goal, yes? For now, I want to see if we can just find the entrance to the hidden room."

"Uh, yeah. Right. I got it!" Kamijou took a deep breath, trying to somehow calm his nerves.

After that, he took one final look around the cafeteria.

Suddenly, all eighty students in the room had their eyes on Kamijou.

At first, Kamijou mistook this for him having raised his voice.

"This... could be bad.... Are we going through checkpoint number one or what?"

So even when he heard Stiyl's urgent voice, he couldn't react to it.

"Uh, huh?"

"Don't space out. There's no way people on the front of the coin can see the sorcerer on the other side. I see. This means there are automatic warning systems in place near the hidden rooms like this."

"..."

Kamijou looked around him.

The students, eighty in number, were definitely staring at the two of them. Gone were their humanlike gestures; they simply stood there like poles, their eyes like lenses—inorganic.

"C-could they———"

He glanced around... at the dozens of students who were now unmistakably standing on the back of the coin. If they were on the back of the coin, then what that meant was———

"———Sorcerers!"

Stiyl had already taken a step back without him by the time Kamijou shouted in incredulity.

However...

"The seraph's wings are a shining light, the shining light is the immaculate white, which exposes sin———"

A single student, stiff as a pole, alone, started to murmur something he didn't know the meaning of.

"The immaculate white is the 'proof of purification, that proof is the result of' motion———"

A second person's voice overlaid the first.

"The 'result is the future, the future' is 'time, time is' uniform———"

And along with the second person, a third person, a fourth person, a fifth person, a sixth person, a seventh person, an eighth person, a ninth person, ten people, eleven people, twelve people, thirteen, fourteen, fifteen, sixteen, seventeen, eighteen, nineteen———!!

"Uniformity is all 'things, all things are created by the past, the past is the' origin, the origin is 'a singularity,' the singularity is 'sin, sin is man, man' 'fears punishment, fear' is 'crime, crime is' within the self, if 'within the self lies something to be avoided, then by the seraph's wings' 'the crimes of the self are' exposed and must burst out from within——!"

A grand chorus, eighty strong, arose—nay, it was a vortex of words born of every human in the building, more than a thousand people, that could shake the entire battlefield itself.

A bluish-white light about the size of a Ping-Pong ball appeared at the brow of one of the students. Maybe it really was a ball—it flew through the air, its aim unclear, and dropped to the floor right next to Kamijou.

Fshhhh. It made a noise a strong acid might produce and a chemical smoke rose slightly.

Maybe you could get away with only a burn if it were just *one* of those…

"All right, Imagine Breaker, you're up!"

"What?… Wait?!"

He turned back around, and suddenly **there were hundreds of bluish-white orbs coming at him so that they blotted out his vision.**

"Uh, ahh————there's no way I can deal with all of this!"

Kamijou ran toward the exit to try and beat Stiyl there. The sorcerer pursued him, flustered, and they burst out of the cafeteria. He had thought Kamijou would be his shield.

"Wha…Hey, don't run! What do you think your shield is for?! That right hand can defend against Dragon's Breath, but you're not even using it! You're turning your defenseless back to them! Are you insane?!"

"What the hell?! How dare you say that when you tried to use me as a shield, asshole! I don't care how strong those are, there's a hopeless number of them! I can't deal with them all with one hand!"

It was like a boxing match with a four-armed opponent. Even if you put up a defense around your face when looking out for two arms, the other two would penetrate through to your wide-open stomach. This gang was too big for a loner to handle.

Roar! Tons of spheres surged out of the cafeteria toward them.

Like the cafeteria had been filled with water and a door was opened, that's how it looked.

The two of them had no choice at the moment but to flee down the hallway.

"Damn. All things considered, he managed to make a Gregorian Choir, albeit a fake one...I may have underestimated this Aureolus Isard creature."

"What the heck is a 'gregorio' whatever?!"

"It was originally the ultimate weapon of the Roman Orthodox Church. They'd assemble 3,333 monks into a temple and gather their prayers for one huge spell. It would cause the magic power to skyrocket, just like focusing sunlight through a magnifying glass." Stiyl gritted his teeth. "There were only what, two thousand students here? It's like that expression this country has. Dust that piles up can become a mountain."

Kamijou was startled.

He was aware that he didn't understand half the things Stiyl said, but in the end——didn't that mean they were surrounded by and fighting, like, two thousand people?

His brain knew that this building was a battlefield and that they had assaulted the very center of the enemy's camp. But as soon as he thought about two thousand people turning on him all at once, his despair inflated.

"There's no way I could win against them all at the same time!! The building may be big, but we're still *inside* it, you know! You're gonna get caught eventually if you play hide-and-seek with two thousand people!"

But Stiyl, still looking forward, answered, "That's not for certain yet. The core...You need to control all two thousand people at once, or else the spell will fail. If we can destroy the key to that synchronization, we'll be able to put an end to the Gregorian Choir."

They continued to run down the long, straight hallway. When they finally got close to the stairwell, they could see another flood of blue orbs coming to attack them from the front.

They had been caught in a pincer attack.

"The stairs———Let's go!"

Kamijou and Stiyl promptly dove into the stairwell next to them. Kamijou tried to ask for Stiyl's opinion on whether to run up or down, but all of a sudden he noticed something out of place.

"You…! You've been looking awfully relaxed this whole time! You've got some kind of plan, don't you?!"

Yes—despite basically walking the line between life and death at the moment, Stiyl was far too calm.

"Hmm. I do have a secret plan, but I'm not sure I should use it at a time like this."

"Wha—? If you did, then use the damn thing already!!"

"You think so?" said Stiyl, turning a deeply mischievous grin at Kamijou.

The smile was way too ill suited for the situation; he took caution and unwittingly gulped, but at that moment…

Thump! Stiyl shoved Kamijou down the stairwell to the flight below.

"Wha…"

Before Kamijou could even think, he lost his balance and hurtled down the stairs. A searing pain ran through his body as if he were being beaten by four or five people. He couldn't even scream. If he did, he'd bite his tongue.

"Bad luck, scarecrow. ♪"

So came Stiyl's cheerful voice from overhead. In a daze, he looked above and saw Stiyl dashing up the stairs—in the exact opposite direction.

Right after that, the flood of orbs rushed in as if to split off the upper levels from the lower ones. Like a raging river, **as if completely natural, they settled their sights on Kamijou and stormed toward him———!**

"That bastard…!"

Kamijou forced his aching body to move and ran farther down the stairs.

Stiyl's words popped up in the back of his mind.

This was Aureolus's base of operations, so it was apparently chock-full of the guy's mana. Supposedly it was like a picture painted only in red; if Stiyl was to use his blue-colored magic, Aureolus would detect it happening.

However, he'd notice nothing as long as Stiyl didn't do anything.

On the other hand, Kamijou's Imagine Breaker was progressively erasing the red paint. Unlike Stiyl, who had an on/off switch, he essentially had a transmitter hanging from his waist at all times.

The important point was that Stiyl had brought him all this way just to use as a disposable decoy.

He knew Stiyl had far too little in the way of plans to be attacking an enemy fortress, but he actually had this up his sleeve the whole time.

...Damn it! But wait. Isn't that strange?

An alarm was blaring inside Kamijou, but he couldn't figure out what it was indicating. He didn't even have any ideas. If there was something he had no idea about as an amnesiac, then that meant...

The Kamijou from before he lost his memories was...

His "knowledge" was warning him about something.

As if to cut his thoughts short, a new set of footsteps came into earshot.

And they were from downstairs, like they were obstructing the way.

"...!"

The torrent of spheres was approaching him from above. He couldn't stop running at this point. He checked what was down there as he sprinted downstairs at full speed.

There was a lone girl, standing there like she was waiting for him. He'd never seen her before. He also didn't know where her uniform was from, but she was probably a student preparing for exams and one or two years older than him. With round glasses and black hair tied into braids, the girl looked far and away removed from sorcery, let alone a fight.

"Crimes are punished by flame. Flame is governed by purgatory.

Purgatory is made to burn sinners. It is the only violence recognized by God—"

However, what escaped from those sweet lips was an unpleasant voice that sounded like rusted gears.

Each time she formed a word, the pale blue orb at her forehead grew larger. The ball waited, eagerly and anxiously, for the moment it would exceed critical mass and shoot off like a balloon whose mouth was released.

The front and back of the coin must have been reversed. This girl should have been on the front, but now she stood on the back as a sorcerer. That probably applied to every student currently inside Misawa Cram School. On the other hand, that meant if he moved immediately, Kamijou would easily be able to take her down.

I can do it...!

Kamijou clenched his right hand. He wouldn't be able to keep up with dozens or hundreds of them, but one or two orbs wouldn't present any threat. He gripped his fist as tightly as he could as if to reaffirm his power, the Imagine Breaker—

Bazzt.

The girl's cheek blew off like a firecracker had exploded underneath her skin.

"Wha—?!"

As Kamijou stood there dumbstruck, the girl's fingers, her nose, and inside her clothing all made small bursts, one after the other. Each one of the ruptures was small, and they were ripping a few centimeters of skin off at most. However...

"Violence is...affirmation of death. Affir-matio—is, awareness. Awa——re...ne——"

The girl's body ruptured with every syllable she formed. The very lips forming those words ripped, and blood dripped from her mouth because even her insides might have been bursting apart. In spite of that, the girl didn't stop saying words. No—she *couldn't* stop. It was like she was a frog being shocked with electrodes, and its leg muscles were moving independently of its will.

Could that be...

The dread inside Kamijou nearly got up out of his stomach. His knowledge was speaking to him. He didn't know where he had learned it, but this strange knowledge was saying something.

Espers cannot use magic.

It was stating that supernatural abilities and magic were both abnormal powers, but their substances were entirely different. Espers have different brain circuits than normal people, so even though they do the same things as sorcerers, they can't perform sorcery.

However, this was Academy City.

Every student living in this city, no matter who it was, would be undergoing a Curriculum for Ability Development.

So, what if…

What would happen if an esper, who can't use magic, was forced to utilize it anyway?

"St…op———"

Kamijou mumbled in spite of himself, forgetting what situation he was in.

Their circuits were different. That's what his knowledge told him. He didn't know jack about the inner workings of the occult, but maybe it would be like trying to force a battery-powered Walkman to connect to a wall socket?

Since electricity *was* passing through it, the circuits would activate, but…

Wasn't that just unreasonably forcing the circuits to function while burning them out?

"———Stop it! Hey, you must understand that your body is being ruined!"

At this point, he was forgetting to clench his fists. He forgot everything, despite looking down the end of a metaphorical handgun barrel, and darted all the way down the stairs.

"…ss, is——inside, yourself. Inside, is——the world. Connect, your inner self with, the outer world."

The girl went on muttering something and then was suddenly silenced by a sharp splitting sound.

Her forehead split open, and the light blue sphere she had called forth vanished. What remained in its wake was only an open wound, out of which flowed crimson blood.

Maybe that did it. Her body shuddered, angled itself toward the steps of the staircase, and began to decline.

Something inside him whispered.

The human body is heavy, even if it belonged to a petite girl. If it turned into *luggage*, things would be different. It told him that he wouldn't be able to escape from the deluge of orbs while carrying dozens of kilograms along.

Something inside him whispered.

Besides, this girl was the enemy. He'd get nothing in return for saving her, and it would also put him at risk of getting shot in the back. It was insisting that if he wanted to save himself, he must leave the enemy behind here.

Something inside him whispered.

And above all, it said, there was no more saving someone who had sustained all those injuries. Her wounds were fatal by anyone's measure, and the scientific religion had tainted her very soul.

...

Kamijou silently chewed on his back teeth at the echoes of the voice in his mind.

"Shut...up!!"

In spite of all that, he used all his might to reach a hand toward the girl about to tumble down the stairs.

The girl was certainly heavy. There was no reason he'd be able to escape the flood of orbs with a person on his shoulders when he *already* couldn't get away. He knew she was the enemy. He knew her body's wounds were deep and her heart's wounds graver still. That all went without saying.

But still...

There was absolutely no reason to allow this girl to be dumped into the deluge of globes approaching them from the rear. There would never be a reason for that no matter where in the world you looked.

She obviously wasn't doing all this because she enjoyed it.

She had enrolled here thinking it was just a prep school, and before she knew it, the scientific religion had corrupted her. In the end, she was being treated like a disposable tool before she understood what was going on.

Kamijou remembered the knight collapsed at the elevators.

If he had learned anything back there, it was that he couldn't possibly abandon someone about to die, whether they were an enemy or not!

"Guh…Damn…!"

The girl who fell into his chest with a *thump* was lighter than he had expected. However, he meant that in human terms. As an encumbrance, she was quite heavy. Adding to that, they were in the middle of a flight of stairs, so the footing was bad. He was about to plummet down them.

As he tried to hurry down the stairs holding on to the bloodied girl, he threw a quick glance behind him.

There was…

…

Fwshhhh. Like a surging flash flood, the rain of orbs was right in front of his face.

Kamijou immediately deflected the orb in front of his nose with his right hand, used his left to grab the girl's waist, and dashed down the remaining stairs all at once. Well, he *tried* to run down them. Unfortunately, the unconscious human body was surprisingly weighty. It was like he was being told to swim with an iron ball attached to his feet.

He thought to just jump, but gravity pinned his body down.

Not letting that slight loss of time escape, hundreds, *thousands* of orbs came swirling toward him…

"……!!"

Kamijou shut his eyes tightly out of reflex.

I'll at least be a shield for her. Okay, fine. But while he could defend against one or two of the spheres, hundreds of them would be a different story. His body would be eaten alive by the innumerable orbs, little by little, as if by countless insects, and he would melt like they were a strong acid—

"...?"

———He wasn't being melted. No matter how long he waited, nothing happened. He was under the illusion that time had stopped. He could no longer open his eyes out of carelessness. The strange delusion imprisoning him said that time would resume the moment he did.

But if he didn't open his eyes, nothing would happen.

He cracked them open, with all the terror and caution of snipping a wire on a time bomb.

"...Huh?"

His eyes were now open, but he couldn't comprehend what he saw.

He was under a weird illusion that **time had halted.** Because that was the only explanation. The balls had come right up to his nose. He was about to be swallowed up by hundreds of them. So **why exactly was the deluge of orbs stopped dead in midair like a paused video?**

At last, the orbs resumed their movement, like taut strings attached to them had been cut.

However, they didn't move to swallow Kamijou up in their fierce current. Instead, every one of the countless orbs fell straight down as if they were apples being slowly released from a hand. When they hit the floor, they melted into the air and completely evaporated.

Click-clack came footsteps.

Kamijou didn't know what was going on...but the noise was coming from the lower level. At any rate, he looked down from the landing toward where he heard them, as if he was investigating for an answer.

Downstairs, there was an exit to a hallway, and the light of the evening sun was shining into the poorly lit emergency stairwell.

And there...

...stood Deep Blood, Aisa Himegami, as if she were looking up at him from the bottom of a well.

6

At that time, Stiyl Magnus watched as his used-up flame sword disappeared.

A single rune card bobbed through the air like a petal of a cherry blossom.

This was the hallway on a floor higher than Kamijou. It was a straight, long passage, and nothing about it was out of the ordinary, but Stiyl had figured out that the core of the Gregorian Choir was concealed here.

He was a sorcerer. With that being his own expertise, he could easily see the flow of mana. Despite the students here having a meager amount of magic power, the core was gathering and controlling the mana of two thousand people. It was hard for him *not* to pinpoint its location.

"...I see, so that's how he 'hid' it."

Stiyl spoke under his breath, fiddling with his cigarette, relaxed.

Hiding something on the front of the coin equated to **absolute defense** on the back of the coin, because those on the back could never even tear the wrapping paper on a Christmas present if it was on the front.

For example, sealing the core inside the ordinary walls would give it an impenetrable bastion.

Even if an enemy sorcerer found it, he thought there would be no problem if he couldn't *do* anything about it.

"However, that's only ***if* he was able to completely cover it up**."

Stiyl exhaled smoke with a lack of interest. His flame was formless. If there was a hole less than a millimeter wide born from the slightest warp in a wall or window, for example, flooding through it with 3,000 degree Celsius fire would be a piece of cake.

Common sense on the front of the coin didn't work on the back. If he had wanted to perfectly protect the thing, then he should have stuffed it into a vinyl bag or something and bound the opening shut.

Thus, Stiyl decided he'd try and destroy the core without even having seen what it was.

As a result, it seemed that he was able to stop the Gregorian Choir.

"...Still, though," he said to himself, waggling the cigarette in the corner of his mouth. "This is his way out? Alchemists really have twisted since the last time I saw them. An escape route should be made by shedding your *own* blood, not that of other people."

The brain wiring differs between espers and sorcerers. If you force an esper with different neural pathways to use magic, the mana would run rampant, tearing their blood vessels and nerves to pieces.

In actuality, even in this hallway, even at his very feet, there were numerous students collapsed on the floor. Some were still moving, and some were no longer able to do so. In addition, a dense, metallic smell wafted over to him from somewhere. If he peered into one of the rooms around him, there would doubtlessly be a hell dozens of times worse there to greet him.

The fact that his own words made mention of the young ones surprised him.

It was like there were still humane parts of him left to do so.

...Is he contagious?

Stiyl remembered the face of a certain young esper and grimaced.

Then his ears began to pick up the sound of very audible footsteps from the other side of the hallway.

They were not in a hurry, nor were they trying to be silent. They were not concealing malice, and yet they weren't trying to assassinate him with a single, certain strike from the shadows.

If he had to describe it, it was like an opponent knocking on the door to his house before attacking. The smell of bold fearlessness, of absolute confidence in certain and total victory, was a declaration of war and a triumphant proclamation.

The footsteps spoke.

"It was inevitable. No matter where you might have hid yourself, I had conviction that I could lure you out to the core by utilizing the Gregorian replica." The footsteps did not cease. "It is obvious. There were two intruders... Where is the other? It is manifest. Has your familiar been swallowed by the Gregorian replica?"

"If he *did* get swallowed up, that'd be a load off *my* shoulders," Stiyl sung back. "Unfortunately, he's quite a bit more stubborn than you'd imagine. And he's not really cute enough to be called a *familiar*, either."

The footsteps stopped short about ten meters down the passage from him.

Stiyl grinned once. Then he focused directly ahead.

Those eyes were not smiling in the least.

The footsteps' identity was the soles of a pair of Italian-made leather shoes. The tall legs stretching out from them and the slender body achieving two meters in height were both arrayed in an expensive, pure white suit.

His gender was male, his age was eighteen, and his name was Aureolus.

The color of his hair was green. The dyed color was a symbolic one representing earth, one of the five elements he controlled. His combed-back hair was the only thing that made the man, whose skin and clothes were both white, stand out.

His outfit was gaudy enough to be an object of ridicule. However, it was transformed into something very natural by the androgynous beauty the man possessed.

"Anyway, what's a guy not even meant for battle trying to lead me here for? You do know you wouldn't even be able to slow me down, right? Or are you perhaps hiding some dozens of magic items in there today, Curio Dealer?"

"..."

That was close to taboo for Aureolus.

Alchemists weren't meant for combat in the first place. In order for one to stand on the front lines, he would need to strengthen himself with weapons or Soul Arms. Aureolus had to use dozens, if not hundreds of magical items to finally be able to stand face-to-face with Stiyl.

"That is incorrect. Can you not even discern, knave, that at present, I bring no magic items with me?"

"I'll bet. After all, this building is a sanctuary in and of itself. It's one huge lump of a magic item. The environment supplements you on its own, so you don't even have to use any to power yourself up. Hmph. So what? What is it you want to do? Even if you stay quiet, the sanctuary will fight for you on its own. You just have to borrow its power to get rid of party crashers. So just what did you come here to do? Or, should I say, **what *can* you do?**"

"You cur!"

"Your face is telling me that rubbed you the wrong way, but unfortunately, **I have no need for you**. So get out of my way. Your parenting style does irritate me somewhat, but there's no point in blaming you, is there? After all, it's the *sanctuary* that committed that sin. It would be cruel to demand retribution from you, wouldn't it?"

"You blasted knave———!!"

Slip. With a motion like a snake slithering out of a hole, a golden blade leaped forth from the right sleeve of Aureolus's suit.

An arrowhead…?

Stiyl furrowed his brow. It was certainly shaped like an arrowhead, but it was as big as a smallish knife. The moment he concluded that it was a hidden weapon made for throwing…

"Limen———"

Aureolus's right hand swung upward. The edge of the blade stared Stiyl in the face like a viper raising its head.

"———Magna!!"

Instantly, the thing shot out to attack Stiyl, flying straight as a bullet, aimed right at his eyeballs.

"…?!"

The only reason he was able to instantly twist his body and avoid it was that he had guessed it was a throwing weapon but a moment prior. Had he thought it was just a knife, it would have pierced his skull.

Likewise, a golden chain was attached to the tail of the giant arrowhead.

As he swiveled, he looked at where the knife, now more like a giant golden snake, was headed. The chain was coming out of Aureolus's suit sleeve, cutting through the air, and passing right by Stiyl's face.

Shlick.

The tip of the arrowhead stabbed into the back of a fallen student with a sound like fruit being sliced.

. . .

Before Stiyl could think of something. . .

. . . *?!*

Pop. As if he had thrust the knife into a water balloon, **the student's body turned into fluid and exploded**.

It almost looked like the body had been melted by a strong acidic solution, but no, that wasn't just any fluid. It sparkled in a golden color—it was none other than pure, smelted gold.

The chain rewound itself with a *voosh*, and the arrowhead danced back to Aureolus's sleeve.

"It was natural. Do tell me what surprises you so." Aureolus raised his right hand again. "My position is that of an alchemical master. Of course, I shall not allow you to claim ignorance of my name's origin."

Stiyl could not speak.

The very technique that symbolized alchemy, the transmutation of lead into gold, certainly existed. But even if you were to use modern materials for such a grandiose technique, it would cost close to seven billion Japanese yen and would require more than three years to perform. It was truly a hyperbole of magic.

But right before his eyes, Aureolus had brought it to fruition in less than one second.

It was the fastest ever— No, it was *godlike* speed, like a track record no one would ever be able to break again.

"My Instantaneous Alchemy, Limen Magna, automatically transmutes anyone it harms, even slightly, into pure gold in the blink of an eye. Any defense is ineffective, and any escape is impossible. Now bring out your weapon, Innocentius, scoundrel. I have strong interest in learning whether or not it can transmute that formless incarnation of flame of yours."

The golden blade poked its head out of the alchemist's right sleeve like a cobra.

"..."

However, Stiyl did not give a reply.

He stood there frozen in place, like he was struck dumb by what he had just seen happen.

"Hmm. It is inevitable; you must be amazed before my Limen Magna, but do not end it here. I have not yet had my fill. Ten thousand deaths are not enough to repay your attitude five seconds ago, knave."

"...Don't be surprised? Well, that's just impossible," murmured Stiyl Magnus, dazed, like a child who had just seen a ghost.

"Why on earth have you been doing something so pointless?"

"Wha...?" The alchemist stopped moving.

"What are you surprised for? Sorcery is all in the *experiment*, not the results, right? Hmm. For example, let's say there's a craftsman who creates medicine in five seconds. But there's still no variation whatsoever in the effects of that medicine." Stiyl sighed at him with ridicule. "That's what you're doing. Limen Magna? How pathetic. My point is, what does something like that do any differently from spreading strong acid on a human and melting them?"

"...It is inevitable."

"I get that you've tried really hard, but setting Innocentius on this would practically be bullying a weakling. Besides, it's at home. I don't have the free time to use it in a place like *this*."

"...It is inevitable. You make me laugh!"

As if to erase Stiyl's scornful voice, Aureolus fired the Limen Magna from his right suit sleeve. His roar in itself could have supplied the force at which he fired it. It turned into a golden laser and left a stream of afterimages because its launch-rewind speed was just too fast. He may have been a sorcerer, but Stiyl still had a human body. He could never follow the storm of bullets. It was reaching ten shots per second. As a result, six shots out of ten penetrated through him all over, from his face to his ankles, like a sewing machine.

The rune cards he was holding scattered and blew through the air.

However...

"And what is this? **Don't you realize that you're just one of the magic items yourself?**"

Despite his upper body being littered with holes, despite the arm-width hole straight through his face, he kept on speaking like he was bored.

"Wh...at...is this?"

Aureolus, stunned, fired yet another Limen Magna. His bladed bullets, firing at ten per second, aggressively carved up not only Stiyl's already-shredded upper body but also his lower body, which was holding it up.

However...

"Yes, a telesmatic clump using a Celtic cross for a focus is indeed an obscure model. Certainly fitting for a former Roman Orthodoxy bishop. But the one I'm looking for is Aureolus Isard. I'm sorry, but could the dummy Aureolus please stand down?"

Stiyl flickered. His body was now transparent enough that it seemed like it would disappear at any moment, but nevertheless, he was still standing.

"What do you mean? It is natural. I shall dissect your argument, beginning with its premise. It is obvious: The Limen Magna is my alchemic technique, and one I developed. It is evident; if that was not the case, then what would you say was the source of my power?"

"The real Aureolus Isard, of course. Though I think it's about time you yourself started to realize that something's wrong. Well, it's of no consequence. Then I have one question for you, Dummy Aureolus. What exactly was your reason for studying alchemy?"

"...That is simple." Aureolus readied his Limen Magna. "The purpose of alchemy is nothing other than an investigation into truth. My own particular specialty is humans. How high can a human climb while maintaining his human form? It is to search for that I knocked at the gates of the schoolhouse."

If one were to paint his body with the illusory plant belladonna, then he could raise his spell building and incantation speed by several degrees in exchange for destruction. He could even live for thousands of years if he buried himself in the Antarctic permafrost.

However, Aureolus pursued alchemy not as a way to exceed his limits via this abandonment of humanity, but instead to search for how far someone could ascend while retaining his shape and dignity as a human.

Aureolus was a descendant of Paracelsus, the magic doctor. He made that his raison d'être and wore it proudly.

The sorcerer, though, broke all that to pieces with his next words.

"Then why are you trying to make contact with something as inhuman as a vampire?"

"..."

"Hmph. See, you don't know. You don't know anything. You *really* don't know anything—what Aureolus Isard is doing or what Aureolus Isard is trying to do. You are a dummy who was only input with data beforehand. It's impossible for you to comprehend the *error* that's making the real thing twist around his own beliefs for.

"Could you call something like that Aureolus Isard a true alchemist?" he asked.

He should have been completely destroyed, but for some reason, the sorcerer asserted this like he had already beaten the alchemist.

"And that Limen Magna. Even though it's a magical experiment for performing research, Aureolus Isard would never boast about the experiment itself instead of the results. Taking medicine makes a cold go away, but only children can rejoice at just that fact, no? Wasn't it the duty of an alchemist to investigate which ingredients inside the medicine cured the cold?"

"Ugh, ah..."

If he wanted to deny it, he could have done so at any point.

Aureolus, however, had made the mistake of listening to him. Each of the sorcerer's words fit perfectly inside him like pieces of a jigsaw puzzle. He found himself unable to ignore them.

"So I'll say it as many times as I need to, you fake. The one I've got a bone to pick with is Aureolus Isard, **not you**. It would be easy to break one or two of his security devices, but doing so to something with the same face as an acquaintance puts me ill at ease. If you would leave, then you should do so quickly."

Dummy Aureolus couldn't take this anymore.

At this point, **he didn't even care** if he was a fake. He had finally acquired this one and only trump card by his own hands, and yet even *that* was borrowed goods? That's what he couldn't stand.

He readied the Limen Magna in order to wipe the enemy before him off the face of the earth…

"And besides, you actually understand, don't you? You know that the alchemist Aureolus Isard isn't weak enough to lose *this* easily."

He heard the voice from behind him.

In that moment, he felt warm air, like that of a heater, stroke his cheek. **Suddenly, Stiyl Magnus appeared out of nowhere.**

A mirage…?!

Aureolus immediately attempted to back away.

A mirage is a phenomenon in which air is heated and expands, changing its refractive index. It's possible to hide yourself like melting into the air and, vice versa, to appear where there is nothing, like an image coming up on a screen.

The one at the mercy of Limen Magna the whole time was a fake. The real one had melted into the air to hide himself and had moved in behind Aureolus.

At that point, he perfectly saw through Stiyl's tactic.

If he had spaced himself properly, he would have been able to avoid the attack.

However…

The fake illusion he impaled with the Limen Magna. Feeling empathy for that being, even for just a moment, not even a second, was his mistake.

Blank spaces in a person's thought processes leave fatal openings.

By the time Aureolus finally snapped out of it, Stiyl had already created a flame sword in his right hand. Not only that, he had also brought it straight down on him, cutting off his left arm and left leg altogether.

The smooth motion cut into his flesh like a knife slicing through butter.

Roasted by a 3,000 degree Celsius flame, the surface of his skin carbonized. It couldn't even bleed.

"Ugh, gah…"

But something other than the physical pain was dominating Aureolus's mind.

"And besides, you actually understand, don't you? You know that alchemist Aureolus Isard isn't weak enough to lose this *easily."*

The sorcerer's words rattled his brain like a giant bell had gone off in his head. Yes. That's how it should have been. Aureolus Isard *should* have been absolute, should have been invincible, should always win, should utterly crush his enemies, should know nothing of fleeing, should be devoid of the very concept of escape—he *should* have been an overwhelmingly perfect saint.

Then what was *this* unsightly display?

This was a coward. Hiding behind countless instruments, being frightened every time it's poked.

"Ga-aaaaahhhhhhhhhhhhhhhhhhhhhhhhhhhhhhhhhhh-hhhhhh!!"

That was the end of Dummy Aureolus's reasoning mind.

While missing an arm and a leg, Aureolus whipped the Limen Magna around.

"?!"

Stiyl readied his flame sword to guard against the golden arrowhead. However, the Limen Magna flew off in an unexpected direction and stabbed through the students collapsed in the area one after another.

Splosh. The entire floor was awash with golden lava.

Aureolus thrust the Limen Magna toward the melted pure gold once again, and then he swung it around from there. As if it could also be used to manipulate that gold, the liquid was shaken from its singular pool by centripetal force and splashed out in all directions, much in the same way that a magnet can attract iron filings.

Of course, that included where Stiyl Magnus was standing.

"Damn!!"

He brushed away the golden spray flying at his face without much thought. At the same time, he made his flame sword explode. The hundreds of drops of pure gold were far too many to take down one by one, but the force of the explosion blasted them all away in one go.

He sliced through the smoke that screened his surroundings with a newly created flame sword.

But Dummy Aureolus was nowhere to be found—he had escaped, likely taking advantage of the explosion. Stiyl thought to follow him but gave up on it a moment later.

Because the superheated gold he had swept aside was lying across the hallway before him like a puddle of magma. It was only about five meters long, but he'd be set on fire if he failed a running jump.

It seemed his only recourse was to find a way around it. Fortunately, the Misawa School was made up of four buildings, each linked by raised walkways. *There's nowhere I can't get to if I take the long way around*, Stiyl thought to himself rather calmly.

7

"It only looks bad. Her wounds aren't deep. She'll be fine if we treat them," said Deep Blood, Aisa Himegami, calmly to Kamijou after he dragged the Misawa Cram School student, the girl with glasses and braids, through the corridor with him.

"B-but she's all covered in blood!"

He shouted back before he could think, staring at the girl lying on the hallway floor. He couldn't tell what school her summer uniform was from, since it was dyed over with crimson. On her face, arms, and other parts, skin was visible; there were even places with torn skin clinging to her like a plastic bag.

"Her skin ripping only damaged her capillaries. If an artery had been severed, it would be far worse. Blood would come out like a geyser."

"Wha… Well, but why—"

She's *not even a doctor*—no, *even doctors wouldn't know this without a detailed examination. How can she declare all this so smoothly?* thought Kamijou.

"Regarding blood flow. I know more than most."

Kamijou was dumbfounded. Because he suddenly remembered the name of Aisa Himegami's ability.

"Give me a hand."

But Aisa Himegami didn't even seem to notice him. In order to care for her wounds, she abruptly began to remove the girl's clothes, right in front of Kamijou, a male.

"Wah, wa—"

"Keep calm. It's rude to the injured."

He didn't mean it like *that*, but when he considered it calmly, he thought being conscious of the naked body of a girl is maybe morally wrong in this situation. A doctor would get fired on the spot if he got excited in an operating room, after all.

The subsequent events were truly the handiwork of a doctor, an emergency responder. Himegami meticulously stopped the bleeding with a handkerchief. For the bleeding on the girl's wrist that didn't look like it would stop by pressing a cloth to it, she used Kamijou's pants' belt to constrict her whole arm and completely cut off the blood flowing from her artery. Unbelievably, she used the wounded girl's hair and a needle from a sewing kit to stitch her torn stomach flesh closed.

Kamijou couldn't do much. All he did were things like lifting the wounded girl's arms to a position above her heart or pressing the handkerchief to the mouth of the wound, all at Himegami's instructions. His hands were covered in blood just from that. It gave him a strange sort of feeling when he thought about it being the blood from someone he was trying to save, rather than from someone he hurt.

"We're done for now."

Himegami made this declaration, paying no attention to the fact that her shrine maiden garments were soaked in blood.

"Hemostasis is complete. Her blood will coagulate in fifteen minutes. Then her wounds will close. But the disinfecting is incomplete. She'll be fine for about two hours. Bringing her to a hospital for further treatment would be ideal."

"..."

Once again, Kamijou looked at the wounded girl lying on her side. She was about the same age as Kamijou, but her body, and likely her heart as well, had been ripped asunder to such an unimaginable extent.

Experiencing joy at the fact that they saved her life wasn't *wrong*, but...

They couldn't avoid the reality that she had lost everything else.

"We did what we can, so now... we just have to leave it to the city's power of science, huh?"

Kamijou made the remark, looking at the girl's face. The tattered skin was hanging from it like torn vinyl from the internal rupturing.

"Plastic surgery will be fine. It will heal if they use skin from her butt."

"..."

Well, Aisa Himegami *had* only given an answer based on modern medicine, but Kamijou wasn't quite in agreement with it being okay to bring the skin on her butt to her face.

"Anyway, that was some serious skill right there. Are you some famous, unlicensed doctor or something?"

"I'm not a doctor."

Before Kamijou could ask, "Then what are you?" she said:

"Actually. I'm a magician."

"..." *I feel like I've heard that before*, thought Kamijou, but it was true that she did rescue the wounded girl, so he brought to bear the biggest compromise he could manage. "Err, which part of you is a magician?"

"I have a magic wand."

"Uh-huh... Hey! Isn't that a nightstick with a stun gun buried in it?!"

"It's made with a new material."

"No, no, no!"

Kamijou cried somewhat stupidly before finally realizing something a moment later.

The injured girl in front of them had healed to the point they could take their eyes off her.

* * *

Flop.

It was something so simple, but it caused Kamijou's entire body to drain of strength. It felt good. It felt so good he wondered why he wasn't crying.

People had died. There were probably a lot of people who died in places he couldn't see. For every one or two they saved, the jaws of hell were unquestionably open and waiting for many times that number.

Despite that... it should be okay to feel proud about having saved just one person.

"Well, then..."

Whatever the situation, he couldn't leave this girl to die. Before doing something about Misawa Cram School and Aureolus Isard, he should leave for a moment and call an ambulance.

"I'm going home. Can't leave a wounded person in a place like this. And it'll probably be easier to have an ambulance waiting outside."

"Okay. That sounds good. There is more than one wounded. If you prepare an ambulance ahead of time, you can make their trip to the hospital shorter."

"...Don't talk like it's someone else's problem. You're leaving here with me!"

"?"

Himegami looked at Kamijou, pure mystification plastered on her face. Was it because she had been imprisoned for so long? Maybe she couldn't even think about running away anymore.

"Sigh. I said, 'Let's not stay locked up in a place like this; let's go outside.' Actually, that's the whole reason I came all the way out here!"

Himegami didn't say anything.

She only stood petrified, like she was surprised.

"What? Did I say something weird?"

"..." Himegami asked quietly, "...Why?"

"Why? Do I need a reason to save someone?"

"..."

Once again, Himegami stiffened in bewilderment.

Only this time, was her face getting red?... He was seeing a weird illusion.

"But I..."

Aisa Himegami tried to say something.

But then she was cut off by the sound of something slippery being hauled across the floor coming from the direction of the stairs. Ragged breathing, too. He couldn't hear a voice, but he could feel negative emotions like hatred and fury just from its breath, like they were nails being hammered through his ear into his brain.

"Damn it, damn it! What is this *weight*? It is not acceptable. To think this mere *raw material* is dragging my feet... Keh-heh, feet? Have you come to drag me by the feet, Aureolus Isard?! There aren't even any feet left on me for you to drag! Aha-aha-ha... If every single damned one of them is making a fool of me, then it is inevitable. I will melt them all...!!"

It was the voice of a man gone mad. It was grating, like the audio feedback caused by extreme volume.

Then, just like that. *Slosh.* Along with that dragging noise, the man walked out of the stairway entrance and into the hallway.

"Uh..."

Kamijou couldn't help but be speechless. It was a foreigner with green hair in a white suit. However, his left arm and left leg were missing from the sockets, and some kind of twisted golden poles had been forced into the open wounds to serve as fake limbs. He must have been experiencing a great deal of pain, but there was no sign of suffering on the man's face. It was as if the floodgates of endorphins and dopamine had been opened in his brain. He wore a magnificent and oily expression, which mixed fury with anger and ecstasy with insanity, all to prevail over the pain.

The man's right hand and the distorted prosthetic left arm.

They were holding the napes of the necks of a baffling six bloody boys and girls, like he were carrying garbage bags, three in each hand.

"Hah, what is this?" The man looked at Kamijou with bloodshot eyes. "Why are you *here*, boy? Only sorcerers should be *here*, right? Are you an intruder as well? Perhaps a friend of that flame?"

The man shouted from three meters away, as if he was spitting. Kamijou, however, didn't move.

"You... They're..."

"It is obvious. They are only *materials*. Alchemy requires materials. So why are you looking at these *materials*? How strange. You are within the sight of my Limen Magna. I should be perfect. Why do you have such composure? Am I at fault for something?"

Kamijou jerked back at the words "Aureolus Isard," which formed in his mind.

But next to him, Aisa Himegami's expression didn't change.

With the one who was holding her captive—the alchemist who should have been the very symbol of absolute terror.

"How sad."

She spoke, her face still perfectly stony.

"If he hadn't realized it. He could have stayed as Aureolus Isard."

"Guh...?! Y-you wench!!"

Aureolus's howl was accompanied by a giant, somewhat gold arrowhead flying out of his right arm's sleeve. The arrowhead quickly revolved around the alchemist, and the strung-out golden chain stretched out to form something that looked like a shield——

——as it pierced through the bloodstained students Aureolus had been carrying.

The gold arrowhead melted the six pierced students into liquid in a flash, and their bodies turned into a yellow fluid. It wasn't just any liquid. It boasted a metallic sparkle reminiscent of mercury and released burning-hot vapor into the air with a bestial *hiss*, proving it was metal smelted by high temperatures.

"Wha... What the hell?! Do you have any idea what you just did?!"

But. Even faced with that sight, Touma Kamijou was **only** looking at the melted students.

Aureolus shuddered at the fact that the boy wasn't even noticing his killing move.

"It is only natural—death!"

With a shout, the arrowhead and chain spun swiftly around the alchemist again. The golden mud surrounding him whipped up into the air as if by the violent gale winds of a tornado.

It was both a wall and a tsunami. It created a blossoming tidal wave moving in all directions and reaching up to the ceiling, with Aureolus in the center, like a meteorite dropped into the sea.

Suddenly, in his peripheral vision, he saw Himegami move.

She crouched down on the floor without a sound, then proceeded to retreat, holding the collapsed girl. She was wobbling unsteadily, but she was not in a panic. It was like she knew just backing up a few meters would put her out of range of his attack.

Fortunately, the melted metal was more viscous than a liquid; it was like melted chocolate. He got the impression that it wouldn't spread around the floor very much if the tsunami was to crash.

Kamijou followed Himegami, who was holding the girl, and took a step back.

But just then, the arrowhead pierced through the heart of the golden tsunami, leaving a perfectly circular hole behind. It rushed toward him with incredible force.

"...?!"

He wanted to avoid it, but his body was already in the process of backing up. At this point, he couldn't recover his posture. The only method he had of dealing with the attack shooting right at the middle of his face was to use his right hand to immediately grab hold of it.

The sound of flesh ripping came from inside his hand.

Not wanting to be caught, the golden arrowhead withdrew back into the golden tsunami again. His right hand, sliced into two layers, felt as hot as if a cooked sheet of metal had been held against it.

A moment later, the tidal wave fell apart and surged toward him at a stretch.

He leaped backward and rolled onto the floor, and somehow he managed to escape from the scorching sea of metal.

Kamijou and Aureolus—the golden lake separating them was roughly three meters long.

...Damn... it. I can't feel my hand...!

He ground his back teeth at the pain; it was already difficult for him to ball his fingers into a fist. It could nullify God's miracles, but it couldn't even compete with a freaking hobby knife.

"It is... disheartening. What... is that?"

Standing beyond the drawn curtain of golden tsunami, Aureolus was actually even more flustered than Kamijou. It had gone beyond confusion and into the realm of stupefaction.

The golden arrowhead in the man's hand broke to pieces like a crumbling sand castle.

It had reacted to the Imagine Breaker in Kamijou's right hand.

Did that blade contain some kind of unnatural power? If that was the case, then Kamijou's palm would have been wounded because of the slight time lag between when the blade responded to his hand and when it crumbled apart.

"It is impossible. What is that right hand? It should be unmistakable. Why is it not transmuted? It is evident. My Limen Magna is the ideal form of the many variations of alchemy. Even the schools of Bohemia and Vienna gave it up as hopeless, impossible to realize. Then it is utterly peculiar. By what *illegality* does it reject my theories?"

Limen... Magna...?

Kamijou thought vaguely, scowling at his open wound pulsating to the rhythm of his heartbeat. The alchemist said "transmute." Was he talking about the golden, metallic lava?

"Hah, what pleasure. Ha-ha, what pleasure! You interest me, boy! Just what mysteries hide within that body? Allow this magic doctor to open up your body and reveal everything about it!"

Aureolus waved his right hand horizontally and produced a new golden arrowhead.

Eyes sparkling with animosity, the alchemist aimed the tip of the bladed tool right between Kamijou's eyes.

Here it comes...?!

Kamijou instantly readied his right hand over his face; the arrowhead had already closed to within a hair's breadth of his forehead. He had wanted to hit the thick of the arrowhead right away, but an acute pain shot straight through his fist.

"Tsk!"

In an attempt to at least deliver a counterattack, he tried to grab the golden chain, but before that, it reacted to his right hand and shattered like a glass ornament.

The apex of yet another golden arrowhead appeared from out of Aureolus's right sleeve.

Before Kamijou could even think of escaping forthwith…

Aureolus began to fire a continuous stream of the blades, as if his sleeve were a machine gun.

They were fast. The time it took for Aureolus to fire, the arrowhead to break, and for him to ready the next shot was under a fifth of a second; it was impossible for a human to keep up. But Kamijou couldn't carelessly flee, either. He knew that averting his attention for a split second, to speak nothing of turning his back on it, would give the arrowheads the chance to puncture vital spots on his chest and face.

Fortunately, their speed was ridiculous but their trajectories were simple. The rapid-fire arrowheads could only shoot in a straight line. They were easy to read compared to a boxer mixing hooks in with straights.

"Ggh-ahhhhhh!!"

Therefore, Kamijou had no alternative but to use his right hand to rid himself of the arrowheads, even though it meant he would be slashed. As far as he could tell from the previous "transmutations," he'd just turn into melted gold if he used anything but his right hand.

As a result, it didn't take long before Kamijou found himself surrounded by the wreckage of broken arrowheads and chains.

"Ha-ha-aha-ha-ha! What a delightful specimen you are. It is neither a magic-devouring curse nor equipped with the Lance of Longinus. You really do use just your bare hands to crush my Limen Magna!"

On the other hand, Aureolus was laughing from the bottom of his soul, without caring that he couldn't annihilate his enemy despite swinging at him his best move ten or twenty times. He was like an explorer who had arrived in an untrodden, uncharted land.

"Not enough. Ha-ha! Boy, I do not have enough moves to measure *your* limits!"

As one was crushed, another one formed anew and accelerated toward Kamijou. It sliced through the air, trying to pierce his body.

Kamijou's right hand was already covered in blood; he couldn't even clench it properly.

This... is ba—!

It could cleave off a finger. He stiffened up as fear crawled down his back, but the golden arrowhead unexpectedly drilled right past Kamijou, who was late on his reaction.

Had Aureolus missed? No, he had no such optimism.

Aisa Himegami was standing behind Kamijou, holding the wounded girl.

"Hime—"

He twisted around immediately and started to shout to her, but he was far too slow to counteract the passing bullet. The arrowhead was already on a precise collision course with the center of Himegami's forehead. Deep Blood should have been the object of Aureolus's ambitions, but he must have lost his ability to tell who was who in his delusional state.

He saw Aisa Himegami's face before him, surprised at something.

Kamijou tried to call to her...

Squish. The sound of the golden arrowhead tearing through flesh rang out.

"Ah—" Did that voice come from Kamijou himself? Or was it someone else's?

Even that was beyond his comprehension—that was how gruesome and unexpected the sight before him was.

The golden arrowhead didn't strike Aisa Himegami.

The tattered girl Himegami had been supporting... It seemed difficult for that wounded girl to lift even a finger, but she had immediately reached out her hand to defend Himegami's face.

The golden arrowhead was stabbing deeply into the palm of her soft hand.

And yet the girl lightly tapped Himegami's chest with the other hand without showing a hint of pain. The shrine maiden faltered a little, then took a step away from the girl.

The girl whispered something quietly. It was very weak, and he couldn't tell what she was saying.

But she was smiling.

It wasn't a smile for herself—it was a weak smile made to reassure someone else.

And just like that, the girl whose name he didn't even know was transmuted into melted gold.

In that moment, Kamijou yelled.

He didn't even know what he shouted. The roar was enough to tear a hole in his throat. For better or worse, the alchemist stopped what he was doing in surprise and took an extra moment to rewind the golden chain.

Kamijou grasped it with his hand.

Yes—**not with his right hand, but with just his left.**

His intuition. It was telling him that the arrowhead was the only part that performed Limen Magna. The chain wouldn't have the kind of power to transmute anything into gold. If it did, then he wouldn't be launching the arrowheads straight at him—he'd be swinging the chain around. He could cover a much larger area that way.

"Nuh…?!"

Naturally, Aureolus tried to pull the chain back to his hands. It was pulled taut like a game of tug-of-war. In a crazy twist, Kamijou stomped his foot down onto the tense chain.

Thomp. Aureolus was pulled a little bit toward him.

And in front of him was that which he had made himself—the sizzling lake of melted gold——————!

"Graaahhh!!"

Aureolus had involuntarily taken a step into the golden puddle,

and he immediately tried to jerk away. But he couldn't. The chain had become a chain to bind him, and it wouldn't let him back up.

Screaming, he extended the long chain hidden in his suit even farther. In doing so, he finally succeeded at removing his foot from the gold lava. His foot had only been buried for two seconds. However, his right foot—the only one he still had—had already been burned so much that everything from his ankle down was emitting hissing smoke.

Kamijou released the golden chain from his bloody hand. Perhaps he realized that it no longer bound him.

Would it be wiser to flee or to attack?

It was only for a moment, but Aureolus hesitated—and in that moment, he witnessed something unbelievable.

Kamijou lowered his body slightly. It was like he was trying to spring as far as possible on his legs... to vault over the golden pool, then to rush at the alchemist.

He had let go of the chain, but that act had nothing to do with it holding him down or not.

It was only to clench his fist, so he could beat down his enemy. He had forsaken it just because it would hamper that movement.

But no matter how you looked at it, that would be impossible. A straight line drawn across the pool would be three meters long. It would be one thing if he got a running start to leap the gap, but he could never cross it without that.

Despite that, Kamijou's eyes did not waver.

It was as if he was asserting that even in the case of failure, even if his body was to sink into the golden lava and burn up, he would spend what was left of his time tearing his enemy apart.

Those naked emotions, driven to a peak, alerted Aureolus to the danger...

A moment later, and without hesitation, Kamijou bounced into the air.

While his leap looked like self-destruction, it wasn't aimed at Aureolus.

A window frame in the hallway, letting in the setting sun…
He placed his feet on that tiny ledge and dashed straight for him!
"…!"
Aureolus immediately attempted to respond, but Kamijou had already leaped off the window frame, from the very highest position, as if to fall upon him.
His survival instincts screamed, *Intercept him!* They implored, *Shoot him down with a golden arrowhead right now!* The alchemist immediately aimed his Limen Magna—then realized.
Touma Kamijou had jumped overhead and was about to crash down.
If he shot him down with the Limen Magna…the boiling golden lava would rain down upon him!
"How dispiriting! A mistake…!!"
He had no time to pay any mind to how he looked, his pride, or even the burn on his foot.
Aureolus instantly rolled back, dodged Kamijou's attack, and turned to run.
He felt pain at turning tail on an ordinary person, one who wasn't even a sorcerer. However, that was entirely overshadowed by an even bigger sense of dread. He fled for now, tumbling on his ravaged feet into the darkness.

8

The dummy Aureolus slowly bumbled down a long, long hallway that seemed to go on forever.
The boy grabbing the Limen Magna was all it took to make it lose power and break to pieces. However, that wasn't the issue. The golden arrowhead was nothing more than a terminal, a body of hardened aether; the actual Limen Magna was the fortress Misawa Cram School itself. Even if a terminal's mana stock was depleted, the fortress just needed to resupply it and prepare a new aetheric form.
Therefore, that was not the reason Dummy Aureolus was running away.

It was that boy's right hand. He couldn't see the bottom of its power. He felt like no matter how much mana he poured from the main body to the terminals, it would all be eaten. If the arrowheads kept breaking like that, then would it not drain the fortress of all its mana at some point? *That* was how strong the danger at his back felt.

"Damn... it..."

However, Dummy Aureolus could still think. Both Stiyl and that boy, despite Limen Magna being ineffective against them, were avoiding the golden lava itself.

"...Which means **I need enough gold so they cannot avoid it, even if they understand where it's going**. Hah, I have 1,982 people on hand. It is evident. There is no reason that wouldn't defeat them."

However spacious it happened to be, they were still inside a building. It wouldn't be hard to wash a large amount of gold down from the top floor, causing the lower floors to all be swallowed up by the muddy stream, just like a dam break.

He enjoyed that image. The mere act of imagining it seemed able to drive away his unpleasant mood.

"Ha-ha. Destruction, destruction! Destroying destructive destruction with destructiveness! Yes, I shall not die yet. Deep Blood—yes, with such a splendid research specimen within my reach, I cannot possibly die! Ha-ha, no! Not only that—there are still thousands of people worthy of investigation, hiding in this world, are there not?! Ha-ha, how wasteful it is that that boy must die before I unveil the truth behind the mysteries of his body!"

Fortunately, he had already called all the school's students onto the back of the coin. All he had to do now was assemble all that material into one place. *I can pierce them all at once after that*, he thought, before suddenly realizing something. The core of the Gregorian replica, which had been manipulating the students, had been destroyed by Stiyl's flames.

"Lord. Wherever I go, there's something in the way...!"

His roar cut through the air like a heated sword.

But then, he heard the *click-click* of footsteps from behind him, and they were even sharper than his cry.

"...?!"

If there was someone watching, they would have seen the illusion of Aureolus's back shrinking visibly in the blink of an eye.

In normal situations, human psychology will cause one to avert one's eyes from fear. Of course. Nobody wants to be close to something unpleasant or painful, nor do they want to accept it. So they try to pass it by, even avoiding letting it into their sight.

However, *these* footsteps would not allow even the most natural of physiological reactions. An almost hopeless murderous intent dwelled within them. If he averted his eyes and displayed weakness for but a moment, he would end up dismantled into a hundred pieces.

Therefore, Aureolus's only choice was to turn around. He wanted to run for his life. He couldn't endure any more pain—and yet he was forced to turn around with a *creak*, as if someone were manipulating him like a puppet.

There...over there was...

Ten meters away stood Touma Kamijou, like a wild beast who broke out of its test cage.

"What...on————?"

Aureolus couldn't comprehend it. He believed he was flawless. He could never comprehend a human with the power to hunt him into a corner like this.

However, Touma Kamijou was truly there.

"...Give it a rest already, bastard."

Aureolus scowled at the words falling out of Kamijou's mouth—his voice sounded like he had been struck with cold rain, you wouldn't even know which one of them had been cornered.

He had seen hell. He had seen off someone dying right in front of him, and he knew that many people in other places had died as well. And despite all that, he was able to save just one injured girl. But this alchemist had swiftly melted that one redemption, stealing it from him.

Yet Kamijou didn't talk about any of that. He stared down the enemy—if he had time to say anything more, then he had time to do something more important first.

His malice was like burning steel.

"Eek."

He immediately readied a Limen Magna. Not out of any desire to fight but out of fear. Unfortunately, his reaction gave Kamijou the last push he needed.

Silently———Kamijou's feet exploded off the ground toward him.

Aureolus, his face twisted in terror and panic, fired off the golden arrowhead to at least prevent him from advancing. The attack was aimed at his face, but Kamijou brought his body low, like a spider, and effortlessly dodged it. He didn't even slow down in the process.

"?!"

Aureolus's panic ballooned even further. But even while panic was affecting his abilities, he could still keep up the pace of firing and rewinding six Limen Magna in one second. He easily withdrew the arrowhead into his hands and fired a second shot aimed at the face of the ducking Kamijou.

He was already crouching. There was no available way out.

But this time, he swung the back of his right fist up and batted away the body of the arrowhead. It and the chain both shattered to pieces like an ice sculpture. It was such an accurate interception that it seemed like he'd known from the start the arrowhead was coming there.

Lowering his body had been bait to lead the opponent's aim. By showing a fatal opening like that, **Aureolus would be forced to attack there**. It was much easier to deal with a straight assault whose trajectory he already knew than the lawless back-alley fights where he didn't know *how* many fists would be flying at him.

There were ten meters between them. Kamijou had based his ingenious move on the assumption that he wouldn't be able to close that distance by dodging just one strike. But on the other hand, it wasn't a distance far enough for him not to be able to close after two———!

"Wa—"

Aureolus, twisting in surprise, shouted out as he tried to fire for a third time. But before that, Kamijou's right fist landed a direct hit on the alchemist's face. Kamijou didn't slow down yet. He continued, driving his own forehead into the jaw of the enemy who was a head taller than him.

Aureolus's brain was knocked around by the hit and he helplessly crumpled to the floor. He tried to roll on the floor to evade the situation, but Kamijou wouldn't allow that. He stamped down on Aureolus's fake golden right leg. Then he twisted his foot and ripped it off.

Splurch. A sound like a fruit being crushed resounded from the open wound into which the gold had been jammed.

"Ga—aaaaaaaahhh!!"

Screaming, Aureolus fired a Limen Magna at Kamijou's face as the boy tried to straddle him. But unbelievably, he latched onto the chain with his **left hand. Not to break it—only to grab it**, never giving the slightest thought to the possibility that he'd be turned into melted gold if he made one wrong move.

Kamijou swung his left hand around farther and wound the golden chain around his own arm. After completely blocking the Limen Magna's movement, he looked down at Aureolus from above.

It is astonishing...At this rate, I'll be ki—

Aureolus made a decision quickly. He let go of the golden chain hidden in his suit. Kamijou had been balancing himself with that opposing force, so he staggered back a bit. Aureolus used that opening to roll along the floor and get out from underneath him. His mind was screaming. The Limen Magna hadn't been destroyed. He had *willingly let go* of the very proof of his own existence. That fact was trying to crush his heart into pieces.

He should have been able to keep his life in exchange for everything he was. No—it wouldn't be fair if it didn't. But he couldn't move any longer. Now that his fake leg had been yanked out, he could barely even walk.

"..."

As he crawled away, Kamijou then slammed the golden chain into him with all his might like a whip. The heavy blow drove all of the air out of his lungs, and he writhed in agony on the floor.

Kamijou was silent.

Without a word, he closed in and put his foot on Aureolus's back. He took the golden chain and wrapped it around the neck of its owner. All he had to do now was to pull on the chain, and he would strangle the alchemist. It would be impossible to break the bone with his nondominant hand, though.

Kamijou felt nothing about his own actions. Rather, he wasn't *able* to. His mind was white-hot and empty, and it was like reality itself was losing its color. However...

"I...want...to...—he...lp..."

With those words, the boy's brain was robbed of all its heat like he'd just been drenched with cold water.

He knew it was a selfish desire. Just how many people had he killed with this body? That question led him to only one choice. Even a children's live-action hero wouldn't feel any kind of hesitation.

But Aureolus was weeping, and his face was wracked with tears.

He knew he would never be able to escape, but he still exerted himself to reach out with his arm and to try and crawl.

Kamijou remembered then—the knight they had left behind in the lobby; the students, whose bodies were bursting while they recited the incantation as they became parts of the Gregorian Choir; the one girl whose name he didn't even know who had shielded Himegami and was turned into burning hot gold.

He should know the path he must take.

Silently, he channeled strength into the hand gripping the golden chain...

But all he could do was let go.

Aureolus slithered across the floor and crawled away from him—as if fleeing from a human-shaped natural disaster; as if lamenting the misfortune that had befallen him, while at the same time giving thanks to the fortune that had allowed him to live through the day.

The boy was *human*. Killing was something he just couldn't do.

* * *

Dummy Aureolus no longer knew which floor of the building he was on.

He had tumbled down a few flights of stairs, but he couldn't even do that anymore. He had no strength left. He rested his back against the wall of the dimly lit emergency stairwell and stared stupidly at the one hand he still had.

It was ever since that boy punched him. It felt like every bit of the power that had supported him until now was being stolen. The exhaustion felt like an energy cable supplying him from a different location had been altogether severed.

At that point, Aureolus actually figured it out.

That he was not human. Without the external barrier supplying him, he couldn't even stand up.

That he was the same as the Limen Magna: mass-produced and easily expendable.

"Ah…"

Groaning at the dulling sensation in his fingertips, he was, at the same time, *fulfilled*.

Why is that? The Limen Magna aside, my body aside, just what in God's name is that right hand, which can erase magic just by touching it? he thought, eyes sparkling with the intellectual curiosity of a boy looking through a telescope for the first time.

His question. How far could humans rise while retaining their human bodies and their dignity?

He had a notion that he had seen that limit. Not only in that extraordinary ability, but in the boy himself, who could still feel human anger and human sadness, despite possessing that sort of power.

Thinking about it that way made him able to accept this humiliating end.

There was no reason for a scholar to keep living after he learned the answers, after all.

Click came the sound of footsteps.

Aureolus sluggishly looked up at the staircase and saw Stiyl standing there.

"It is dispiriting...Are you not through killing me?" The alchemist laughed at himself. "Leave me be, and I shall naturally waste away. You have no reason to kill me in the first place, do you?"

"That's right. To put it bluntly, I have no use for someone like you, since you're not particularly involved with ***her***," Stiyl told him in a disinterested tone. "Ah, right. One of the Thirteen Knights was near the elevators before. But that wasn't something you did, was it?"

Dummy Aureolus looked up at Stiyl atop the stairs from his resting place on the wall.

He wielded Limen Magna. Even if it could melt any physical material into gold, it couldn't hope to physically crush the Surgical Armor of one of the Thirteen Knights.

"...Hah. If you put it that way, then it is evident. You know I have killed not a single person."

"What?"

"It is obvious. It's just a loser's boast. Struggle to understand what I said." The edges of Aureolus's mouth turned up. "So? Why have you appeared here, beside me, for whom you have no use? Can you not allow me to rot away naturally?"

"It's the opposite, moron. I'm placing offerings at a grave. Could you stand rotting away like this?"

"..."

Dummy Aureolus looked at Stiyl blankly for a few moments.

Then he chuckled.

It was unusual for this man, but he undoubtedly chuckled.

Despite being a dummy, Aureolus was a scholar. And now, having found the answer to the greatest question—having completely investigated the limits of the human body—he was brimming with an unparalleled satisfaction.

But he still had a little bit of time left.

His life would expire within no more than ten minutes.

However, Aureolus was a scholar. During that empty time, he

would notice something. A new mystery. The next question. The unimaginably sweet and beautiful research material lying beyond.

He didn't have time to absorb himself in research, though.

As a scholar, noticing a mystery and then dying without being able to put effort into researching it would be the equivalent of hell. It would linger. It would be a regret he couldn't get away from.

That's why Stiyl was saying this:

Shall I send you on your way before you discover that sweet mystery and writhe in agony?

Shall I send you to heaven while you still have the satisfaction of having accomplished your goal?

"Heh." So Aureolus chuckled. "You knave. I cannot tell whether you are angel or demon."

"They're essentially the same thing anyway. The only difference is who they follow."

Stiyl slowly descended the staircase.

"I prove here the reason my name is the mightiest—Fortis931."

He bared his jet-black robes. Runic cards fluttered out of them like flower petals.

"Your magic name is it," Aureolus lazily noted under his breath as he watched Stiyl come down the stairs. *Now that I think of it, what was my magic name?* He remembered it.

"Ah, yes."

My honor for the sake of the world—Honos628.

The name he had charged himself with. The name he had constructed himself with. He finally remembered it and narrowed his eyes slightly.

"Shall I say a last prayer as a priest, alchemist?" asked Stiyl Magnus. He had come down the stairs and walked up to the alchemist.

"Do not sing, you damned sorcerer."

The moment after Dummy Aureolus answered, Stiyl's flames shot into the alchemist's mouth.

They entered the alchemist's body quickly and completely scorched his insides. If there was a hole on his body, fire spouted from it. But it didn't stop there—he split into an upper half and a lower half, and the flames that came out of him from there blasted his upper half away like a rocket.

9

Meanwhile, in one room of the student dormitories—or to be more precise, in its bathroom—the runaway girl (or rather, Index) was staring down the stray cat (or rather, Sphinx). It seemed like this tortoiseshell cat had been raised by someone before. In other words, it had no charm. If you threw a ball of yarn, it wouldn't chase it down. If you said its name, it would just stay curled up under the table. If you were trying to eat, it would snatch some of your food. Well, that last one was serious business. The food Touma Kamijou made meant a lot to Index—or rather, the girl with the bottomless stomach.

With this and that, Index figured she should completely retrain it. She did away with her collusive mood and was in the process of covering the cat with bubbles. Incidentally, she had just dreadfully tried out the bathtub's automatic water-heating function, following the friendly instructions Kamijou had left her.

...But I wonder where Touma went?

There were a few questions on her mind. The first was about the phone call. It wasn't that he'd only wanted to know if the phone was connected, it was his attitude—she'd selfishly eaten his pudding, and he let it go with just a "whatever."

And speaking of his attitude, it was the same story with this uncharming cat bristling its hair at her.

Fundamentally, Kamijou would never do something he didn't want to. He was the kind of person to try and work out his own solution, even if there was no other way.

And yet, he let two things he found undesirable pass. It'd be weird if she *didn't* think something was up.

Okay! nodded Index. She got out of the bath and wrapped herself in her habit, the Walking Church, and then made her way to the front door. Without thinking, she opened it—and *then* considered. Even if she asked Kamijou, she still wouldn't be able to find out where he was. She hadn't even thought about calling him on the phone. She'd admit it: Using the telephone was a concept far beyond her understanding. Especially the one in the Kamijou residence—it was the kind with the fax machine built in. It had so many buttons on it that she didn't even know where to start.

I guess I have to give up, huh, she thought. But as she turned to reenter the dorm, she suddenly caught something out of the corner of her eye.

Something like a tarot card was hanging on the wall.

It was one of the runic seals that the sorcerer Stiyl Magnus used.

"..."

Index stared at it silently.

Something had happened. Something was definitely taking place somewhere she didn't know, and she had been left behind again.

She thought back to that transparent boy she had been reunited with in the hospital room just a few days ago. The same despair and panic that she felt back then started to burn its way through her heart.

She ran. The only thing she could do was to chase him.

Thankfully, Index had 103,000 grimoires in her head, so she knew what kind of magic Stiyl's sorcery was. Runic seals were a variety of magic where the sorcerer needed to keep sending magic power back to them or else they wouldn't work.

Putting it simply, there was a line. A slender one, like the sort connecting the body and soul during an out-of-body experience. She couldn't use magic, but she could detect it. There was no reason she wouldn't be able to follow it.

With that, Index darted toward the battlefield, forgetting to even close the door...

...without realizing that she would actually be the one to ignite more trouble.

CHAPTER 3

The Master, Like a Closed World's God

DEUS_EX_MACHINA.

1

Stiyl Magnus was heading for the topmost floor of the north of the four buildings.

The decoy he had set loose, Touma Kamijou, might have drawn the enemy's attention more than he anticipated, because no one was coming to yell at him. The sorcerer had gone full hermit mode, confirmed the locations of the doors to all the secret rooms, and succeeded in learning something important.

Deep Blood, Aisa Himegami, was apparently *not*, in fact, being locked in one of those rooms.

As far as he could tell from the dust and remnants of mana at the entrance to all of the hidden spaces, there was no trace of anyone going in or out of them, whether on the front of the coin or the back of the coin.

Aside from Aureolus, he also hadn't run across any personnel, like subordinates or soldiers. This didn't seem like the kind of environment made to imprison someone who could run away at any moment.

That made things troublesome in their own right. If Aisa Himegami wasn't being confined against her will, and she *was* following and cooperating with Aureolus Isard, then that unknown Deep Blood ability might be turned on him.

...Good Lord, there isn't a single decent esper out there.

As he thought that far, Stiyl suddenly recalled the boy whom he had used as a decoy.

Stiyl personally felt like there wouldn't be a problem if he were to die back there. He had informed him that they weren't allies right from the start, and he had even declared he would use him as a shield.

But in that moment after he shoved the boy down the stairs, he had made a betrayed face.

He looked like he'd been backstabbed by a trusted ally.

"..."

Stiyl slammed a flame sword into him upon their reunion and then dragged him into a war zone of swirling death against his will. Despite all that, that boy considered Stiyl to be trustworthy?

That fact dug into Stiyl somewhere in his heart.

Though it was a small thorn, it made him pretty irritated for some reason.

...Good Lord, there isn't one single good, decent esper——!

That's why Stiyl was running up the narrow emergency stairwell.

It was really no use to think this, but...Now that the boy was his decoy, some stinking *human* part of him was whining that he needed to achieve something worthy of that, and...

"It is unclear. Why in the world do you hurry so?"

All of a sudden, a cold voice flew at him from behind.

"..."

Stiyl halted.

He was running up a narrow emergency staircase. He obviously couldn't have missed passing by someone, so what was that voice at his back?

It was as if the man's voice had suddenly materialized out of thin air.

"..."

He turned around slowly, realizing deep down that the fact that someone got behind him without him knowing already foretold lethal consequences.

There, he saw…

"Hmm. So this is the place."

As the purple hue of night began to blend with the evening orange, Index arrived at Misawa Cram School. It *looked* like a totally normal building, but that was weird in and of itself. She had followed the mana from that rune sorcery set up in the dormitory back to its owner, and it brought her here. And yet, the thread of magic cut off right at the wall of the building.

If she were to say it, then it was clear as day that it was *abnormal* inside the building, but something was forcing it to appear ordinary.

Just as mana exists in people, so too does a "power" exist in the world.

Crossism calls this "God's Blessing." Though the model society of modern western sorcery, Stella Matitina, calls it Telesma, the nuance is closest to the concept of *chimyaku* or *ryuumyaku* in eastern feng shui thoughts. As those names imply, it is *myaku*, or veins, that spread out like blood vessels and run throughout the world.

Of course, just as with the gasoline-like mana refined from a person's life force, this "world power" isn't very strong by itself (though, from the huge discrepancy between the life span of a planet and that of a human, you understand that *this* power is just a little bit more than a person's magic power). It is transformed into the gasoline-like "rays" via shrines and temples and turns into a vast source of energy.

This power filling the world is the same as air in that normal humans (sorcerers included) cannot perceive it. The only ones who can are those who specialize in the field, such as diviners and feng shui practitioners.

In the four buildings towering over her, however, there was none of that force.

The normally undetectable world power is like air. But in the same way one struggles to breathe when placed in a vacuum, Index was struck with an indescribable feeling of wrongness.

To put it simply, the force everything is filled with was absent in those buildings.

It was like a giant headstone for the world cut into a square—a tower of dead magic.

The building probably had a barrier to prevent mana from leaking outside, but this was going way too far.

Kamijou's right hand tirelessly and continuously destroys this world power, but that wasn't anywhere near this bad. His destruction was in harmony with nature—almost like a dead tree returning to the earth and forming the roots of new life. That's why Index hadn't caught onto it until he had actually destroyed her Walking Church.

But this "magic tower" was different.

It was a man-made abomination, where the forest had instead been razed to build a city of stone and steel.

Didn't that rune sorcerer notice the incongruity?

Maybe he couldn't sense it because he was a runic sorcerer who was himself a furnace for vast amounts of mana. Kind of like how if you're used to thick, flavorful foods, you lose your ability to notice slight variations in taste.

But Index wasn't able to temper a single bit of mana. For that reason, this subtle, mild difference of taste was enough to give her goose bumps.

"It's not a barrier to protect oneself against enemies entering, it's a barrier of *death* to prevent enemies who have entered from escaping…Hmm, the model case for that is kinda like the pyramids in Egypt…"

As she muttered to herself, the nun in white passed through the automatic doors.

She had no reason to stop there.

It was bizarre, and that's why she had to bring the boy out of there as soon as possible.

The second she took a step in, the air around her changed entirely. It was like walking into an air-conditioned store after being in the boiling-hot sun. The bustling, peaceful city streets had suddenly been switched with traces of an empty battlefield overflowing with death. That certainly wasn't incorrect. In the back of the wide lobby, on the wall with the elevators, there was a knight armored with Roman Orthodox ritual implements lying dead.

Index drew near with trepidation and inspected the knight.

The ritual implement, the Surgical Armor, used mana to absorb and disperse the impact from physical attacks. Since that was the main feature of the armor, it was in turn weak to magical attacks... but this one had definitely been deliberately rocked with something physical, in spite of that.

...Did they not know anything about magic, or did they do it because they had a taste for that kind of thing?

Of course, looking at this building that replicated the grave of King Kufka, she knew that the former was out of the question. The latter presented its own set of problems, though. How had someone broken through a Roman Orthodox Surgical Armor with brute force? Had they summoned an archangel via Telesma, or were they skilled at creating metallic golems?

In any way, she couldn't leave the boy in a place like this. It smelled too strongly of death to let a magic-ignorant amateur get lost in here.

Then she heard something being dragged along, coming from her side. Index looked in that direction. There was an entrance to the emergency stairs next to the wall the elevators were on. From there she heard the ***slither, slither*** of something being pulled across the floor, in addition to ragged breathing.

"Wh—"

—*o is it?* She wasn't even able to ask, because then she saw **it** crawling out of the stairway exit.

There was something there. Not some*one*, but some*thing*. It clearly wasn't a person. Its bottom half had been ripped off, its left arm was missing from the shoulder, the right half of its face had been blown away, and the remaining parts had been carbonized, toasted to a crisp by high temperatures. Something that could still be moving despite all that couldn't be called a person.

Creeeeaak. She could swear the half of a face faltered for a moment.

For some reason, it looked like it was tilting its head in confusion…and the instant Index thought it was out of place, *it* used its one remaining arm to slam on the floor and fling itself at her.

"…"

It'll bite my throat. When Index immediately went to back away from the cannonball shooting toward her, she tripped over the collapsed knight with her leg. Her body toppled over with it. The thing, having momentarily lost its target, was about to fall from its position and land atop Index, and—

"Shatter."

Suddenly, the frozen space resounded with a dignified male voice.

It was instant. The elevator wall across from her crumpled like a paper door, and a man's hand reached out from it. The large fingers grabbed the *thing*'s carbonized, half-destroyed head like it was grabbing a ball.

Right then.

Before Index's upturned eyes, the *thing*'s body shattered, just as the voice had declared.

The scene looked like hardened ash falling apart. *Crack.* Three fissures split the *thing*'s body first, then scattered it into the wind like powder snow. Before it all came down on Index's face below, every bit of it melted into air.

"Open."

The voice again. The door torn from within opened to either side. **It was distorted. There had been no pockets for the metal door to fit into.**

The ultimate magic, which would overwrite the nearby reality according to his own words.

"Was that…," Index whispered, flabbergasted. As if he paid no mind to her, a tall man stepped out of the elevator. He had combed-back green hair and wore a stark white Italian suit and expensive leather shoes.

"Well, well. We meet again, though I suppose you do not remember even if you hear that. It is unavoidable. You would have no recollection of the name Aureolus Isard. No—in fact, for me, that must be none other than a godsend."

There were many marks that looked like bugbites covering the neck of the man seemingly trying to make small talk or something. The concept of acupuncture needles—those eastern medical instruments—would at first seem to be out of place with a westerner, but that wasn't actually the case. There was that story about the founder of the western sorcerers' society, Stella Matitina, willfully adopting Buddhism.

"Well, even should you not remember, I shall not go without saying it. We meet again, Index of Prohibited Books. As always, you appear to remember nothing, and as for me, I am most pleased to see you haven't changed."

The man reached out his hand as if to blind Index, who was looking up at him, dazed.

The magic hand—the one that had smashed that *thing* that was neither human nor monster in one fell swoop.

However, Index couldn't move a muscle. She only said:

"Are you... maybe... the golden Ars Magna?"

The man smiled softly in reply.

2

"Let's go back already."

After Kamijou joined up with Himegami by going all the way around the four buildings for lack of a way to cross the golden lava, he expressed his opinion to her in an utterly exhausted voice. "I beat that Aureolus guy. I didn't kill him or anything, but he's done for. He definitely can't fight anymore. It's not his physical wounds— His soul is dead.

"So let's go back," he said.

He had lost something he needed to protect. He couldn't save the students being used for the Gregorian Choir anymore. He had settled the score with the alchemist. He didn't have a reason to keep fighting. He wanted to go home as fast as he could and be away from this whirling death zone.

I want to go home. I want to go home now and have dinner with Index. Everything is fine if I'm with her. If I can see her again, ***I can still go home****. Before I get pulled back into this war zone... before this world where death and slaughter is normal takes me prisoner... If I don't go back to my world, my everyday life, I will lose it all.* Kamijou's thoughts were vague, but he was certain of them.

But evil shadows were settling into his weary head.

One was that, according to Stiyl, Index had been losing all her memories every year.

One was that, according to Stiyl, Index found a new partner every year.

One was that, according to Stiyl, Index forgot about that, too, every year.

It was obvious when he thought about it, but there, Index was smiling...

...and all around her were so many people who needed her.

He hadn't said it out loud, but Stiyl Magnus had been saying this between the lines:

Don't get the wrong idea. That girl isn't your property or anything.

"...Ugh...Kh!"

Dizziness assailed Kamijou all at once, and he put his hand on the wall. The thought that he was looked at here as one of those many others around her gave birth to the sensation that his path back to a normal life had been cut off.

...What a sick desire to have a heroine.

Kamijou knew that glimmers of self-hatred in extreme situations can slide into self-destructive wishes, like self-sacrifice and feelings of suicide. He intentionally took a deep breath and calmed himself down, then decided not to think about any of it—he realized that if he walked any farther down that road, it would inevitably destroy him inside.

For now, let's take Himegami and get out of here, he thought with a sigh, but...

"That Aureolus Isard. He was probably a fake."

Aisa, unimaginably, said this like it wasn't a big deal.

"Wha—"

"Body double. I can tell, since I've met the real thing. The real thing doesn't kill people so rashly."

Himegami's words slowly but surely sank into him.

She was right. Now that he thought about it, it was strange. He knew that the alchemist was using Misawa Cram School as cover—if he had all the students destroy themselves for his Gregorian Choir, that cover would be blown.

Nevertheless, Kamijou's mind jammed on the brakes. He wasn't thinking clearly. He'd already decided to go home. That's why he was able to keep his cool. Reentering the battleground despite that was an order he just couldn't comply with at this point.

"Wait, just wait! What are you talking about? I definitely took down Aureolus Isard!"

"I'm saying that was a body double," Himegami maintained definitively. "The real one always uses acupuncture needles. He didn't have any, so he was a fake. And besides. The real one isn't that crude."

Kamijou couldn't accept that. He didn't want to. His logic developed from the basis of his desire to go home, so he couldn't possibly concede the existence of any more enemies right now.

"However. That one has no interest in anything but his own goal. If you want to leave, he wouldn't stop you."

Himegami's words were just too calm, and they finally put a stop to his internal complaining.

But she just said something odd.

"Wait a sec. You're coming with me, you know? Aureolus would never let us leave as long as he's intent on keeping you, the Bloodsucker Killer."

"Why not?"

"What do you mean 'why'?"

"I didn't mean, 'Why wouldn't he let us go?' I meant, 'Why am I coming with you?' "

"Wha—?"

That put him at a loss. This late in the game, now that they'd finally evaded the enemy for the time being, Himegami apparently still wasn't thinking of getting away from this school.

"Don't take it the wrong way. I have my own goal. It isn't to get out of here. I can only realize it if I'm here. Or rather. It would be more correct to say that the goal is impossible without that alchemist."

Her words were decisive. It even sounded like she viewed Aureolus as an acquaintance.

What the heck? thought Kamijou. In psychology, it was mentioned that it was possible for an odd sense of solidarity to develop between a criminal and his hostage in extreme situations like kidnappings and barricading incidents—was this like that?

"But whatever your goal is, I'm pretty sure he doesn't see you as a friend or anything. If he did, he wouldn't be locking you away and barricading himself in here."

"That was before Misawa Cram School was hijacked." Himegami's eyes were resolute. "Did you hear what kind of treatment I got here originally? Like why there are hidden rooms all over the building? You are probably too normal to be able to endure it."

"..."

"After that alchemist came. The hidden rooms stopped being used. I've just been here. I haven't left only because I don't feel the need to. If I just left the barrier, I would call *them*."

Kamijou thought back to Stiyl's ramblings from before they entered the Misawa School.

This place was a barrier, perfectly concealed to look like a featureless, ordinary building from the outside.

Deep Blood.

Vampires were a legend among sorcerers, and she had the power to kill them instantly. Was she...

"Then what is it? Are you telling me you've been hiding here the whole time in order to avoid needless battle? Since you didn't want the vampires or whatever to notice you?"

"...My blood. It doesn't just defeat them. It lures them with a sweet scent. It invites them. It gathers them. It kills them. My job is that sequence of actions, like a vividly colored bug-eating plant. It's who I am."

Kamijou's eyes widened.

Vampires—they caused even Stiyl to shiver at the taboo of just speaking their name. Aisa Himegami—she had an immense power that could smash even vampires to pieces with one blow. But when she said that, her voice had the loneliness of standing out in a cold rain.

"Vampires. Do you know? What kind of creatures they are?"

Even if asked, Kamijou didn't know. What came to mind was a mental image of an evil creature that attacks people in picture books, and besides, the word *vampire* didn't even strike him as *real.*

"They're not different from us," Himegami said, however. "They're no different. They cry. They laugh. They get angry. They get happy. They smile at others. They can take action for others. They're people like that."

Himegami smiled softly, as if she was remembering something pleasant.

"But," she continued, her smile vanishing instantly. "My blood. It kills them. There's no reason. It's because they're there. Without exception. Without exemption. They cry. They laugh. They get mad. They get happy. They smile for others. They can take action for others. Those people. Without even one exception———**it destroys them**."

Her words dripped with blood.

It was the voice of someone who had crushed every enjoyable memory before her eyes.

"Academy City is a place to control powers. So I thought they would know the secret behind this power, too. I thought if they knew the secret. Then there would be a way to remove it, too. But I didn't find any of those things," she told him. "I don't want to kill anymore. If I must kill someone. I decided I would kill myself first.

"So it's fine this way," she finished.

The one girl, named Deep Blood, said this all by herself.

"But just because..."

"Please don't say anything. Besides. It's not all bad. Aureolus said he could create a simpler barrier. It's called the Walking Church. It's a barrier in the form of clothing. If I wore that. I could walk through the city without calling them to me anymore."

"..."

"I have my goal. And Aureolus has his. We can't accomplish our goals. Without each other. So I'm okay. Aureolus cannot do me harm. As long as Aureolus wants to grant his own wish. If you want to leave this battlefield by yourself. I'll lend you my aid. I'll explain to Aureolus."

Kamijou could not say anything anymore.

He didn't understand what suffering this girl was going through. He didn't understand how to save her. He didn't know what he was supposed to do.

"...Just...tell me one thing." He didn't know, so he asked her. "When we first met, if you didn't want to call vampires, why did you leave here and binge eat?"

"It's simple. The reason Aureolus wants me. Is because he wants vampires. If I'm always inside the barrier. I can't summon them."

"But isn't that exactly what you *don't* want to do? You don't want to hurt vampires anymore, right? Then why would you listen to some stupid order telling you to summon—"

"Yes. But Aureolus promised. He wanted vampires. But he definitely won't hurt them. He just wants them to help."

"...The hell, man. And here I thought I had barely escaped Misawa Cram School with my life for sure."

"...A question. You said you were running. Why did you come all the way here?"

"I came to rescue you, duh. Do I need a reason for that?"

Kamijou's expression turned sulky, making Himegami's eyes grow large.

She was making a face like she got a present for her birthday when even *she* had forgotten about it.

"That is strange. But nothing's wrong. Because I'm not being locked up. So you can rest easy and go home. No problem." Himegami smiled a little. "Aureolus said. He has someone he wants to save. But his own strength isn't enough. No matter how much he tries. He needs their help. So I promised him. I would help Aureolus. To use my power. Not to kill but to help. For the first time in my life."

"..."

Was that true? Even if *she* wasn't telling any lies, it was more than possible that Aureolus was. After all, he was a murderer. This vortex of death and slaughter was something he created. There were too many places where what she was saying and the reality in front of him didn't add up.

But even so, if...

If Aureolus Isard *was* the person Aisa Himegami said...

"...He can't do that."

"?"

"If Aureolus Isard really is how you say he is...if he still hasn't become a complete monster and has even a little humanity in him... then I can't let him **make any more mistakes**. I'm not gonna say that people who mess up once are beyond all help, but if you let Aureolus go on like this, you're really going to regret it."

Himegami didn't say anything.

She should have actually realized it, too. There was a gap forming, separating the ideals Aureolus embraced from reality. It was plain to see just by looking at this battlefield. His very ideal to do no harm was going down the drain.

"This is criticism. By what thoughts would you offer objection to my ideas?"

However, just then a man's voice befell them, cutting his thoughts short.

Ring. The voice was like a sanctuary in itself. It disrupted Kamijou and Himegami's chat and brought forth silence.

It was a soft voice, like someone had whispered in his ear. The voice's owner, though, was nowhere to be found. He could only express it as a voice that did not use air as a medium, completely violating the laws of physics.

Click came the sound of footsteps.

They were from behind Himegami, but they were at least thirty meters down the straight hallway.

There shouldn't have been anyone there.

There shouldn't have been anyone there, but when Kamijou blinked once, someone was indeed there.

There was nowhere he could have hidden.

He stood there placidly, as if to say he hadn't been concealing himself from the beginning.

"You..."

Kamijou doubted his own eyes.

From out of the void appeared the Aureolus Isard that he should have already beaten, and with all his limbs attached—in fact, he didn't seem to have a scratch on him.

Did he use some special technique to heal his wounds? Kamijou wondered. But that would be strange, too. No matter how he recovered from his injuries, humans couldn't change in *quality* like this. Though he had the same form, the "person" inside didn't feel the same, as if Kamijou were looking at a twin brother with a different personality.

And this overpowering presence...

Despite Aureolus being thirty meters down the hall, the very fact that he was *there* weighed down on Kamijou to the point of despair, like he'd already slid a knife between his ribs.

A human incarnation of the term *the real thing*, along with all its connotations—that's what was standing there.

This is dangerous, thought Kamijou on the spot. *He's dangerous. He's the game master. There's no way I can beat him by his rules, inside this barrier.* That's why, however, Kamijou tried to move around Himegami to cover her—for him, there was no option to sacrifice her and run.

But then...

"I am tranquil. Without impediment, **I head there now.**"

Before Kamijou could take a single step, Aureolus **had already closed the distance of thirty meters** to cut between Kamijou and Himegami.

"Wha...?!"

Any understanding Kamijou might have had of the situation went out the window as he froze in the presence of Aureolus, now right in front of him. The alchemist didn't have quick feet. It was like he just cleaved space and *appeared* there all of a sudden.

It was as if Kamijou were watching a movie that skipped a frame.

"It is clear. I am sure many questions come to mind, but I have no duty to answer," the alchemist stated calmly. "The blood of Himegami is something very important to me. I have no intention of handing her over to *you* without resistance; therefore, I have come to pick it up."

Pick it up. The phrase somehow succeeded in reigniting Kamijou's thought processes.

"...Damn you!!"

He couldn't stand down after coming this far. For now, he would tear the mastermind, Aureolus, away from the captive, Himegami. Thus, he ran forward. There was less than two meters separating them in the first place.

However...

"**You shall not—**" declared the alchemist in an unhurried voice, "**—come any nearer to me.**"

In that instant, a dramatic change occurred.

An onlooker wouldn't have seen any alteration. **But that lack of change was the bizarre part.** Kamijou had been running at full speed trying to join the two meters...but he wasn't getting anywhere. It was like he was chasing the sun setting on the horizon—run as he might, the distance never shrank.

He was under the illusion that Aureolus and Himegami were sliding away from him in a hallway that went on forever.

He panicked. He considered the Imagine Breaker in his right hand. It had the ability to erase any abnormal power, even God's own miracles, but...

Then...what the hell am I supposed to punch?!

"It is unavoidable," Aureolus said without emotion. "What about me do you claim would cause her regret?"

A chill ran down Kamijou's back and he stopped moving. He couldn't get close. While he understood that, his body had apparently judged it dangerous to even *try* to get any closer.

Aureolus stared intently at Kamijou's expression with eyes devoid of feeling, like he was staring at an insect on a specimen table and was stabbing one pin after another into it.

Suddenly, Aureolus brought a single, hair-thin needle out of an inner pocket of his white suit. Kamijou's nose detected the faint scent of disinfectant. He put the needle he had picked against his neck, then casually stabbed it in. The motion was like he had flipped a switch for hypnotic suggestion.

Everything about that movement screamed "execution order." Kamijou flinched and tried to leap back.

However, Aureolus flung the needle he had stabbed into his neck to the side, saying:

"It is unsatisfying. Boy—how boring you are."

Kamijou, still trying to back away, immediately found himself unable to open any more distance between him and Aureolus, no matter how much he withdrew. He was shocked at this queer reality. It wasn't displaying a millimeter of change, whether he advanced or retreated.

So, unable to do anything about the enemy in front of him, he felt like his heart would burst out of sheer nervousness. Aureolus stuck out his right hand without a word, stopping just before Kamijou's chest—as if to grab something... as if to gouge out his heart.

And the alchemist sternly—

"Blow—"

"—Wait."

—tried to declare something, but Himegami suddenly squeezed between them and her voice interrupted his.

Kamijou was speechless. Himegami was standing between him and the true alchemist with such overwhelming power, without any preparation, positioning herself as Kamijou's shield.

You... moron...! Don't be doing this!

Kamijou desperately tried to push Himegami out of the way, but he couldn't draw even a millimeter closer to her. His entire body trembled with a sense of danger, like a clueless child walking up to a robber with a handgun…

But just then, he remembered what people referred to Aisa Himegami as.

The Bloodsucker Killer.

Vampires could make Stiyl start shaking in his boots, and in turn, the power of Deep Blood could crush those vampires in one blow. In this situation, her presence was the trump card joker—the kind that can overturn a game's balance with a single shot.

A chance to win…?

…Is there one? If not, then she wouldn't be doing something crazy like this, he thought.

However, Aureolus looked at Kamijou with an expression of boredom.

He didn't even spare a glance toward the joker, Deep Blood.

"It is clear. You may embrace a meager ray of hope, but Deep Blood is not my enemy." There was no sentiment in his voice. "It is natural. Why does Aisa Himegami possess the name Deep Blood? An ability so strong it can kill a vampire—ah, yes, I see. While true, if she had a power to that *extent*, the nickname 'Bloodsucker Killer' wouldn't fit, no? If that were the case, I believe a name like 'Overkiller' would not be inaccurate."

…Does he mean…

The panic trying to steal Kamijou's last hope rapidly closed in around his thoughts.

"It is inescapable. Deep Blood, whose blood lives to reject, is a power used only against vampires. It is not a variety of superhuman strength; its identity is nothing more than her blood. It lures with a fragrant aroma—a red color, one that will return to ash any and all who drink of it. Terrifying is its brutal level of seduction. But he shall still die, for he must drink. It is obvious, however. It brings no harm to humans. Only the descendants of Cain revert to ashes when bathed in the light of the sun."

Aureolus said all this while taking another needle out of his pocket and stabbing it into the back of his neck. Kamijou couldn't tell what sort of effect it had on him, but a glint of uplift appeared in the alchemist's emotionless eyes.

"Hah. You planned to denounce me with that attack, but it changes nothing. At the very end, you cling to, rely on, and pray to Deep Blood, not Aisa Himegami. How is that different from me?"

Slash. Those words stabbed deeply and mercilessly into Kamijou.

With those words, he ruined the spirit of someone who kept trying to struggle, even though knowing that it was pointless, useless.

However...

"That isn't true. This person did not even know what Deep Blood meant. He also didn't know what vampires really were. This person only came here because. He simply wanted to save another person he had just met today. We haven't even exchanged introductions. He just couldn't leave me here."

The one pleading with him was not Kamijou but Himegami.

She spread her arms wide as if to become a shield to block him from Aureolus's words. "Aureolus Isard. What is your goal?"

The alchemist's eyebrow moved ever so slightly at Himegami's words.

"He is neither a sorcerer nor an alchemist. You got an ordinary person involved. Is your goal to punish him unjustly and satisfy yourself with his death?"

"..."

"If something that petty is your goal. I'll take my leave. I know that I can't hope to beat you. But even I have the option of biting my tongue to end my own life."

"..."

"I don't want to kill any more vampires. You are necessary. For my goal. If you say I cannot have your assistance. Then I have no more reason to live. Now, then. What will you do? Can you keep on living? Without my assistance?"

Himegami's eyes were rock solid.

Her straightforward, equal stare almost made *her* look like the master of this castle.

Aureolus took yet another needle out of his pocket and thrust it into the back of his neck.

"It is obvious. I have no time to spare in a place like this," the alchemist answered without interest. "I have things I must deal with. I suspect I should focus on dealing with the Index of Forbidden Books rather than this intruder. It would be easy just to crush her, but to be frank, I cannot get used to how to treat *that thing* no matter how much time goes by."

Aureolus's mutterings were casual, but Kamijou's breath caught in his throat.

... Wait. Index of... Forbidden Books? Could this guy have—?!

Kamijou tried to grasp at Aureolus in a desperate attempt to overturn the situation. But he didn't come even a hair's width closer. The alchemist's hand, which he had lowered before, turned to point at him again.

Himegami took a step toward Aureolus as if to challenge him, but the alchemist continued without feeling:

"Fear not. **I shall not kill him.**" He removed the needle from his neck. "**Boy, everything that has happened here—**"

Damn it, this is no joke! I can't retire here now! Not like this!

But the alchemist smiled faintly, as if he was reading his mind, and said:

"**—Forget it all.**"

3

It was now night around him.

"?"

Kamijou rose from his seat and took a look around. *Seat?* When he glanced about, he realized he was inside a school bus. He looked at the route map, but it wasn't going anywhere close to his dormitory. He followed the line back to the name of the previous stop. The words "School District 7—Misawa School Front" were written there.

In general, the last trains and buses in Academy City were all aligned with the curfew, 6:30 PM. It was out of the ordinary for a bus to be running at night like this. Maybe it was a private bus the prep school had arranged.

"Misawa Cram School?"

Kamijou tilted his head. *Is that the name of a cram school? Why was I sleeping in a place like this?* he thought. He had no idea. He'd never be commuting to a prep school in the first place. He was Touma Kamijou—he wasn't even "suited" for the summer holiday homework, much less studying for exams.

For a moment, the word *amnesia* popped up in the back of his mind, giving him a chill. He thought at first that it was just that his memories of the past had disappeared, but maybe he was in a more serious situation.

"...I'm going to the hospital," he told himself, deciding to get off the bus whose destination was unknown. He'd see where getting off at the closest stop took him, but he still didn't recognize any of the neighborhood.

His sense of balance was fine, and he wasn't bothered by any weird urges to go to sleep. He seemed to be healthy at a glance, but having a gaping hole in his memories of the last few hours meant that he should definitely go to the hospital and get a proper checkup.

Which means I'll need my insurance card, I'll need to go back to the dorm first...No, wait, is the hospital still receiving patients this late? Well, this is an emergency, oh, but how will I explain to Index? She will definitely think something's up if she knew I suddenly went to a hospital, besides that, she's probably pissed that she didn't get dinner...

His head a jumbled mess, Kamijou decided to go back to the student dorms for now. The buses going through this station wouldn't pass by the dorms. *What rotten luck*, he thought to himself, when...

...he turned around suddenly, feeling like something had called him...in the direction of Misawa School.

"?"

Kamijou craned his neck to the side. *That's weird. I feel like I'm forgetting something important.* It was a sense of irreversible danger, like he'd left to go on a vacation but forgot to shut off the gas. The back of his head felt like it was steadily burning up. *But why?* thought Kamijou, mulling over the faraway Misawa School **he couldn't see yet**.

"Well, I guess if I can't remember, it's just not worth remembering," he said noncommittally, resuming his walk.

He hadn't eaten in a while, but he couldn't very well avenge himself for the food. At the moment, he needed to find a way to soothe Index's nerves. *Probably with one of those Kuromitsu House puddings that are seven hundred yen a pop or something.* The unanticipated cost hit him. *Damn, why did I buy that stupid 3,600 yen reference guide?* he thought, sighing, scratching his head noisily.

...With his right hand, which could cancel out all supernatural forces, even miracles.

Bagrikk. The events of the day came storming into his mind with a sound like his skull was being split.

"...!"

Kamijou turned around in alarm.

Night had already fallen on the city. Maybe it was because he was one bus stop away, but he couldn't even see Misawa Cram School from here. How many hours had passed since then? Stiyl was nowhere to be found. Himegami wasn't here, either, nor was Aureolus. And———neither was Index.

"Forget it all." With just those words, Aureolus had **actually made him forget everything until just now**. He forgot about the Misawa School, which was now a battlefield; about Himegami, who had been kidnapped by Aureolus; and...him saying something about obtaining the Index of Forbidden Books.

"Shit!"

He didn't know what had happened in those few hours. Stiyl was still in the school by himself—was he okay? With all those thoughts bouncing around in his head, he ran toward it.

Highly confused and sprinting at full speed, he didn't catch on at first. To the fact that he wasn't running into anyone, despite dashing as fast as he could...to the fact that there wasn't anyone to hamper his path in the first place...**and to the anomaly that, even though it was nighttime, Academy City's shopping district was empty.**

...*What?*

By the time Kamijou finally realized how strange that was, he was already in sight of the Misawa Cram School buildings, towering into the night sky.

He was downtown, but the space was devoid of human presence. He recognized this particular out-of-place feeling. It was the same sensation he had gotten when Stiyl brought out the Opila barrier this afternoon.

But this time, it wasn't that *nobody* was here.

In a far stranger twist, there was a handful of people standing, encircling the school.

...*What?*

Kamijou stopped and turned back. There was someone standing a little ways off from him. He didn't even know if they were male or female; they were attired completely in silver armor, right from the top of their head down to their toenails.

No passersby were in the area. That made the bizarreness stand out even more. From his viewpoint there were three of these armors, and if they were actually trying to surround the four Misawa School buildings, there would be many more than these.

...*What is this? Those people are wearing some weird outfits...Are they from the Church?*

It bugs me. He figured that he'd try and talk to one of the people in armor first. The situation may have changed in some way while he bumbled around without any memories.

"Hey, what's going on? Are you people friends with that Church or whatever?"

He asked suddenly, remembering the knight who had passed away near the elevators.

One of the corpse-like suits of armor gave a start at the word *church.*

"—I am Bittorio Cassela, 'the Lancelot' of the Thirteen Knights of the Roman Orthodox Church." If anything, he seemed troubled. "Hmph. You're that civilian who left the war zone by coincidence. We've already seen you leaving that fortress. You sure do have some good luck. If you don't want to die, then evacuate at once."

What is this jerk talking about? he thought, observing the full suit of armor very carefully.

"We said that we do not wish to cause unnecessary deaths. We have judged that there is no need to broaden the casualties without purpose, even if we were to conduct a prayer bombing using the Gregorian Choir."

Kamijou was stunned.

The Gregorian Choir was the thing being used inside Misawa School, being performed by using a huge number of students. According to Stiyl, **it had originated in the Roman Orthodox Church.**

"*——It was originally the ultimate weapon of the Roman Orthodox Church. They'd assemble 3,333 monks in a temple and gather their prayers for one huge spell. It would cause the magic power to skyrocket, just like focusing sunlight through a magnifying glass.*"

Stiyl's words came back to life in the back of his mind. If a *replica* had that much power, then just how much destructive power did the *original* contain?

"Bombing…That's insane! How powerful would that be?! You'd get swept away just for being in there?! You can't be planning to blow away the entire building!"

"That is exactly what we will do. Our divine art has been prepared in the Great Temple of the Vatican, the highest hallowed ground in the world, using the prayer of 3,333 people. It can revert any zone on the planet precisely into ash. Leaving that apostate's tower be would surely affect our dignity."

"That's…nuts. Wait, there's a ton of unrelated students in there! Stiyl and Himegami, they might still be in there, too, and even Aureolus———"

———Aureolus apparently only wanted to summon forth vampires in order to save someone.

"And if you just blow up that humongous building, where do you think the debris is gonna fly?! Huge chunks of stuff'll shoot all over a six-hundred-meter radius like cannonballs!"

"A righteous end justifies the means. Consider the blood to be shed the cornerstone for the future."

Those words nearly pushed Kamijou over the edge.

What he said one moment before and what he said one moment after were completely different. They told Kamijou, a civilian, to flee lest he be caught up in it, and yet here they were, not giving a damn about the people inside Misawa School. It was too inconsistent.

"You're insane! One of your own comrades is inside that building!"

"...Percival has been martyred in a foreign land and has let his own blood flow to become the rock upon which tomorrow will be built."

Kamijou thought back to the dead knight near the elevators.

The words of this fully armored person trembled and were filled with madness. He had lost all ability to think rationally.

"Damn it, wait! Then just give me time! One hour—no, thirty minutes will do!"

"I will not listen to your words! Begin the attack!!"

The knight calling himself Lancelot raised the long sword at his side toward the heavens. It glowed in pale red. *It's like some kind of antenna*, Kamijou thought.

The armored man swung down the "antenna" before Kamijou could leap at him.

"A reading from the Revelation of John, chapter eight, verse seven—"

As if to signal something.

"——Recreate the sound of the first angel sounding his trumpet here!"

He didn't know if it was an effect of the magic, but like a howl, the glistening sword sounded a trumpetlike noise throughout the night sky...

All of a sudden, every sound disappeared.

* * *

The thinly sliced clouds floating along in the night sky appeared to be completely blown away.

To others, it would have probably looked like a giant bolt of lightning. A huge pillar of light, coming from the heavens down onto the world below. But the bolt was red like blood. Hundreds, if not thousands of bundled red arrows of fire all fused together to form a single, enormous lance, and in one fell swoop, it stabbed into one of Misawa School's four buildings.

The holy spear of crimson struck through from the roof of the building to its basement in the blink of an eye.

Just like stepping on an empty soda can, the building was squashed down to half its original height nearly instantly. Its glass all shattered, and interior objects came hurling out of the windows.

The detonation didn't stop. Only one building had taken the hit, but it was connected to the buildings next to it via raised walkways. The first building dragged the two adjacent to it down by the bridges joining them, forcing them to collapse. The last building remained standing like some sort of tombstone.

Kamijou was dumbstruck at the lunacy.

People fell out every time fissures ran through the crushed walls of the building, like a beachgoer shaking the sand out of his trunks. It didn't end there. Tons of debris were raining down like meteors, even destroying some of the neighboring structures. The only saving grace was that no one was around due to the Opila.

"Damn it, this is nuts..."

Kamijou clenched his teeth. Stiyl was in there, Himegami was in there, and lots of other students and teachers, and Aureolus, too—and even Index might have been in there.

"You goddamned lunatic!!"

Kamijou sprang into a dash. Not toward that armored guy—there was no time to waste on something like that. He charged straight at the site of the bombing.

A sandstorm of fine particles assailed him as if to obstruct his way. He couldn't see in front of him. He mustn't open his eyes. But he still ran, thinking that the reality he was presented with was some kind of joke.

But suddenly, a change occurred.

"?"

The first thing Kamijou felt was the building particles blocking his vision being pulled back. The storm of particulate matter began to flow forward as if whipped up by a gale—right toward the demolished school.

"?!"

No—it wasn't only the particles. The fragments flung all over floated into the air, and collapsed walls rose up. The connecting pieces fitted together like a jigsaw puzzle, and their damage began to close up as if being fixed up with a spatula and clay.

It was like he was watching a video rewinding. The fallen building lifted itself up. The people who had been tossed out and had fallen began being sucked back into the fissures, and the damage to the building started to repair as well. The next thing he knew, like nothing had happened, Misawa School's four buildings were standing there again. Even the buildings nearby that were destroyed by the blown-away cannonball debris were back. It was enough to make him think that even the contents of his memories had been altered.

Wait, thought Kamijou.

Rewound... That means...?!

Kamijou looked up into the dark sky, and at that moment, a crimson holy lance fired out of the school's roof as if drilling through the heavens. It was obvious where it had gone. As the rest, it **rewound** back to the caster.

"A-ah..."

He promptly looked to his side and saw the owner of the dumbfounded voice, the fully armored man. He was sitting on the ground, his legs having given out. Was it because he knew all too well the power of the real Gregorian Choir?

What is this? thought Kamijou, speechlessly looking up at the night sky. Even the seven Level Five *Superpowers* in Academy City couldn't pull off a nonsensical miracle like that.

That's... our enemy.

Aureolus Isard.

That's... his true strength...

How am I supposed to fight someone that ridiculous? he thought, standing there speechlessly.

"Damn it!"

Kamijou ran toward Misawa School for now, as if trying to shake off the fear.

When he arrived at the automatic glass doors, he froze, stunned.

What he saw on the other side of the pane of thin glass was *normal*, and he couldn't sense a single trace of destruction.

With dread, he passed through the door and reentered the battlefield.

Inside the school, it was the same as always, but the very fact that nothing had changed almost made Kamijou's hair stand on end. That wasn't all. The students within were unharmed and were taking classes like usual. It was like everything, including having been wounded by the Gregorian Choir and melted into puddles by the Limen Magna, had been undone.

As he ran past one of the classrooms, something caught his eye and he stopped.

That's...!

A single female student was sitting near the back of the wide classroom. He knew her. She had braids and glasses—she was the one who had shielded Himegami and was melted by Aureolus's Limen Magna.

There she was.

Copying down notes from the blackboard, rubbing her sleepy eyes, leaning on her hand.

There she was.

Living in a totally normal world, as if nothing had ever happened.

"...!"

The scene was incredibly peaceful, but it instead filled Kamijou with horror. If involved with Aureolus's sorcery, everything would be reset this easily—life and death, fortune and misfortune, ordinary and extraordinary.

But for now, he still ran through the building. He wanted to make sure everyone was safe as soon as he could.

He didn't know where he ran or how far.

He finally found a familiar face when he dashed out into a straight hallway on one of the floors.

"What's up? You look pretty rattled."

It was the voice of Stiyl Magnus, who had abandoned him, then used him as bait, but with a carefree grin on his face. Kamijou should have hated him, but at the moment, it reassured him more than anything else.

"Hmm. If you're here, that means——this is definitely Japan, then? I mean, there were Asians everywhere so I thought so, but what's going on? This strange barrier construction...I remember the scent of this magic, but..."

Stiyl went on rambling to himself, disregarding Kamijou in front of him. It seemed like his memories had been erased, too, just like Kamijou's. Wait, not exactly like them. He didn't know why he was in Misawa School, which meant Stiyl's memories had to have been erased going much further back than his.

He only needed to touch Stiyl's head with his right hand to restore his memory. But when he thought that, he suddenly got worried. Wouldn't the very fact that he was "brought back to life" from that bombing attack before be erased, too?

When Aureolus told him not to come closer, his right hand didn't work at all. However, with a life on the line, he couldn't take any chances.

"Hey, which of these buildings have you been in until now?"

"What?"

"Just tell me."

"??? The north building, pretty sure. Why?"

Kamijou breathed a sigh of relief. The north building. Three of the four buildings had collapsed, but the north building continued to stand there awkwardly. Stiyl hadn't been revived or anything in the first place.

Now that he knew that, things were simple.

"Hey, Stiyl, I'm gonna teach you a special prayer that will get rid of all your troubles."

". . . I think Kanzaki *is* the one that specializes in eastern spells, but sure."

"Just listen. It's simple, just shut your eyes and stick out your tongue. Say *ahh*."

"???"

Though genuinely suspicious, Stiyl did as he was told.

Kamijou declared, "Congratulations! This is to commemorate you using me as a decoy and running away, you jerk!!"

". . . Huh?"

Right after that, Kamijou let go a right uppercut to Stiyl's chin, knocking it upward.

Stiyl Magnus simultaneously regained his memories, bit his tongue, and tumbled down to the floor.

4

Aureolus stood for a while on the top floor of the north building.

This uppermost story was a giant space using the entirety of the level, called the "principal's office." Perhaps due to the place being a preparatory school, though, its impression was closer to a *president*'s office than a principal's.

Aureolus wasn't directing his gaze to its extravagant interior.

He was staring out the window with his back turned to the glittering room, but he still wasn't looking at the nightscape spread out beneath him, either.

He was peering at his own face reflected in the glass.

. . . How unforeseen, that they should have walked here from such a distant place.

He contemplated as he stared at his visage, which wouldn't even twitch an eyebrow at seeing buildings lift themselves up like living creatures from his one statement—really only two words: "Go back."

My old self was not like this, he thought.

He was the sort who had trouble expressing his feelings, but he thought he was once a *human* who was able to express everything from joy to anger, from grief to delight.

The skin on his face didn't move an inch, and the light in his eyes didn't waver a millimeter; it wasn't out of serenity or composure, but simply because he didn't have the flexibility to create expressions.

Even that I care not about, thought Aureolus.

Achieving his own mission meant all the world would be engulfed in an unremitting war, and that his emotions would be whittled away. He understood that.

Aureolus Isard just wanted to save one girl.

Behind him there was a large desk made of ebony, and on it was a girl who had been placed into a sleep.

Index Librorum Prohibitorum—the archive of forbidden books.

It had been three years since meeting the girl, who hadn't even been granted the minimum requirement to be human: a name.

Aureolus Isard was a Cancellarius of the Roman Orthodox Church.

As one who penned grimoires yet still belonged to the Church, he was an exception among exceptions. He would reveal the evil ways of the witches around at the time, find methods to deal with them, put them into words, and make them into books—all the while believing his works would protect the innocent from the witches' threat.

The volumes recorded by Aureolus had actually saved a great many people.

However, the Roman Orthodox Church made them into their very own trump cards. They did not tell anyone unrelated to Crossism, nor did they inform even other people of Crossism, like those of the Church of English Puritanism and the Russian Catholic Church. They implicitly declared that if they desired salvation from the witches' threat, then they should convert.

As a result, many fell to the hands of the witches even though the alchemist had led them to solutions.

It was unreasonable, like not being able to give a sick person even the simplest of surgeries and watching him die.

Aureolus found it unforgivable. He had faith that the trump cards he devised would save *everyone.*

It wasn't long before he made the decision to bring one of the books he authored outside the confines of the Church.

It was England, which had enough harm caused by witches that it was called the "land of magic." With the utmost care, he wrapped himself in two or three layers of camouflage and succeeded in secretly establishing contact with people of the English Puritan Church.

There he discovered hell—in the form of a girl who could never be saved.

He knew it at first sight. It only took one glance for the alchemist who wished to save the entire world to understand that he would never be able to rescue this girl, even if he rescued all else.

The one girl carried 103,000 grimoires taken from around the world. Just one of those evil, wicked volumes could drive a normal person mad, and she carried as many as the stars in the sky—and even though she was aware she would never know salvation, she still smiled like a young girl.

In reality, the girl really couldn't be saved. A human is not fundamentally strong enough to carry 103,000 grimoires. The girl's body was violated by their poisonous knowledge, and her mind was trespassed by their poisonous insight.

It was so bad that her memories needed to be wiped annually to flush that venom.

That's where the alchemist witnessed the end of his ideal.

She could still smile for others' sake, despite all that misfortune being forced upon her by others.

The alchemist began to write grimoires in order to rescue just this one girl, continuing to trust that his books would save all the world, without exception. Whenever he finished writing one, he would go over to the English Puritan Church. And even if ten or twenty of them ended with failure, Aureolus never gave up, he still continued to write them.

At some point after he had forgotten how many grimoires he had completed, Aureolus took a moment to think about why his will never broke and why he continued to write them.

Doing that caused him to finally realize something.

From the moment he first saw her, he had considered her to be beyond salvation. "Providing grimoires" was but a front as to why he never gave up—the truth was that **he only wanted to see her**.

Nothing special.

The alchemist's wish was to save her, and instead, she had saved *him*.

Once he knew that, the end was near. Aureolus got to the point where he could no longer hold a pen. Now that he realized he couldn't even rescue one person, both his mission and his confidence were completely shattered.

She can't be saved, she can't be saved—**no one can be saved with these methods.**

If he still desired this girl's salvation, his only path was to fall from grace.

He had but one reason for his fall.

If God had the power to save the entire world, then why couldn't the girl in front of him be saved?

With that, Aureolus Isard made an enemy out of the Roman Orthodox Church, of Crossism, and indeed of the whole world. Even then, she couldn't be saved. He dabbled in the Zurich school of alchemy, a type of Hermeticism, and even then, she could never be saved. He came to believe by fully decoding the human body, he could heal any sickness. He had believed that if he fully explored the human mind, he could heal any soul. Even then, she absolutely couldn't be saved.

She was alone. Neither faith nor technology could save her any longer.

And that was why he thought...

Just why would it be wrong to rely on the power of the descendants of Cain, who have strayed from the path of man?

He would betray anyone for his purpose. He would use anything. He would even subdue Deep Blood with his own two hands.

That was how the alchemist wandered from the straight and narrow. What was left behind was the tragic wreckage of a man who wished for the salvation of others above his own.

"..."

However, there was one thing Aureolus Isard did not realize.

The person silently looking at his back—the girl named Deep Blood—was *also* here because she wanted to help someone.

Salvation was distant.

There were still no signs of the coming of a messiah.

"Aureolus reflected the Roman Orthodox Church's *real* Gregorian Choir...? That's impossible!"

Having finished chasing Kamijou around with a flame sword in hand, Stiyl was dumbfounded by what Kamijou told him.

"No, I'm serious. The busted buildings all got fixed like it was some kind of videotape rewinding," answered Kamijou, running down the hall.

Stiyl seemed to have been able to probe more deeply into this place than Kamijou. Apparently, after locating Aureolus's headquarters, his memory was erased, and he'd been wandering around the building since then.

"...That would mean...But that's impossible for current alchemy...," muttered Stiyl, annoyed, giving a puff of cigarette smoke.

"He said stuff like 'don't come closer' and 'forget it,' too. What, is that kind of crazy stuff all over the place in the magic world or something?"

"...Of course not. Magic is an academic field—a world grounded firmly in theories and rules. If something that rule-breaking existed, the whole thing would be ridiculous, and no one would bother studying sorcery."

"Then what the heck *was* that? He's *actually* saying one word and the world changes into the way he wants it."

"The way he wants it...Hmm. I don't like the sound of that. It reminds me of Ars Magna."

Kamijou briefly frowned at his odd reaction to the words "*the way he wants it*," but then he remembered.

The power to warp the world into whatever you want—**it was the ultimate objective of alchemy, and no one has yet accomplished it.** Didn't Stiyl explain that to him before?

"Wait. Then doesn't that mean he mastered alchemy?!"

"That doesn't make sense!" Stiyl shot back with unusual roughness. "I explained before that this Ars Magna isn't a technique that humans can carry out. Even though the incantation itself is complete, just one or two hundred years wouldn't be enough to recite it, even without sleep or breaks. There's no excess that can be eliminated to shorten the thing, and if you tried passing down the work from parent to child to grandchild, the ceremony itself would be messed up like a game of telephone. Therefore, a human with a finite life span cannot use that sorcery!"

If Kamijou had studied magic, Stiyl's argument probably would have sounded pretty sensible.

But the sorcerer's voice was trembling—almost like he had witnessed something unbelievable.

"...Oh, I guess so." Kamijou tried looking at it from a different angle. "If he can change the world to the way he wants it, then it's kind of weird that we're alive in the first place, huh? If he just thought *die*, that would be it. He wouldn't have to use the Gregorian replica or a body double or anything."

He wouldn't need vampires or Deep Blood in the first place. If he needed them, he could just make them himself. And if he could change the world into whatever he wanted anyway, he could cut out the vampires entirely and just grant his wish through his own power.

"But jeez, what's that guy trying to do, anyway? He wants to rescue someone or something, but then he just casually kills other people, and all of a sudden Index gets caught up in this... I wonder if all the unexpected stress from this incident is making him lose his mind."

"What, that girl is?"

"He just mentioned something along those lines. I haven't actually seen her. Maybe he was just going crazy and seeing things," Kamijou replied lightly to reassure him—and to reassure himself.

However, Stiyl's face fell even further than when they were discussing the alchemist. He spat out his cigarette like it tasted bad.

"Damn, I see. I get it now. If you're away from civilization for three years studying magic, anyone'd be out of touch with the world." As he held a new cigarette in his mouth, he finished, "I figured out what he wants. It's Index."

"Wha…?"

Kamijou didn't get it. Index shouldn't have been involved in this incident from the beginning.

"Listen up, Touma Kamijou. Index used to need her memories erased once a year. In other words, her human relations would all be totally reset annually, and a new partner would be at her side each time. That's the kind of situation it caused."

"Yeah, but…So?"

"This year it was you, two years ago it was me—" said Stiyl, truly exasperated, "—and three years ago, the name of her partner was Aureolus Isard. I believe he acted as her teacher."

Kamijou was speechless.

"All her partners in the past ran into the same dead end. They all struggled desperately to put an end to her memory problems, and they always failed," Stiyl growled. "Of course, he would have arrived at the same dead end…I see. So even when the results came in, he didn't accept them."

"…Meaning?"

"It's simple. We, her past partners, haven't been *rejected* by Index or anything. **She just doesn't remember.** So it's easy. If you could somehow heal Index's mind and have her remember, **she'd turn back to look at us again**."

Kamijou's heart felt like it had been struck with a nail.

He didn't know why the shock hit him. It would be great if Index's brain was cured, right? He didn't understand, and this hazy jolt didn't seem to want to go away.

Her smile…

He didn't think it would be this shocking to consider it being directed toward someone else.

"...But besides, that kind of thing is completely unacceptable," Stiyl said quietly to himself. "If it's wrong to erase someone's memories, then it's equally infernal to tamper with their memories. Is he really so far gone that he can't understand that?"

His voice was low, so Kamijou looked at his face to try and hear.

But he gave a puff of cigarette smoke and shook his head, bored.

"It's nothing. I was just saying **that it's absolutely impossible for him to save her**."

"What?"

Kamijou wasn't sure what he meant. If the man could fix buildings, steal memories, and even rewind people's lives, was *anything* impossible for him?

"This is another easy one—you're the one who brought it all to nothing."

"?"

"You saved her, didn't you? **You can't save someone who has already been saved.** That's all there is to it. No hidden meanings here."

"Oh," said Kamijou, finally figuring it out.

Aureolus Isard was Index's partner from three years ago. It had been three years since he lost her; without any communication with the outside world, he would have no information.

In other words, Aureolus was—

"We're here. How polite; the door is open for us."

Stiyl looked ahead.

The giant door to the principal's office, the entire top floor of Misawa School's north building, was ajar, as if to welcome them in.

5

It was a wide-open space.

This was the room in which the branch school principal and the founder of the scientific religion once sat. The room sparkled in beauty, but it had no class—fitting for such warped ambitions. A sense of revulsion was the only thing that stood out, as if they had wandered into a restaurant concerned with etiquette alone, ignorant of the proper way to wait on customers.

Himegami made a surprised face when she saw Kamijou enter into the room. On the contrary, Aureolus showed no emotion whatsoever. Something natural had naturally happened. That was all his expression said.

The air around them was terribly hollow. It was as empty as a timeworn, faded photograph.

That void likely reflected the alchemist's own soul.

As a man who could manipulate the entire world, there probably wasn't anything he couldn't obtain.

But because of that, there was nothing *certain* for this man.

A skilled puppeteer—an esper with brainwashing abilities—would never think that just because everyone around them was smiling, that it was out of happiness. A puppeteer can create those very smiles with a single fingertip. Even when presented with the brightest of laughs, they could only think of it as what they could do just by moving a finger.

He was the same.

For someone who can create anything, he would never find meaning in what he created.

The mood here was not the kind that hangs over the field of a decisive battle.

This place in which Aureolus Isard stood would change into an empty and hollow war zone—that was all.

"Hmph. From your eyes, I can see that you comprehend my objective," the alchemist started in a bored tone. "Then why, I ask, must you try and stop me? Your own objective, for which you engrave runes—is that itself not for the sake of defending and rescuing the Index of Forbidden Books?"

Aureolus glanced down.

In front of the alchemist, atop a garish desk, laid a silver-haired girl, put to sleep quietly.

Kamijou automatically tried to run toward her, but Stiyl's long arm cut in from the side and prevented him from doing so.

"It's pretty simple. That girl can't be saved with those methods. She's too important to give to a surgery we know will fail, got it?"

"Nay, I say. Your reasons are born from envy. It is natural. You cannot be satisfied, for you and I are kindred spirits who have lost their dreams and despaired, and yet I have outwitted you. I shall not call this *worthless*, because the fundamental truth of my own delusions is one and the same."

Stiyl knitted his eyebrows a bit.

Aureolus Isard had said that smoothly, with no hint of sarcasm.

"Until this point, due to the all-too-extensive volume of information in the Index's brain, she required her every memory to be erased each year. This is an unbreakable rule, and a fate the likes of man cannot hope to oppose," Aureolus declared sternly. "However, this only means that one must make use of that which is not man. Now that I have arrived at this conclusion, it is instead a mystery—why has there not been a single soul to propose the use of vampires until now?"

"..."

"Vampires are that which have eternal life. That which continue to store memories, like humans, ad infinitum. However, never have I heard of such a vampire whose brain ruptured from too much information," the alchemist said. "The vampires—they have it. **They have a 'technique' to never losing themselves regardless of the quantity of information they collect.**"

"Hmm, I see. So your plot is to jump in bed with vampires and have them teach you that method, then?" Stiyl wiggled the cigarette in the corner of his mouth. "A question, if you will. If that method turned out to be impossible to use on another human body, what would you do?"

"Obvious. If impossible for the body of a human—then one must only remove the Index's body from humanity," Aureolus answered without skipping a beat.

In other words, he meant—

"**You'd get her bitten.** Tsk. I doubt there's a believer in the world who'd rejoice at being made into a plaything for one of the descendants of Cain. I'm gonna tell you something I have to tell all her other past partners as well—if you want to save someone, it's vital that you remove yourself from the picture and learn what that person is feeling. Well, *that's* something I **only learned recently**, too."

"... Worthless. That is truly hypocrisy. This child said at the very end that she did not ever want to forget. She *said* she did not ever want to forget the memories in her heart, even if it should violate the scriptures, and even if she should die for it. She said this while her body was incapable of turning a finger, without even noticing the tears flowing from her eyes—and smiling all the while."

Aureolus Isard looked somehow to be holding in his temper.

What was he remembering? What was he looking back on? Kamijou was in no position to know.

"So that won't change your thoughts no matter what, eh. Well then, allow me to use my trump card. It's a bit cruel, though." Suddenly, Stiyl looked in Kamijou's direction. "Go on, tell him, **current partner**. Tell this *wreckage* in front of us what his fatal flaw is."

"... What?"

Aureolus looked at Kamijou for the first time.

What part of that line had touched a nerve? He couldn't tell but said:

"Just what time period are you talking about, anyway?"

"Wh... at..." This time, Aureolus Isard stared at Kamijou intently.

"That's how it is. Index was saved a long time ago—not by you, but by her current partner. This guy managed to achieve what you couldn't." Stiyl grinned in honest cruelty. "About a week ago, was it? Ah, well, I guess you wouldn't have heard. After all, you weren't at her side for three years. Of course you wouldn't have gotten the message that she had actually already been saved."

"Impossible..."

"Yeah, I can understand why you can't believe it. I watched it happen directly myself, and *I* still don't. Or maybe I just don't want to? Since I've basically been confronted with the fact that **she will never look back and *see* me again**."

"Impossible, infeasible! There is absolutely no method to save the Index! Pray tell, what do you claim a human could do when he is neither a magician nor an alchemist?!"

"The specifics are tied to the good name of Necessarius—or rather, the English Puritan Church itself—so I'll stay silent on that, but let's see." Stiyl exhaled smoke with spite. "His right hand is called Imagine Breaker. Putting it simply, he's the owner of a power that is more than he deserves."

Astonishment.

The alchemist looked at Kamijou with an expression that made his serenity until now seem like it was a pipe dream.

"...Hold. That means..."

"Yes, good work, man. You've been hiding underground for three years since betraying the Roman Orthodox Church, but it was all a wasted effort. Well, I get your pain at your hard work not being rewarded, but don't worry! Right now, **just like you wished for, she seems very happy with her partner, you know?**"

"————Ha..."

That sentence was all it took.

Auroelus Isard began to laugh madly, as if everything supporting him had been destroyed.

"Ha-ha-ha-ha-ha-ha-ha-ha-ha-ha-ha-ha-ha-ha-ha-ha-ha-ha-ha-ha-ha-ha-ha-ha-ha-ha-ha-ha-ha-ha-ha-ha-ha-ha-ha-ha-ha-ha-ha-ha-ha-ha-ha-ha-ha-ha-ha-ha-ha-ha-ha-ha-ha-ha-ha-ha-ha-ha-ha-ha-ha-ha-ha-ha-ha-ha-ha-ha-ha-ha-ha-ha-ha-ha-ha-ha-ha-ha-ha-ha-ha-ha-ha-ha-ha-ha-ha-ha-ha-ha-ha-ha-ha!!"

...There's no going back for him now, Kamijou thought vaguely, yet with confidence. But he was wrong. To his broken clock–like eyes, light returned. In front of the alchemist, atop the large desk, something had started to move. The lone, sleeping girl Index had reacted to Aureolus's insane mirth and awoke in a haze.

The last pieces of Aureolus's final stronghold broke, and it began to sink.

Index opened her eyes slightly and, with the delicacy of raveling a thin strand of thread, queried:

* * *

"...Touma?"

Her eyes, however, did not look at Aureolus Isard, who was so close to her.

She didn't know where she was, how long she'd been there, who had done this, or how she'd been brought here. She hadn't even checked her own body, and she ignored the unease at thinking of what could have happened while she was passed out.

But she smiled. Her eyes narrowed as if she was very pleased.

Just because Touma Kamijou was in her sight.

"...Ah..."

Kamijou took a step back in spite of himself.

Index's manner made him quite happy. She looked at him and him alone, rather than the rest of the world. The action felt irreplaceable, like a kitten who had just opened its eyes.

But at the same time, it was very sharp and cold.

Behind Index was the alchemist, who would have certainly been the main character once upon a time. He had been completely forgotten by the girl he needed to protect, and he was frozen with a face like he was watching the end of the world.

Kamijou couldn't look directly at that reality.

Aureolus Isard—once the hero. He betrayed the Roman Orthodox Church, abandoned his faith to become an alchemist, and yet he still exhausted all his might trying to save just this one girl.

And yet a bad end awaited him.

If Touma Kamijou had made one mistake, this ending could have come to him as well.

She was a pure and saintly heroine, loved by everyone in the world...

But because she was the heroine, her kindness couldn't be for anyone other than the world's one protagonist.

That was all, and yet it was everything—those cool, realistic eyes of purity bared their fangs here.

* * *

"I should be perfect. Why do you have such composure? Am I at fault for something?"

Suddenly Kamijou remembered the words of the body double he defeated.

That was not some shoddy, poorly made copy. In fact, it was a mirror image of Aureolus Isard's very essence.

"Kh..."

Aureolus Isard could no longer even form words.

He just smiled... with his face frozen in distortion and his breath escaping a little at a time like he had hiccups.

He raised his arm above Index's head.

His stance was akin to a guillotine blade about to fall. Index, despite that, didn't take her eyes from Kamijou. That seared through the alchemist's mind excessively. He gathered strength into his uplifted arm.

"Index...!!"

Kamijou instantly tried to run to her. He was so panicked he didn't know which foot to put in front of the other. The alchemist grinned like a madman. He looked at Kamijou, who indeed seemed like the protagonist.

He reached out with his right hand. But it was too far. He wouldn't make it. With force, the alchemist...

...didn't bring down his arm.

Kamijou stopped and watched in spite of himself.

"Ugh..."

Aureolus quaked, his arm still positioned above Index's head like the blade of a guillotine.

"Uuh-uuuuuuuurrrrrgh!!"

Yet he still couldn't move.

He had lost everything he had and even attacked former companions, all to try and save this one girl. A complete stranger had already saved her, and to make things worse, she didn't even grant one look at the man who had abandoned everything for her sake.

In this situation...If it were Kamijou, would he be able to retain his faith in Index?

Could he stop himself from feeling like he had been betrayed?

Nevertheless, Aureolus Isard still couldn't bring himself to harm Index.

The alchemist gave that much import to the archive of forbidden books.

"..."

Kamijou could not move.

He had no memories. He'd heard from others that he had apparently rescued Index, but he didn't know how he did it or what feelings he'd had at the time.

He'd saved someone without knowing and had won her trust completely unaware.

With this man before him, he thought again: Just where was his *right* to monopolize her trust?

Keen. Aureolus set his glare upon him, even granting him the illusory sound of a sword being drawn.

This man could kill people with but one word. He knew that his glare was one of death, but somewhere in his heart, Kamijou was completely convinced. Aureolus's furor had by no means been quelled. He was a raving madman with nowhere to go now that he couldn't aim the angry outburst he wanted to let out at Index.

Then where exactly would he point the tip of his blade first?

It was incredibly obvious when he thought about it. He knew that this much would be completely natural.

"——Grovel, intruders!"

A roar exploded from him.

Suddenly, Kamijou felt like dozens of invisible hands were holding him down, forcing him to kneel like a bank robber whose gun had been stolen. The word *intruders* probably included Stiyl, too—out of the corner of his eye, he could see the red-haired sorcerer also being beaten into the floor.

"Guh...gah...!"

Kamijou struggled for his life, fighting back the urge to vomit that came from the feeling of all his organs being pushed on. Little by little. He slowly brought his right arm toward his chest; it felt like it was bound by a strong electromagnetic force. One millimeter at a time. *For now I just need to touch my body with my right hand. If I do that, then I might be able to get back my freedom of movement, just like when I got my memories back.*

"Ha-ha-ha-aha-ha-ha-ha! **I shall not kill you that easily. Allow me to take my time and enjoy this! I have no intention of laying hands on the Index of Forbidden Books, but if I do not take this out on you, I will lose myself!**"

The alchemist removed a slender acupuncture needle from an inside pocket. Then, with trembling hands, he pressed it to the back of his neck and thrust it in. It was as if he were depressing a button in his body.

He threw the needle aside like he was batting away an insect biting his skin.

That was the trigger for the start of his attack. Aureolus glared at Kamijou and…

"Wait."

Aisa Himegami stood in his way.

It was the exact same position she had taken once before, when she shielded Kamijou. But the situation was distinctly different. Aureolus had clung **not to Aisa Himegami, but to Deep Blood**. Now that his goal, Index, was no longer attainable, he didn't need to pay any attention to a mere means to an end…!

"Hime—"

And yet, Kamijou couldn't say it.

He could feel it from looking at her back. She was seriously worried—about Kamijou, of course, but also about Aureolus, who was steadily falling to pieces. Wordlessly, she was telling him that she somehow needed to set things right again before this came to an end they couldn't take back.

He couldn't possibly tell her a cold truth like that to her back.

"You are in my way, wench———"

But that in itself was his failure.

Kamijou looked at Aureolus's eyes; they made him think of gun barrels. Those eyes were serious. He moved his right hand in urgency. No, he *tried* to. If he didn't stop this, then Aureolus would definitely get Himegami involved. Little by little, inch by inch, he forced his right hand to come up off the floor and pulled it to his face. He touched his index finger of his ultimate right hand to his tooth and bit down on it.

Crash! It sounded like all his bones had broken, and with it returned his body's freedom. *Now's my chance*, Kamijou thought, getting up. Now he had to push Himegami out of the way and make Aureol—

"———Die."

In that moment, his words made time stop.

Stabbed to death. Strangled to death. Poisoned to death. Shot to death, sliced to death, bashed to death, publicly executed, crucified, incinerated, suffocated, crushed, run over, frozen, drowned, bombed. He compared it to every single way of killing he knew, and yet it didn't give him any insight as to the cause of Himegami's death.

There were no wounds. There was no blood loss. There clearly wasn't sickness.

She just died.

It was just like her batteries had run out. If such a thing as a soul really existed, it was like it had been removed from her body, leaving an empty shell.

She didn't even scream.

Her body swayed heavily. It leaned backward, faceup—as if to show Kamijou her face—and she started to fall. Slowly. Slowly. Himegami's face began to come into sight.

Himegami's face was wrinkled and twisted into a smile.

One that seemed about to burst into tears even now, yet never showing a single drop. It wasn't from sudden surprise or shock.

That smile said that she was prepared for this, but she wasn't able to change the outcome.

Aisa Himegami understood from the start that standing before Aureolus would bring this about.

But she had still clung to one last hope, smaller even than a ray, and tried to stop him.

No one had wanted her, and she was treated like an object until the very end.

In the same way the alchemist wasn't able to become the hero, the death of Aisa Himegami "Deep Blood" was decided simply, as if removing a piece of humanoid scenery.

There was no way…he could just watch this silently.

Don't you…

With the alchemist no longer in his sights, Kamijou darted toward the falling Aisa Himegami without a second thought. He didn't have a reason. It just felt like if she hit the floor, that magical death would come into reality and never again be changed.

"—don't you fucking give me that!"

Somehow, he was able to grab her body with both hands just before she crumpled to the ground. Her body was extremely light… like something very important had fallen out of it.

In his arms was the girl's body, strangely soft.

But though weak, a pulse could definitely be felt…**through the right hand he caught her with.**

"Wha…**Has your right hand annulled my Golden Forge?**" The alchemist's eyes froze. "Impossible. **I have surely decided the death of Aisa Himegami. Does that right hand incorporate some heavenly mysteries?!**"

"…"

Kamijou didn't respond.

Whatever. I don't care about your stupid logic. Just like when you got your stolen memories back by pure coincidence, ***you only***

canceled my order to "die" with that right hand. *I don't care about any of that stuff at all.*

Kamijou couldn't forgive this man.

He pitied him. He even sympathized with him. When he saw him unable to harm his precious Index after she had left him behind, he had even nearly lost sight of the reason he had to clench his fists.

But now that was out the window.

Even if he was betrayed by the most important person to him before his eyes. Even if he witnessed the moment the most important person to him was stolen. Even if he was tortured with rage, with nowhere to go, unable to even blame himself.

She was someone who had thought of him as truly important...

...and he had pushed his rage onto her to satisfy himself. He could never condone the way his brain was wired.

Kamijou didn't understand a thing about the Touma Kamijou before his amnesia.

What memories did he have, what past had he journeyed through, and what feelings did he have as he pursued the future? What did he like, what did he hate, what on earth did he protect, and what in creation did he want to keep on protecting?

However, there was one thing he could say for sure.

Touma Kamijou could never accept this alchemist—no, this *human.*

That was how **the two disjointed Touma Kamijous** came together at last, after coming all this way.

"Fine, Aureolus Isard. If you think you can make anything go the way you want—"

Touma Kamijou slowly lowered Aisa Himegami from his arms to the floor. Then he stood back up. He was silent, and yet he did not hide his anger, which was so great that it could have given you a static shock if you touched him.

"—then first, I'll crush your goddamn illusion...!!"

He made this declaration in the voice of Touma Kamijou, the one and only Imagine Breaker.

INTERLUDE TWO

——That's why I wanted to be a magician.

This story is from ten years ago. One day, one evening, a mountain village in Kyoto was attacked by vampires. It was completely sudden and unheralded, abrupt and illogical.

Though peaceful enough that even a police station would have been unnecessary, the small village was transformed into hell in a single night. The young ones who took up the mantle of fighting back against the vampires were buried one after another, and the remaining villagers gathered in one building. Those who attempted to escape from the village, unable to endure the terror, never returned. At the end, it was impossible to know **who was a human and who was a vampire**. The situation degraded into a quandary of promised companions killing one another.

Before dawn broke, the villagers were only divided into two categories: corpses and vampires.

Then how come I survived by myself? Who am I? thought the girl in her youthful mind. Vampires were surrounding her. They were the familiar older men and women she had just said good-bye to this evening.

The vegetable grocer who said, *It's dark now, so you should go home quickly*, came to bite the back of her neck.

——The moment he bit her, the vampire returned to ash.

Yuzuka, the girl who said, *Let's play again tomorrow*, came to bite the back of her neck.

———The moment she bit her, the vampire returned to ash.

Her mother, who pushed her out of the way and said, *Run away quickly*, came to bite the back of her neck.

———The moment she bit her, the vampire returned to ash.

Soon, everyone began to notice it. If a vampire bit the girl's neck, they would be extinguished, as if it was some counterattack. The girl's wishes had naught to do with it. Vampires would melt away and disappear just by taking her blood into their mouth, as if it had become sulfuric acid.

In spite of that, no one stopped biting her.

One by one, the villagers turned into ash, lost their physical forms, and were blown away by the wind. The girl watched it silently.

Because of course she couldn't say it.

Because all the vampires kept saying:

"I'm sorry."

One said he didn't want to become a monster, and another cried that she didn't want to turn someone else into the same monster as her. They went on having faith that they had but one salvation: to return to ash.

The vampires returned to ash.

Saying, *I'm sorry*. Saying, *I'm sorry for making you carry this sin all by yourself*. Crying until the end. Unable to smile until the very end, without being saved until their very last moments.

When she noticed, the village was covered in a blizzard of ashes.

The village was at peace. No one was around, so it was at peace. Even the culprits, the vampires who had wandered into the village, were no more. She didn't know when she had actually been bitten, but they apparently turned to ashes at some point.

The girl understood something in her gut.

Even the vampires who had attacked the town were victims. The vampires were probably very scared of the girl who had the power to kill them in one fell swoop, she thought. They trembled day after day, and they couldn't take it anymore, and they decided they needed to kill her at all costs, and yet they didn't have the power to do so.

After worries piled upon worries, they tried to assemble their forces by turning the entire village into vampires...

...But even that plan was easily annihilated by her power.

That's why I wanted to be a magician.

To rescue those who couldn't be rescued and protect those who had been abandoned. The kind of magician from storybooks, without rules and removed from common sense, who was able to save victims *and* criminals, and even drag the souls of those already dead back from the pit of hell.

At all costs. No matter what anyone said. She thought this for a long time: that she wanted to become a magician. This was all she wanted, and when she met the alchemist, the dream that she knew couldn't be granted suddenly seemed to be just down the road, and she was bewildered. She was so nervous that day that she couldn't sleep. It wasn't an uncomfortable nervousness.

And now, in front of her, was the one alchemist.

"**You are in my way, wench—**" said the dream she strived for, the corners of his mouth twisting with malice.

"**—Die.**"

She didn't know what she thought at that moment. Her consciousness didn't last. While she didn't know what she was thinking, her consciousness fell, slumping into a deep darkness.

But right before that...

"——don't fucking give me that!"

She could swear she heard a boy cry out.

Neither sorcerer nor alchemist, the boy shouldn't have been any more than human.

The boy was really angry.

But it **wasn't at** what the alchemist did. It was because she was going to die.

His figure somehow appeared blindingly radiant.

For some reason, she got the feeling that he was looking at her dream, which she could never hope to reach.

CHAPTER 4

The Sevens of Murder

Deadly_Sins.

1

In this space, lifeless but certainly vast, stood two people.

"..."

Kamijou didn't spare a glance at Himegami, breathing shallowly at his feet. He *couldn't* spare it. He didn't have that kind of time. She had risked death and used everything she had to try and stop some-one. If he cared about her for even a second, there was a man in front of him he had to stop as soon as he could.

Ten meters strong separated them.

Against a man who could distort the world to his bidding with a single word, it was a hopeless distance.

"..."

He stepped forward despite that.

He didn't have to stop. He didn't need to turn back. He wasn't fighting because he just happened to get involved, he set foot onto the battlefield with his own two feet.

"..."

Therefore, without a word, without a signal...

The esper and the alchemist quickly began their battle, each to defeat the other.

"————*Sh!*"

Kamijou exhaled slightly and tried to burst into a sprint toward Aureolus. Aureolus did nothing about it. All he did was take a single acupuncture needle out of his clothes pocket and insert it into his neck.

There were ten meters between them. If he put his back into it, he could close that in four strides—

"———**Suffocate.**"

But after Kamijou took the first step, he suddenly lost all momentum.

Grrrk. It felt like a steel cable wrapped around his neck, and he flinched and bent over at the pain. He grabbed his neck with his own right hand like a person suffering from imbibed poison might.

The memories lost to Aureolus had been revived like that, and Himegami, ordered to die, avoided death like this.

However, his breathing didn't return to normal.

He wasn't able to take a breath; it was like instant glue had hardened in the back of his throat.

Calm down… Calm down!

As Kamijou gasped for breath, he dislodged the fingers of his right hand from his throat.

What was it he said? Bind my neck with a rope?… ***No****. It was more vague, more simple. He was just saying* ***my breath should stop*** *and I should die, wasn't he?!*

So he took his fingers from his throat and forced them all the way into his mouth. Like someone trying to throw up something they just ate. His fingertip touched the back of his throat; as the urge to vomit jolted through him, he heard the *crash* of glass breaking, and his breath returned.

This all happened in a mere five seconds.

But Aureolus, who could use one word as a weapon, still had time to play around in those five seconds.

Disinterestedly, Aureolus threw away the slender, hairlike needle he had stuck into his neck and announced:

"**Electrocute him.**"

An instant later, Kamijou found himself surrounded by pale blue electric lights from all directions.

Before the muscles on his spine could freeze in terror, the vortex of sparks burned through the air and scrambled toward him.

...?!

He immediately thrust out his right hand, though it wasn't a calculated move.

However, like a lightning rod, the electricity gathered only to his outstretched fingers. The sparks that touched his hand recoiled back like a snake at deadly poison, but they began to quietly disappear.

I can erase them...

Kamijou's heartbeat, though, quickened from excitement more than nervousness.

In contrast, the alchemist narrowed his eyes slightly. He took another hairlike needle and jabbed it into the back of his neck.

"Strangle him. In addition, crush him to death."

Dozens of ropes flew at him from the floor, creating waves in it like the ocean surface. At the same moment they wrapped themselves firmly around Kamijou's neck, an abandoned car fell from the ceiling, also creating waves.

I can erase them...!

But with a simple swing of his right hand, the ropes ripped apart like strips of wet paper, and the lump of steel descending on him crumbled like a sugar cube and disappeared into the void.

Aureolus threw the needle aside as if a poisonous bug had crawled up his neck.

I can erase them. I can do this. I can avoid his attacks. If he gives orders with a word, that also means he can only throw one attack at me at a time. If I keep a cool head and deal with them, he's nothing to be afraid of!

Though Aureolus's means of attack involved giving commands using words, it also meant that Kamijou could predict the attacks as he heard those words. It was the same concept as taking cards quickly in karuta. If he said, “electrocute him,” he could guess just from the four letters *elec* what kind of attack was coming.

It only gave him a split second.

However, having a second to spare during fistfights didn’t happen in the first place. In boxing, punches can fly at you every 0.3 seconds. Though the force of each and every one of Aureolus’s blows was tremendous, the speed of his attacks wasn’t much different from human fists.

Understanding it would let him extinguish his fear of the unknown. The gist was that this was the same as punching it out with delinquents pulling out-of-place knives on him, despite it being a children’s tussle.

Aureolus scowled a bit, possibly having caught on to the composure in Kamijou’s expression.

“I see. The true explanation—your right hand must erase all, including my Ars Magna.”

Kamijou had a slight doubt at the alchemist, whose own composure didn’t crumble.

“Then it means this. **Is it impossible to erase an attack that cannot be touched by your right hand?**”

This time, he thought Aureolus’s words would freeze him alive.

“A gun in my hand. Load out: magic bullets. Usage: firing. Quantity: One is more than enough.”

The alchemist gleefully stuck a thin needle into the back of his neck.

He lightly threw his hand to the side, and instantly, it was gripping a sword.

At a glance, it looked like a rapier, fit to be held by princes in children’s books, but it wasn’t.

It was a disguised gun—there was a flintlock, like the kind pirates would have used a long time ago, buried in the sword’s guard.

Something is coming! **Kamijou’s body automatically overflowed with tension . . .**

“Begin firing at a speed exceeding that of human kinetic vision.”

* * *

Aureolus's rapier flashed up, slicing the air in front of him—as soon as Kamijou saw it happen, the sound of gunpowder exploding resounded through the room. A moment later, something lightly scraped his cheek, and then a magic bullet shining with pale white light collided with the wall, scattering a roar of sparks.

"...!"

It was simple. He pulled the trigger built into the sword. That was it. But Kamijou couldn't be expected to intercept a magic bullet sailing at his eyes. He froze, his right hand still in place.

It was simple. He pulled the trigger prepared in the sword. That was all. However, expecting the kind of ability that could intercept a magic bullet soaring at a person's eyes was harsh. Kamijou froze, his right hand still in place. It made him tense up more compared to some supernatural ability or sorcery, because he could easily imagine the destructive force of a lead bullet.

This wasn't anywhere near the same speed as the Limen Magna the body double used.

It wasn't a question of sorcery or esper powers; these magic bullets were impossible for a human to avoid or defend against. They spelled certain death.

Aureolus, looking satisfied, tossed aside the needle stuck in his neck.

"Mass-produce previous action. Prepare rapid firing via ten disguised guns."

As soon as the words left his lips, a total of ten sword guns appeared in Aureolus's hands, five each, spread out like steel fans.

If I get shot by one of those, I'm done for. It was definite that Touma Kamijou couldn't dodge or block them.

Run...!

Therefore, Kamijou would try to evade before they were fired. He was about to attempt a roll to the side...

...but he suddenly thought of something.

Behind him were Himegami, right at his feet and barely able to breathe, and Stiyl, collapsed by the wall and unable to move.

"Idiot! What are you stop—!"

Stiyl's stunned shout, and...

"Preparations complete. All ten disguised guns begin firing simultaneously."

...Aureolus's voice and ten blue-shining magic bullets making direct hits on Kamijou's entire body all happened at the same time.

The ten impacts hit everywhere on Kamijou like iron fists.

To say that they "flew at him" wouldn't do them justice. He couldn't feel this crazy, invisible, high-speed assault any more than he could a video that dropped a frame.

"Gh...gah...?!"

His only saving grace was that the magic bullets didn't have enough power to kill him. He was blown backward being pummeled with slow, old-fashioned shells, and he left a trail of blood in his wake. Like a bouncing gumball, he tumbled onto the floor, and then *slam!* He hit something and stopped. When he looked, he saw it was Stiyl's body. It seemed he'd been sent almost seven meters back.

He thought his flesh had torn and his bones had broken, but it was only intense pain. It seemed like he could still move everything fine.

He didn't think he was lucky. The alchemist had said, **"I shall not kill you so easily."**

Aureolus appeared gratified by this result and pointed the palm of his hand toward Kamijou again.

"...Tsk. What is that? As far as I can tell from the earlier memory manipulation and this sequence of attacks, it certainly looks just like you're altering reality to your whims with a few words."

But Stiyl spoke first, as if to block Aureolus from doing so.

The alchemist diverted his attention to Stiyl, lying prone on the floor.

"Hah. Ars Magna is nothing more than the pinnacle of alchemy. It seems to me that it is only sensible that though attaining it is unimaginably difficult, it is the end goal, so one will naturally arrive there if one continues to walk down the path."

"That's absurd. Even *if* the Ars Magna is theoretically complete, the incantation is too long—one or two hundred years wouldn't be enough to finish it. You can't shorten the spell any more, either, and even if you split the work up by passing it down from parent to child to grandchild, the ceremony would be distorted like a game of telephone…!"

Stiyl shot a brief glance toward Kamijou as he said this.

Kamijou nodded. He understood. If Aureolus was performing these attacks with a few of his words, then it would be safe if he diverted his attention and made him think less about attacking them.

While Stiyl drew Aureolus's attention, he was implicitly saying:

Find a way to beat him somehow with what little time I'm buying.

"It seems like it's something difficult to realize." Aureolus didn't realize it. "Hah. One cannot complete the ceremony in the span of one hundred or two hundred years—**yes, if one should do so alone**. Dividing the work by passing it down through the generations will warp the ceremony like a game of telephone—this is correct, **but it is not necessary to pass it down to one child**."

"…What?"

Stiyl furrowed his brow, and Index talked in a scornful voice.

"It's the Gregorian Choir. If you directly control two thousand people and have them chant the spell, the pace of the work is multiplied by two thousand.…Even if it was a ceremony that took four hundred years, you could get it done in just seventy days!"

An operation done not in series, but in parallel.

Kamijou looked at Index. He thought that what she was saying was knowledge from the 103,000 grimoires in her head…but that wasn't it. No one had ever completed Ars Magna in the first place, so there wouldn't *be* a book in which his solution would be written. She put it all together in her head by combining the knowledge she already had.

"In reality, I was intending to multiply the effect by clashing spell with spell. I accelerated it by only an additional one hundred and twenty times; this cannot be called a success."

Kamijou scraped together the tattered pieces of his awareness and looked around.

His body moved. The distance to Aureolus was only seventeen

meters—not all that far. If he could somehow dodge the alchemist's onslaught, he should be able to aggress on him immediately.

"One hundred and twenty times... You did it in just half a day?!" He got the feeling that the act had been wiped out of Stiyl's words. "But this is a gathering of espers. If you use something like the Gregorian Choir, their bodies would be destroyed, because of their different brain circuits!"

Kamijou looked around once again. There was nothing that looked suitable for a weapon. He groped around in his pocket, and although it wasn't a weapon, he felt something cold and hard.

Two attacks.

If he could block or avoid Aureolus's words twice, he might be able to somehow get in close enough.

"Yes, but why do you not realize it?" The corners of Aureolus's mouth turned up. "**If something is broken, one need only fix it, correct?** In the same way I fixed those destroyed buildings."

Kamijou immediately ground to a halt and looked at Aureolus.

The alchemist continued, without much interest.

"Ah, I have not told you yet, have I? **Those students—today was certainly not their first time dying.**"

"Y-you..."

A scathing-hot whiteness formed in Kamijou's thoughts.

Aureolus stuck a needle into the back of his neck and shifted his gaze back to him.

"Correct. I am not so foolish as to be ignorant of my own sins.... Yes, that's right. I failed myself. I continued to believe in the certain existence of somebody I wanted to save despite. Though I would not possibly have imagined it coming to this!"

He flung the needle away as if he were scraping poison out of his body.

"Bastard!!"

But before Aureolus could weave his "words," Kamijou stood.

He reaffirmed the solid feeling in his pocket.

Like it was natural, Aureolus began to say something that would crush the now-standing Kamijou, but before he could, Kamijou took the cell phone out of his pocket and hurled it at Aureolus with all his strength.

"...Hm?"

Aureolus was perplexed for a moment—and by then, Kamijou had already launched into a sprint.

He didn't think he could finish off the alchemist with a mere cell phone. All he needed to do was create a tiny opening for him to get up close. As expected, Aureolus's attention switched to the cell phone.

"...Stop the projectile. Fall to the ground, meaningless thrown stone."

In that slight loss of time, Kamijou had already closed the distance to half. Just one more attack. If he could somehow block Aureolus's strike, he'd be able to switch to the offensive—!

"The disguised guns in my hand again. Usage: firing. Execute preparations on my mark."

But, **on the other hand, he inevitably needed to get past one more attack to reach him.**

Aureolus disposed of the guns fitted in the ten swords in his hands. As the empty hidden guns hit the floor with a *clatter*, the alchemist's hands were gripping trick guns again, like having used that sound as the signal.

Kamijou's face tightened in tension, and at the moment Aureolus tried to announce his decisive words...

"Innocentius!"

But Aureolus's movements jerked to a halt at Stiyl's shout.

Kamijou looked at Stiyl, stunned. Impossible. He couldn't use that nuisance without hanging up rune-engraved cards around the room. Besides, the Witch-Hunter King was staking out the student dorms in order to protect Index, wasn't it?

It was a *bluff*.

A pointless bluff used to extend Kamijou's life, if only by a moment.

The light of Aureolus's gun barrel–like eyes turned to Stiyl.

"Float into the air, ye priest of London," muttered Aureolus, like he was setting him up for execution. In response, Stiyl floated up near the ceiling as if there were no gravity. Kamijou stopped moving in spite of himself. If he used Imagine Breaker, he could rescind Aureolus's order, but the sorcerer was clearly too far away.

"You fool! **You can't possibly defeat Aureolus as you are now! His weakness is those needles! You should know about medical scie—**"

Stiyl shouted with all his might to thaw the frozen Kamijou...

...and Aureolus, glaring daggers at Stiyl, commanding:

"**Explode, ye runic magician**."

The *pop* sound almost sounded comical.

Just as he had declared, Stiyl's body inflated like a balloon for a moment. Immediately afterward, his body burst out vehemently from within. A jumbled mass of blood, flesh, bones, organs, and muscles splattered all over the nearby surroundings.

Parts of his flesh and blood instantly reached the ceiling, then spread out from there in a dome shape. It covered the vast room like a planetarium—here was a work of art of the sorcerer's very blood and flesh.

"...!"

And the terrifying part was that his blood vessels **were connected**. His organs **hadn't been destroyed**. It was almost like a train map. The red fluid his bared heart was pumping passed through his outstretched arteries, reached the organs that were dotted about, and returned back to the heart.

He still wasn't dead.

Despite being in that state, Stiyl Magnus was very much alive.

In pieces.

The sorcerer's possessions, cards with runes engraved on them, whipped up like a blizzard of cherry petals.

Thump came a sound.

It was the sound of the groggy Index passing out and collapsing atop the desk at the sight of such extremes.

"...Damn...it."

Kamijou frantically worked his thoughts, which were on the verge of being paralyzed by the horrific situation. He used everything he had to kill the shriek rising in his throat. Stiyl hadn't asked for help, even at the very end. The thing he wanted to tell Kamijou, even knowing things would turn out this way... He couldn't possibly put that out of his mind.

You fool! You can't possibly defeat Aureolus as you are now! His weakness is those needles! You should know about medical scie—

He recalled Stiyl's words.

His needles... Medical science?

Now that he mentioned it, Aureolus had been hurriedly moving his hands around as if searching for something for a few moments now. The acupuncture needles he had kept stabbing, over and over, into the back of his neck... Was Stiyl talking about those?

Academy City used even drugs for Ability Development. In this city, apparently knowledge of medicine and medicinal science was beyond that of the norm. His *knowledge* of acupuncture came to him like it was an English vocabulary word on a pop quiz.

Leaving *qigong* and eastern mysteries aside, in terms of **medical science,** acupuncture was basically a way to directly stimulate one's nerves. The stuff could relieve pain or control the functions of organs by triggering excitation. Back before they had anesthesia, it was probably valued pretty highly as an almost-magical way of blocking pain.

...But what about it?

Kamijou mentally tilted his head in confusion. As one might guess from the fact that needles aren't used in modern surgery, the reality was that acupuncture couldn't actually bring about such dramatic effects in somebody's body. It wasn't like narcotics, which could release "limiters" on your physical body or thoughts, either. The most it could do was directly stimulate your nerves, so it couldn't do anything more than spur the release of endorphins, put them into an excited state, and ease anxiety, so—

————Anxiety?

"Change contents. Suspend firing of disguised guns. Prepare for elimination of intruder using the blades."

Kamijou had forgotten to keep running and was blankly staring at Stiyl's end, but he looked back to Aureolus at those words. The trick guns, which should have been staring death at him, spun around and around in the alchemist's hands.

Despite that, he couldn't escape the one question that came to mind. Now that he had one question, many, many others appeared and dragged him down into them.

Yeah. Something is strange.

It happened with both Himegami and Stiyl. They were killed with single words, *die* and *explode*. If he could make everything and anything go his way, why did he need vampires or Deep Blood? If he could make anything exactly how he wanted, **why didn't he create a vampire with his own hands?**

Yeah, something's definitely weird about this——!

No. If Aureolus Isard could *really* make anything and everything the way he **wanted...**

Then why the hell didn't Index turn back to look at Aureolus even one time?

The ultimate Ars Magna, which distorted reality in accordance with Aureolus's words.

That wasn't how it worked.

What if it was sorcery that **haphazardly** distorted reality into whatever Aureolus thought?

"Wa...it. Is that it...?"

Stiyl had said that it wouldn't be hard for Kamijou to beat Aureolus.

Aureolus knew them; he knew Stiyl, Index, and Himegami. Because he was familiar with them, he knew for certain that even with their full power, they would never be able to fight on par with him.

But Kamijou was the sole exception. He had only met Kamijou today—he was a totally unknown quantity.

"Wha... ***Has your right hand annulled my own Golden Forge?*** *Impossible.* ***I have surely decided the death of Aisa Himegami. Does that right hand incorporate some heavenly mysteries?!"***

Of *course* he would feel anxiety at that.

And if everything was aligning with his own thoughts, then that very anxiety was…

"So…That's it…," murmured Kamijou in blank amazement. It was nothing. Now that he had figured out the trick, it was simple.

However…

"Hm. **The source of your excessive confidence…It was that right hand, correct?**"

As he looked at Kamijou, Aureolus pushed the needle he removed from his inside pocket into his neck, looked at him casually, and said:

"Then first, I will sever that right arm. Disguised guns, rotate your blades and fire."

There was no sound.

The moment Aureolus waved his right hand, the afterimages of the trick swords were all over Kamijou, spinning like the blades on a fan at incredible speeds. He had his hands full just barely dealing with *them*.

It was impossible to describe it as "something" had "flown at him."

One moment, the trick swords were in the alchemist's hands…

And the next, they had severed Touma Kamijou's right arm and hit the wall behind him.

Like a hot knife through a stick of butter, Kamijou's right arm was cleanly sliced from his shoulder.

Whoosh, whoosh—his right arm danced and turned in the air.

There was no pain. There was no heat. Kamijou stared dumbfounded—just stared dumbfounded at his detached right arm.

——*He cut off…my arm?*

Whoosh, whoosh—as he watched his arm fly through the air…

——*He can do whatever he wants, he could have just crushed my heart with one word.*

Face not distorting with pain or terror, he had but a single question…

——*But he decided to cut off my right arm first?*

He kneaded all the questions into a single idea and built it up…

——*Even though he should be able to do whatever he wants.*

Fresh blood spewed out of where he had been cut, and as if he was remembering something…

——*Because he couldn't do anything about* ***this power in this right hand.***

Certainly without pain and also without feeling warmth…

——***He couldn't take away my Imagine Breaker if he didn't do something like cut off my entire arm along with it?***

Whoosh, whoosh. His arm spun and dropped to the floor, creating the dull sound of flesh being hit.

In that moment, his idea, born from his doubts, resolved itself into certainty.

Now that he knew what he had to do, the rest was simple.

Crick. He heard a sound like a switch being flipped in his temples.

2

"Aha-ha-ha-ha-ha-ha-ha-ha-ha-ha-ha-ha-ha-ha-ha-ha-ha-ha-ha-ha-ha-ha-ha-ha-ha-ha-ha-ha-ha-ha-ha-ha-ha-ha-ha-ha-ha-ha-ha-ha-ha-ha-ha-ha-ha-ha-ha-ha-ha-ha-ha-ha-ha-ha-ha-ha-ha-ha-ha-ha-ha-ha-ha-ha-ha-ha-ha-ha-ha-ha-ha-ha-ha-ha-ha-ha-ha-ha-ha-ha-ha-ha-ha-ha-ha-ha-ha-ha-ha-ha-ha-ha——!!"

At that moment, Aureolus involuntarily took a step back at the unforeseen event.

He'd cut off the boy's right arm, and yet he was laughing.

He thought for a moment that he'd gone mad from intense pain and fear, but no. This was no more than normal laughter, made in sureness of victory.

But what was truly strange was the fact that he could stay *normal* in this extreme situation at all.

What… is that?

The first thing Aureolus felt was not fear but discomfort. *I know not what that boy is thinking, but this duel was over long ago.*

Therefore, any further discomfort is unnecessary. I shall kill him quickly. With a tinge of irritation, he tossed the needle in his neck aside.

"Disguised gun, to my hands. Load out: magic bullets. Quantity: One is more than enough."

He waved his right hand. In reply, a rapier with a flintlock gun hidden inside materialized out of thin air. Satisfied with his own perfect technique, he continued to give orders.

"Usage: crushing. In accordance with the original objective of a single bullet, fire and crush my prey's skull."

Aureolus pulled the trigger. The gunpowder propelled the magic bullet out, aiming for the still-laughing boy's eyes.

No human could dodge that speed, nor could one block that force.

The boy wouldn't be able to do anything. The inside of his head would simply splatter like a tomato.

That's what should have happened.

"Wha...?"

He couldn't believe his eyes. It wasn't like the kid *did* anything. He thought he had fired the blue magic bullet accurately, but somehow, somewhere, it went wrong, passed by the boy's face, and struck the wall behind him.

Did I judge the distance wrongly? No...

He declared an order once again.

"Copy previous action. Usage: blind fire. Ten disguised guns firing at once."

Aureolus pulled ten of the camouflaged guns out of nothing, and bullets flew from their barrels that looked like a bouquet of flowers.

However...

Of the ten bullets that should have hit him precisely, not one of them could even deliver a glancing blow to the boy.

A misfire?! Impossible...!

Aureolus watched in disbelief—watched the boy who had twice avoided certain death.

Splaaaash. An unbelievably large amount of fresh blood was spurting out of the open wound in the boy's shoulder. The spray was showering his face in blood as well, his face was being painted with blotches of red.

And yet still the boy laughed.

He laughed as if the darkness in his body had all ejected from the gaping hole left by his severed arm.

The boy wasn't doing anything but laugh.

Aureolus started to give a third execution order to the **enemy** before him, but then he wondered:

However, can the Ars Magna even be *dodged not once, but twice by pure coincidence, without some trick?*

The alchemist halted, startled at his misgivings.

He knew the power of his technique the best. It wasn't the gentle sort that could be dodged by sheer luck.

Wait... is he doing something? Do I only not realize it?!

The boy, laughing in earnest jubilation, stuck out a tongue to lick his lips as if they were covered with sauce.

Not even a fallen vampire would do this—it was like he was reveling in the taste of his own blood.

What... is this?!

That was the reason Aureolus couldn't help but feel unease in his heart.

What is that? He can still fight? With that body? Without his right arm? Impossible. The possibility of that is nonexistent. He is already at the point where he would die of blood loss if I left him here. It is fine. There is no problem. There cannot be a problem. There shouldn't be a problem———!

Yes—the very moment that he felt that "unease"...

The boy should have been drained of all his strength after losing his arm, but he muttered something heroically anyway. His face was grinning. He was looking at the alchemist and grinning.

"Kh... agh. You damned knave... **There is no escape from my Ars Magna. Innumerable decapitation blades into position. Sever his head from his body immediately!**"

With those words, many giant guillotine blades came out of the ceiling above the boy's head as if they were cutting through the surface of water. Each one was a blade of execution weighing one hundred kilograms. The hands of gravity pulled them down, but Kamijou simply continued to smile, without attempting to avoid them or defend himself against them.

It is fine. He cannot dodge that. It will make a direct hit without doubt. If it makes a direct hit, then it will naturally finish him. That was my order. I definitely ordered that. I ordered it, I ordered it, I ordered that! Therefore, there is no problem. There is no issue, and thus no need for concern!

Aureolus repeated it many times in his mind. He repeated it again and again. If things proceeded how he thought, in the way he thought, then that boy would die. He should die. He couldn't possibly *not* die...but the more he thought about it, the more his misgivings inflated. It was like those misgivings were saying that all of his words were like prayers meant to suppress the great unease sleeping deep in his soul.

In reality, and just as he thought, the many guillotine blades made direct contact with Kamijou's neck.

He had gotten him for sure this time.

But **all of the guillotines shattered to pieces like sugar cubes just from touching him.**

The boy was laughing.

He was looking at the distressed alchemist—mercifully, cynically, pitifully, disdainfully, pleasurably, as if mocking him for fun.

The boy was laughing...

...with an expression that stated he'd already completely seen through to the weakness in his attack.

Damn...him. By what means...?!

He no longer needed to hold back. Aureolus pierced Kamijou with a sharp, stabbing look.

"Simply die, bo——"

——y, he tried to shout, but then the whispers of his heart wormed their way into his mind like noise.

But will just that one word actually kill him?

He fumbled with his quaking hand to bring out an acupuncture needle, but the many needles fell to the floor in a mess.

But the alchemist couldn't pay this any mind.

As if stricken with horror, Aureolus Isard looked at Kamijou. At some point, the sharp look in his eyes had been chipped into a rusty blade. Even though he wasn't thinking it, his legs strangely started to step back. The sole of his shoe stepped on something and crushed it. He had broken all the needles on the floor.

Ars Magna distorted reality in accordance with his thoughts.

However, if Aureolus was to think *this will not do the trick* or *this cannot defeat him* at the same time, then **even that would become reality—it was a double-edged sword**.

That was the reason he did not create a vampire or Deep Blood "in the way he thought." It was simple—somewhere in his brain he had thought, *I cannot create something like that*, and thus he was unable to.

Aureolus's words were analogous to bullets.

Various ideas would get mixed into one's thought processes. He couldn't give resolute orders with something like that. It would even run the risk of self-destruction. Therefore, he stabilized his mental image into a bullet and fired it by delivering words from his mouth. It worked under the same principle as reciting English vocabulary words aloud to memorize them.

At its roots, his Ars Magna was a sorcery that twisted reality in accordance with his thoughts, not with his words.

However, after coming this far, Aureolus Isard had made a mistake controlling his words.

Vague images in his head were coming into reality by themselves before he could stabilize them with words. It was no different from a handgun spontaneously discharging, completely independent of the user's volition.

Aureolus had an emergency method prepared in case things came to this sort of situation, but…

Damn it, my needles… Where are my acupuncture needles? Why did I drop them? It is so that I won't become like this, so I can kill my unease that I carry them around with me! ***Without them, I am——***

Aureolus gasped.

Without them, what? Halt, stop, do not think any more than that. I must not think thoughts that shall lead me to whence I cannot recover———!

The more he tried to avoid it, the deeper his thoughts fell into the hole. Aureolus was unable to stop thinking despite understanding that. Ceasing his thoughts would mean giving in. Like a snowman beginning to roll down a mountain, Aureolus's misgivings grew without limit and started to lose their purpose.

The boy in front of him spoke nothing.

Wordlessly, silently, he began to walk toward Aureolus.

This conversely plunged Aureolus into the depths of panic.

He could not stop this boy. He did not know how to stop him. Therefore, Aureolus could do nothing. He stood there like a scarecrow, awaiting his visitation. There was no other alternative.

The next thing he knew, the boy was right under his nose.

How ironic this scene was, that he should stand to face him with the desk upon which Index was collapsed between the two of them.

And even despite all of that, the alchemist found himself unable to move, like a snake had glared at him.

I see. Stiyl, Index, Aisa Himegami. Every one of them was familiar. Therefore, I knew their true power and understood beforehand the fact that they could not stand against my Ars Magna. However—what is this boy? This is our first meeting. If I do not know his real potential, then I also do not know whether my Ars Magna will———!

"Hey."

His shoulders flinched at the boy's sudden voice, like Aureolus was a child being lectured to.

The boy spoke.

"You bastard. You weren't thinking that you could crush my Imagine Breaker just by cutting off my right arm, did you?"

He bared his teeth, his eyes with such a glint that they might have fired red light from them.

The boy spoke, sincerely delighted.

Wha— Wait, don't think unease ba————

Aureolus was able to pray. But he wasn't able to stop thinking.

In that instant.

That hole, left by Kamijou's missing right arm... Something strange happened to the flow of fresh blood erupting from it. *Slosh.* Something unknown, something transparent, slowly began to show its form, like scattering blood on a glass sculpture.

Something leaped out of the hole in Kamijou's right shoulder then, and it was certainly not a human arm.

It was a jaw.

It was like nothing he'd ever seen before, save in legends, for it had a length of more than ten meters and a ferocious brutality. It was the gargantuan, gigantic jaw of a dragon king.

He should not have been able to see it, for it was transparent, but it was covered in blood. As if it were the boy's own arm, he slowly opened its mouth, lined with fangs like saws.

As if he was saying that this was the true form of the *power* packed into his right arm.

One of the fangs made contact with the air.

Nothing particularly large changed. However, something he couldn't see had definitely been altered. Though the alchemist's presence had been filling the room, it vanished, as if **his very initiative, the ownership of this area, had been modified.**

Wha...

Aureolus looked up in spite of himself to the distasteful planetarium of human flesh, created with Stiyl Magnus's skin and blood. The carnage spread about the room began to slither toward one point... as if his order to "**explode**" had been canceled.

It... can't be. He is coming back? The same as Himegami, who I already destroyed———!

The moment he thought that, Stiyl dropped to the floor, not a scratch on him.

Icy fear stabbed into Aureolus's back.

Without a doubt, his own insecurity had revived the sorcerer.

Wait, this is no more than my unease, calm down, erase unease and I can erase this ridiculous thing———!!

Desperately biting down on the terror about to claw out his heart, Aureolus attempted one last resistance. This scenario should have been no more than something created by Aureolus's own misgivings. So if he calmed himself down and got rid of this anxiety, the strange power in the boy should also disappear.

But the light of the transparent dragon king's shining eyes was brought to quietly glare at him.

That was all it took to give Aureolus the illusion that his vision was fading from terror alone.

I can't... There's no way.

Immediately after thinking that, the jaw of the dragon king opened as wide as possible and devoured the alchemist from the head down.

FINAL CHAPTER

Deep Blood Encroaches

Devil_or_God.

"I wonder about it every time, your body is strangely *fantastic*, isn't it?" said the middle-aged doctor with the frog face in the completely white hospital room.

"..."

Kamijou couldn't figure out how to respond, and his gaze fell to his own arm on the bed, tightened with a cast.

His right arm had been cleanly and completely severed by Aureolus's Ars Magna. The fact that it was an extremely clean cut was fortune in the midst of misfortune, though. There was no damage to the cells in that cross-section, so the medical staff had performed emergency procedures and stuck his arm back in. As it was stabilizing, the arm was connected completely after only a day.

He possessed knowledge of yakuza having their little fingers reattached after they got cut off, but he had never given a thought to whether you could do the same with much larger body tissue, like that of an arm. Well, if he *did* have that sort of unsavory knowledge, Kamijou would start to seriously begin doubting his past self. Before the amnesia.

"And to add to that, you've had two hospital visits within the last ten days. That will always cause rumors to sprout among the nurses, you know? Could it be that you're into nurses?"

"...What are you talking about? I have no risky ideas about being played around with on the operating table or anything."

"Is that so? That's too bad—I thought I had finally run into someone with the same tastes, you know?"

Kamijou looked at the frog-faced doctor silently. All of his will to be in this doctor's care flew out the window when he considered that he had become a doctor for *those* reasons. *Actually, I want to hit the call button right now.*

"Yes? Just so we don't have any misunderstandings, I'd rather play around than be played around with, all right? And rather than the operating table, I'd rather it be the delivery tab—"

"I'd rather not hear about your obsessions.... Wait, I mean, shut the hell up! Quit making weird gestures as you explain it! You want to be a nurse? Disgusting!!"

His hand really went for the nurse call button this time, but the doctor gave a dejected look, left him with an "I'm leaving," and went out of the hospital room. *I wonder why? I get the feeling that he looked really disappointed...*

Someone else came in as a replacement.

It was the man ridiculously ill suited for modern Japan, Stiyl Magnus.

"I have no intent of cooperating with you for the moment or to make friends. I just, well, came to check up on you."

"...Wait a second. I, Touma Kamijou, would seriously and respectfully like to throw a question out there: How and why the hell are you just gallivanting about?"

Stiyl groaned and scowled in sincerity, then fell quiet.

Speaking of bad taste... There's probably no injured person grosser than what he was. His body was filleted into small pieces of flesh, but he was still alive! I suppose it's not every day you experience that sort of thing, what with your blood vessels intact and still circulating blood to your scattered organs...

"Well, I was thinking of thanking you for your assistance, but... like, when I think about it, this whole thing was absurd. All you ended up doing **was making Aureolus self-destruct**."

"Heh. That's all thanks to the wonderful acting abilities of Touma Kamijou."

That's right—Touma Kamijou didn't have the power to defeat Aureolus Isard.

However, Aureolus used magic that would warp reality to align with his thoughts. In that case, things were easy: He just had to get Aureolus to think a certain way…

To make him think that **Aureolus Isard could absolutely not win against Touma Kamijou.**

That's what his big bluffing scheme was for.… Well, in all honesty, Kamijou didn't remember much about what happened after his arm was severed. It was more like his brain was going haywire from all the pain and the shock rather than him consciously thinking, *I must act.* Excessive blood is said to be linked to sexual arousal by suicide enthusiasts, but that was probably the cause of his mad cackling.

But he didn't breathe a word of that. When humans want to look cool, they do it with everything they've got.

"But, man, it's crazy we both lived through that. I had an arm cut off, and you were a flesh planetarium! I feel like I've been beholden to the mysteries of the human body… Hey, wait. Why are you grinning to yourself?"

"No, no. Listen to you—seems you didn't notice my help." Stiyl's grin was cocky, like he was purely making fun of him. "Twice after your arm got cut off. You stood still and dodged Aureolus's bullets, right? How on earth do you think that happened?"

"… Huh?"

"It's true that your act fooled Aureolus completely. But there was no way your bluff would sink in right away, right? Twice, after your arm was cut off and you started your comedy routine. Wasn't it because you effortlessly avoided his attacks that he started to believe you?"

"… Umm."

Kamijou looked at Stiyl like a fool.

"You still don't understand? Let me spell it out for you. Aureolus's first two attacks didn't fail because your bluff was working. I simply used magic to screw with Aureolus's sense of distance."

"Wha...?!"

Kamijou was startled.

"Is it that surprising? My specialty is fire. It's really not difficult to make a heat mirage, change where light gets refracted and blur his vision," he explained like it was a trifling matter.

"No, not that! I'm not surprised about that! You were a freaking flesh planetarium at the time, all floating in the air! You were still able to use magic like that?!"

"'Flesh planetarium,' eh? Quite a merry way of putting it...But there's no real problem, is there? I was still *alive* at the time, so there's no reason I couldn't temper my life force to refine it into mana. Fortunately for me, the rune cards I had hidden scattered everywhere when my body exploded, too."

Kamijou stared at him, flabbergasted.

This incident had involved vampires and Deep Blood...This guy here wasn't the— Couldn't have been the biggest monster of them all, could he?

"**Leaving pointless things like that aside**, I figured you'd want to hear about your own charges, too. I just came here to explain what happened after Misawa School."

His charges.

Kamijou looked at his right hand, wrapped in a cast. The dragon's jaw. It was nothing more than self-destruction born from Aureolus's anxiety, but he was driven to self-destruction by none other than Kamijou himself.

"Oh, there's no need for faces like that. Aureolus apparently imagined that dragon king to be something mental, rather than something physical. The point is that he accidentally imagined some kind of ghost, which would take his soul without touching his body, or something like that."

"???"

"To put it simply, you didn't injure his body at all. On the other hand, that means you destroyed Aureolus Isard's mind *without injuring him at all.*"

"...Is that supposed to be praise?"

"It's certainly praise*worthy*; in short, you resolved the entire situation just by stealing Aureolus Isard's memories. This was a team battle against a sorcerer holing up in a stronghold, and yet the only casualty was the one from the Thirteen Knights by the elevators. That's only the third time something like *this* has ever happened in the entire two-thousand-year-long history of magic."

So I should be happy about it? thought Kamijou, but suddenly he remembered. He didn't think the Roman Orthodox Church's Gregorian Choir had gotten through unscathed. Stiyl might not remember it, since his own memories were erased at the time.

"...And? What happened to Aureolus Isard after he lost his memory?"

He couldn't possibly be in the same hospital as us, right? thought Kamijou.

"Oh, that's simple. I killed him."

Stiyl Magnus answered outright, with such brevity that Kamijou thought he misheard him.

"What are you making that face for? Listen up. Aureolus Isard betrayed the Roman Orthodox Church and converted to alchemy. He made an enemy out of Academy City the instant he confined Deep Blood and made Misawa School into a fortress, *plus* he's got a bounty on his head for the forces of Crossism that took on Misawa School and ended up being defeated themselves.... And, of course, Index and I—or rather, the witch-hunting specialists in Necessarius—have gotten their own orders, too."

Stiyl was speaking with irritation, possibly because he wasn't allowed to smoke in the hospital ward.

"Look. After making enemies out of this many different worlds, and with all his memories gone, could Aureolus Isard really have opposed them? No—he wouldn't remember anything in the first place, and without anything to protect, do you think he would have the willpower to keep on living with the whole world against him?"

"..."

"Aureolus wouldn't be killed easily. Reprisals are one thing, but on top of that, he's the first sorcerer in the world to succeed at Ars Magna. Of course, many organizations trying to search for that secret method would come looking for Aureolus to torture him—and the worst part is that since Aureolus lost all of his memories, **he'd never even be able to cough it up**," said Stiyl with annoyance. "Look. All Aureolus had left to him was either death or a hell worse than death. If I were told to pick one, I'd recommend the former without skipping a beat."

But still, thought Kamijou.

"I can't... agree with that. Of course I can't. Even if that was the only way... If there's such a thing as a world where people laugh together by taking the lives of others, then why the hell did we even go to that stupid Misawa School in the first place?"

That's right. Kamijou had motivation to fight because he couldn't agree with something. Deep Blood was treated like a playing card, the students were used and thrown away like cogs for the Gregorian Choir and Limen Magna, and Aureolus had tried to kill Himegami just to lash out with the anger he couldn't endure. Kamijou tried to move onto the battlefield without running away from it because he couldn't forgive the *bastards* who thought nothing of human lives, and yet...

If, at the very end of it all, he acknowledged someone's death as *right*...

...then Kamijou couldn't bear the guilt from wielding a fist himself.

"..."

Besides, Aureolus was definitely an unforgivable bastard, but he didn't think he was completely worthless as a human being.

Because if things had really gone according to Aureolus's plans...

Then the reason Index hadn't turned back to look at Aureolus was because **he never wanted to "revise" her**, even if it meant he was rejected—that would have been the alchemist's final act of humanity.

"That's why you're naive," said Stiyl Magnus disinterestedly, looking away.

* * *

"I said 'kill,' but the word has meanings other than taking someone's life, you know."

"Huh?" Kamijou looked at Stiyl.

Stiyl, in a really bored-sounding voice, without linking eyes, continued, "Listen up. Aureolus Isard lost all his memories. What if, in this situation, I were to do a little bit of cosmetic surgery and change the construction of his face? The outside would be different and so would the inside. Look, that person honestly isn't Aureolus Isard anymore. There's no difference between doing that and killing him, is there?"

"..Are you a good person?"

"What's that supposed to mean? I'll have you know that I'm still an English Puritan priest. My specialty is fire, so reconstructing someone's face is an easy feat. I just have to melt it and then fix it back up."

"..You're a good person!"

"Hm? Well, I guess that was an unexpected response, but... Wait, what?! What are you suddenly trying to hug me for?! Stop trying to stand on your tiptoes and pet my head like that!"

As Kamijou and Stiyl raged about the room, kicking and struggling, suddenly the hospital room's door opened without anyone knocking and in burst Index.

"Touma! They're selling cantaloupe-flavored potato chips at the store! They're rare and I want to buy them, so I think I might want some money!... Er..."

Index abruptly stopped moving.

In front of her were the struggling runic magician and Touma Kamijou, currently trying to pet his head against his will because he was impressed with something.

All three of them stopped.

The world froze.

"... Touma. I'm sorry, I guess this was a bad time."

"Wa... wait. You're being weird. Why are you looking away? Hey, you don't just walk out without saying anything!"

Kamijou shrieked and desperately tried to pull back Index before she left. Well, he got the premonition that telling Index, "No, really, I'm very attracted to your childlike body so don't worry!" would *also* be pretty socially unacceptable. *No, wait!* thought Kamijou, his mind collapsing into a wormhole of confusion.

"..."

Stiyl Magnus watched the two of them.

Kamijou and Index were in a heated debate, but it somehow looked like they were enjoying themselves.

It was like the two of them just being there was incredibly natural.

Stiyl Magnus watched the two of them.

Not out of envy nor out of animosity. It was just because he had come all this way to protect Index so she could smile like that. He gazed at the face of the girl he had to defend with a satisfied expression.

Then he sighed. "I've got jobs piling up for after this, so I should be leaving soon." Stiyl's tone of voice was one of boredom, but his face looked somewhat fulfilled.

Index looked at Stiyl once again and quickly hid herself behind Kamijou. She stared at him like a detective trailing a suspect from the shadows.

Stiyl went for the room's exit without having any particular feelings on the matter.

He chose to come all this way so she could be like that.

"Umm..."

Right before Stiyl turned the room's door handle, Index spoke up.

Stiyl turned back. Index was probably angry. Stiyl *was* the one that got Touma Kamijou wrapped up in the Misawa School incident. There was no reason she wouldn't heap all manner of abuse on him for it.

"Well, I'll just say it. Thanks."

* * *

And yet, that's what she said.

"After all, if Touma knew the building was like that, he'd definitely have gone diving in by himself. So I think it was a good thing you were there. So—um, what's the matter?"

It's nothing, said Stiyl's smile.

He didn't say anything more. Stiyl turned back to the exit again and left without a word.

For some reason, Kamijou got the feeling that was the first time he'd seen Stiyl smile.

"Touma."

Kamijou returned his eyes from the doorway to Index. When he did, Index puffed out her cheeks and looked at him, possibly somehow mad at him for not paying attention to her.

He grinned at her in spite of himself. The battlefield in Misawa School had certainly been fierce, but he had been able to make it back home. He smiled because that feeling hit him then.

But... A question he left in the war zone came to mind.

The thing that flew out of his severed right arm—the jaw of the king dragon.

It was nothing more than a product born of Aureolus Isard's anxiety toward Kamijou.

Nothing more, he thought... But at the time, **was Aureolus Isard actually thinking something that specific**—that a transparent dragon jaw would spring out of his right arm?

There's no way, he thought.

It had to have been Aureolus's power... right?

...

Impossible, he thought.

But still. Kamijou thought back to Aisa Himegami. "Deep Blood" Aisa Himegami—the girl with a special power that only worked against vampires.

If such a disturbance was caused by a girl **who could do nothing**

except kill vampires, then if Touma Kamijou's right hand, Imagine Breaker, could even kill divine miracles, then how much must it be worth?

No...

Just what *was* Imagine Breaker in the first place?

"Touma! I said, they're selling cantaloupe-flavored potato chips."

He gave a start and finally snapped out of it after what Index said.

"Uh, right. I see.... Wait, would cantaloupe-flavored chips be sweet?"

Kamijou tried to engage in the conversation that was going on and attempted a vague smile.

This is fine for now, he thought. *Whatever kind of weird power it was, I was still able to protect one girl through the whole thing. I can't ask for more than that.*

So it's fine for now.

For now.

"Touma, Touma! Hey, you know how there was that person named Aisa Himegami in that building?"

Index suddenly began as they were walking down the hallway toward the shop.

"Yeah, that nutso, fake magician. What about h— Wait, what is it, Index? What are you looking at me with suspicion for? You're the one who asked."

"...Touma, you were fighting for Aisa this time, weren't you. Aisa and not me."

"Excuse me?"

Kamijou tilted his head, puzzled. Index was saying some weird stuff all of a sudden, and she somehow seemed really bothered about something—enough to **purposely show Kamijou** her making a pouty face.

"Nothing, nothing really." After Index grumbled to herself a bit, she said, "Yeah. Well, that Aisa person was actually admitted to this hospital. I just went and talked to her."

"Uh-huh," Kamijou said, throwing in an appropriate grunt to keep the conversation going.

Now that she mentions it, what is Himegami going to do from now on? he thought. *She said she didn't want to attract vampires, but the Misawa School barrier doesn't exist anymore. Apparently she can use a Walking Church like Index for it, but Aureolus Isard was the one who promised to make one, and he's gone, too.*

"So after talking to her about lots of stuff, Aisa is apparently gonna be looked after by the Church!"

"...I think I've managed to figure out how this is going to end, so can I just say it first?"

"Gah! Someone goes through all the trouble to do some story-telling and this is what she gets! Touma, saying the ending before the play ends totally kills it! Shakespeare would probably stab you, Touma!"

"Quit saying people will stab me while you're smiling."

Kamijou took one single, quiet breath and threw out the answer that anyone at this point would have guessed.

"You're about to say, 'By Church, I mean the Walking Church!' right?"

AFTERWORD

To those of you who have been reading from the first volume—welcome back.

And to those brave ones who suddenly picked up the second book—nice to meet you.

This is Kazuma Kamachi.

Now then, the afterword. It seems like depending on the person, some of you read this part first. Apparently, the afterword is like a second summary. Or that there are people who read the afterword first, and if it tickles their fancy, they head straight for the cash register.

However, I'd like to advise caution to those of you who dive straight into the afterword. It would probably not be a good idea to read it until you've gone through the story first.

The next thing here is an afterword meant for those of you who enjoy reading the afterword at the end or those of you with the courage to brave spoilers.

The concept this time was a "bad end."

To put it clearly, Aureolus is Touma Kamijou's failed state. I tried to write this book while thinking about what kind of person Kamijou might have become if he hadn't succeeded at the end of volume 1. Even Himegami had the pitiful role of the girl who couldn't become the story's heroine.

So for various reasons, things were pretty brutal this time around. Contrary to volume 1, where even the enemies would at least hear you first, the final boss—to say nothing of the candidate for heroine—never listened to a word anyone said.

Ars Magna was the occult "keyword" everything developed from.

I mentioned somewhere in the story that it was the "true form of alchemy" or something, but that was actually a total lie. Apparently, the first major school of alchemy, the Bohemian school (the one famous for turning lead into gold) appeared in the later stages of the Roman Empire, while Ars Magna didn't come in until quite a bit later, in the seventeenth century. In addition, at the time, the seventeenth century was kind of a dark age for alchemy. It was a fad, where fake magicians would con nobility out of their money. In other words, Ars Magna was just some new-age cult sort of thing that rode the tailcoats of the alchemy boom.

Anyway, the real Ars Magna wasn't something that could create gold or make an elixir of immortality. It was really only something like humans being an incomplete version of God, so if a human was to train and become "complete," then he could become a god. Obviously that all sounds like a mess of cultic hubbub, but as you can see the term *God* in there, you can tell that Crossism got mixed into alchemy.

The thing Aureolus was doing in this book, with the "everything in his head becomes reality" and so on, is actually more the Zurich style of alchemy. This mixed the original alchemy with the psychology of Carl Jung; "doing alchemy in your head" is the gist of it.

There was another version of alchemy from Vienna, but that used some perverted techniques called sex magic, so it's not allowed in Dengeki Bunko (*laugh*).

One explanation for the abundant number of variations of alchemy is apparently that no one knew what it originally was, but the correct answer seems to go more like this: Alchemists would con royalty by saying they could convert lead into gold, but no matter how long they waited, they could never produce that all-important gold. To soothe the nobles that angered, they told all kinds of different lies.

I wrote quite a bit, but well, in the end, this is what I really wanted to say:

Despite all the investigation, the word *alchemy* isn't really used well, huh?

I might as well have given Index a bit more time onstage and mixed in some kind of "easy kitchen alchemy" plot. I wonder how that sort of deep theme would have done in the story?

Now then, here's where I thank everyone involved with this production.

My editor, Ms. Miki, is an amazing person, and one who placed the order for me to write an entire novel in seventeen days. Seriously, thank you for sticking with this book until the end, despite all the holes in it.

My illustrator, Mr. Haimura, is someone I've actually never met face-to-face before. It would sound cool if I called him my "invisible partner," but I really do want to meet him and give him my thanks. For now, I'll just practice it on paper: Thank you so much.

And to all of you readers who bought this book, a huge "thank-you" to you for staying with me the whole way. As I pray that you'll all have the chance to look through the next one, and the ones after that, I lay down my pen for the day.

Mikoto Misaka never got a word in edgewise this time, either (*cry*).

Kazuma Kamachi